NEVER WORN

About the author

Born in Colchester in 1978, Jolie Booth grew up in Braintree, Essex, and studied for a degree in English at Nottingham Trent University. She lived for 15 years in Brighton as well as in Sydney Australia, London and the squats of Berlin, where she ran the  infamous Fischladen squat bar in Friedrichshain, before returning to England.

In her first novel, *The Girl Who'll Rule the World* (2016), we followed the story of a young modern woman finding her way in a tumultuous world, told through a broken narrative and stream of consciousness. That novel, the first in a planned series of books called *Saturn Returns* in which the reader will return every seven years to the world of the heroine Esmeralda, dipping into her life and discovering how it and her ideals have changed, was set in Brighton between 2007 and 2008, during which time Esmeralda turns from 28 to 29 years old and tells the story of a young woman facing her thirties with the feeling that she is going to take over the world. *Never Worn* is the second book in the series.

NEVER WORN

by
Jolie Booth

The King's England Press
2018

ISBN 978 1 909548 75 6

NEVER WORN
is typeset in Book Antiqua,
Castellar, and Franklin Gothic
and published by
The King's England Press
111 Meltham Road
Lockwood
HUDDERSFIELD
West Riding of Yorkshire

Printed and bound in Great Britain by

4Edge Ltd
Hockley, Essex

To my magnificent man,
who teaches me, day by day,
to be a better person

"For Sale: Baby shoes. Never Worn."
- Ernest Hemingway, *Six-Word Novel*.

Critical Acclaim For
The Girl Who'll Rule The World:
Amazon reviews

"You know those chick-lit books that you feel as though you've read before because the 'story' is so predictable? Yeah, this isn't one of those books! It is more of an unputdownable and mind-flipping adventure. I've laughed, cried and blushed when reading this in public but mostly I've thought about how there's a bit of Esmeralda in all of us, we ARE meant to rule the world!"

"I've never heard a voice like this before represented in mainstream media. I say voice. It's more like a scream into the face of the establishment and the power of patriarchy. But then the scream is not even really at them. Esmeralda isn't even bothered about them. She's just screaming because she's not scared to and she can."

"Fresh, original and absolutely unique. I haven't read anything which has made me laugh out loud so much for years."

"It was a pleasure to hang out with Esmeralda. It feels like Booth has given an important voice to a wise woman who we do not hear enough from in this world."

"As soon as you start this book you won't be able to put it down. Beautifully descriptive observant and heartwarming you won't want this story to stop."

"Honest, funny, and – at times – tragic. The author has produced a very readable and entertaining chronicle of the crucial formative years of her character, Esmeralda. Years which see her transiting all sorts of relationships, emotional and otherwise, and getting into some very strange situations, some of which are funny, and some of which are sad. In fact, the skill of this author is often the ability to switch from the comic mask to the tragic mask in the space of just a few lines. I was left with just two questions at the end, firstly who is this woman Jolie Booth, and, secondly, where has she been, hiding her writing under a bushel?"

"A glorious celebration of a powerful woman. Esmerelda is a joy; adventurous, sexually liberated, fearless, razor-tongued, magical, artistic, self-assured and ballsy."

"Rich, idiosyncratic dialogue from the haphazard perspective of a girl on the cusp of womanhood" - Ophelia Bitz

PREFACE

You who never arrived
in my arms, Beloved, who were lost
from the start,
I don't even know what songs
would please you. I have given up trying
to recognize you in the surging wave of
the next moment. All the immense
images in me -- the far-off, deeply-felt
landscape, cities, towers, and bridges, and
unsuspected turns in the path,
and those powerful lands that were once
pulsing with the life of the gods--
all rise within me to mean
you, who forever elude me.
You, Beloved, who are all
the gardens I have ever gazed at,
longing. An open window
in a country house - and you almost
stepped out, pensive, to meet me.
Streets that I chanced upon,--
you had just walked down them and vanished.
And sometimes, in a shop, the mirrors
were still dizzy with your presence and,
startled, gave back my too-sudden image.
Who knows? Perhaps the same
bird echoed through both of us
yesterday, separate, in the evening...

- **Rainer Maria Rilke**

SALUTATIONS

19 West Side Road,
Brighton,
BN1 5LR

21st September 2013

Dearest Jessica,
Thank you so much for your letter. What a relief to hear you are free at last and that prison was not as awful as it could have been. What luck you got on with the other women. I cannot believe you were inside for that long, and for protesting! This world is beyond fucked up. I fear dreadfully for the future. When you went off to that G8 summit there was still some chance that things would be okay and not go completely dark side. Now, well... The dark side is in full swing, isn't it?

Have you kept up with politics whilst inside? Or had you had enough of it? I wouldn't blame you if you had. I stopped reading papers and watching the news some years ago. I have no interest in what Murdoch has to say, or what anyone else has to say for that matter. All I care about is the present moment and the things I can do to make the world a better place in my immediate reality. I think too much media freezes you in a world full of opinions and too much fear. It disables you from being capable of any action at all in the face of it all: how can one work out what one should do next when presented with such a great steaming edifice of bullshit? Best ignore the mountain of woes and focus instead on the few steps of the path just in front of you. Do what you can immediately around you to spread love, serve others and tread lightly upon the earth.

It is great to hear from you. Do you know that all them years ago in Berlin I had this strange feeling, when I said goodbye to you outside 84 Rigaer Strasse, that I was not going to seeing you again. Hopefully that's not true and soon we will be reunited. I should have said something to you at the time, but what sense would that have made? Having the sight isn't particularly useful annoyingly. These flashes of intuition only ever make sense much later, when it's already too late.

You asked me how I've been and what's been happening in my life. That feels difficult for me to answer, because nothing is as bad as being locked up for one's political beliefs, which I think is just about the worst injustice there is. Unfortunately, though, my time over the last seven years has been really, really shit.

I'm in the grip of depression. It has been going on for seven years now and I don't know how much longer I can carry on. It feels selfish, self-indulgent, egotistical and full of shit, but it's a pit of despair that I can't climb out of, no matter how hard I try, and it feels like it will never end. I should be happy. This beautiful life is such a blessing. I haven't just spent the last seven years in prison, for fuck's sake. What a dick I must sound to you. In so many ways I'm living the dream. Here I am, white, educated, sitting in a £550,000 house with a garden (I don't own it, but I rent it), in Brighton (which is one of the most exciting places in the country) in England (which is one of the best places in the world to come from) getting up every day to do a job where I am my own boss (so I'm able to wake up whenever I like) my work allows me to travel and I'm earning a living doing something I love. Talk about first world problems. What a privileged fuckwit.

But on the flip of a coin... I'm completely skint, our rent keeps going up and up and soon we will no longer be able to afford to live here anymore. We don't have rich parents to fall back on. We only just escaped from years of working in an awful job at a call centre where we said the same thing over and over again all day, every day, until we went mad. I cried in the toilets every single day I was there. I feel like I've utterly failed at my dreams. Somehow I need to metaphorically iron out this revolting neural pathway from my poor addled brain and discover my power once more, but I don't know where to start. And to top it all off... We can't have children.

11

In a way, I believe that this has all happened for a reason. I thought I was set for stardom, but in my lifetime stardom has become tacky and devoid of magic. I've been spared from stardom really. Though how do I accept this without feeling like an utter failure? And that was Plan A. I never had a Plan B. There's no chance of making it as an actress if you have a Plan B. Not only did I have to accept I'd failed at Plan A, once I started getting older and Plan A clearly hadn't happened, but I also had to figure out what Plan B was going to be. I got married and tried to have kids. Turned out that we can't have kids. We are now just about to embark on our third and final round of IVF. My hormones are a mess, our relationship is in tatters, we both feel like utter losers and now I'm basically having to accept that I need to start working out what the fuck Plan C might be...

Suicide definitely feels like an option. It pops up in my mind regularly. I imagine throwing myself off of the pier almost every day. Don't worry though, I promise I won't. There are too many people in my life who that would destroy and who I care about too much to do that to. It means I simply have to find a reason to live and a way to make all this shit that has happened be of some value. I've always had a very clear sense of destiny, that my path lies intuitively before me, and in a non-hippy way I think this is down to my ability to turn any situation into a positive. My mum taught me this. It's the most valuable life skill I've learnt. If one can find the positive lesson in everything that happens then you are creating one's life as a possibility, rather than letting it all just happen at you. There is a musical note that only I can make (a pretty awful-sounding note, granted, but certainly a unique one) and without it the symphony of the world would be missing my melody. We all have this note and we all need to sing it loud and clear. I'd attached many baubles to my personal score though, thinking it was going to be more of a leading player in the overall symphony than it has turned out to be. These baubles have been forcibly shaken off though now by the universe and that has been a bitter pill to swallow.

I haven't drunk any alcohol or taken any drugs for over two years, which has been novel. This is because of the IVF obviously. Instead I've had a camera shoved up my fallopian tubes (doctor said I had the best looking womb he'd seen in ten thousand women, which is something, I guess), I've had thirty blood tests, eight up-the-fanny ultrasound scans that are painful, (because one of my ovaries is off on an adventure and hard to find) two simulated menopauses and 150 injections shoved in my belly, administered by yours truly or my dear husband. One operation, one two week wait only to find out that it had all been for nothing, one second attempt that resulted in over-stimulation to the drugs and therefore one aborted procedure, which led to one subsequent hormonal freak-out, rapid weight gain and complete mental breakdown. I spent most of last year in a state best described as a weeping, volatile puffer-fish.

Fun.

This next go at the IVF will be our third and final round. We could try again after this, but it will no longer be on the NHS and will cost us £8,000 a pop. We just do not have that kind of money. And I want my life back. We've been trying for a baby for seven years now... And as you well know, seven years is a fucking long time. The pain of not being able to have children feels like screaming and howling into the wind on top of a mountain at a thunder and lightning storm that's trying to destroy you. I imagine it's similar to what it feels like to lose your parents. Losing your parents cuts you off from a connection to your past. Losing or not being able to have children cuts you off from a connection to your future. And you fantasise about your children all the time when you're trying to conceive, imagining their names and what they will be like. My dream babies die every time I do a pregnancy test. Every period for seven years has felt like a miscarriage. The worst thing is, I keep tricking my body into making my periods come late. That's 72 miscarriages I've put myself through, all thanks to a trick of the mind. It has been horrific. We've also gone through two waves of friends trying to have babies and succeeding. We are the only ones who have failed. We are the only ones out of everyone I know who haven't ended up succeeding in the end. Our lives have become a tragedy. People pity us. Everyone has a tip to share on how to make it happen. They tell us that we just need to relax, or share a tale about how someone they know got pregnant as soon as they stopped trying. I know they mean well, but, my god, I want to scream in their stupid fucking faces every time I hear that stupid fucking story.

This next round of IVF starts next week. I'm therefore looking forward to the next month like a kick in the balls. The scariest thing is, I have a feeling it is going to work this time. And with that will come a whole new set of worries. Here I am, trying to keep a marriage and my mind together, losing my looks, a large chunk of my joy and I've a strong sinking feeling it is going to work and I'm going to end up with a baby. But I feel like a dying pot plant in unfertile soil, like I have a worryingly little amount left to offer the child. I've been in depression for seven years, our economic situation is a breath away from poverty, our relationship is stretched, our hopes are in tatters and the world is unbelievably screwed. I firmly believing that soon we'll be living under a totalitarian regime whose surveillance operations will be running on a global scale like none we've ever seen before, that'll be 'protecting' us from the fighting savages scrambling over the tiny morsels of resources left on this poor planet, and will mean that we won't even be able to fart without the powers that be knowing about it. Human rights are disappearing as rapidly as the frogs and the birds and the clean seas. I believe that seven years from now I will be writing to you from a concentration camp or from a hiding place with a gun. Really hope that's not the case, but this is what I foresee. How much my depression and anxiety need tempering in all this remains to be seen.

How, therefore, can I justify forcing - literally forcing - a child or possibly even two, as they'll be able to put two eggs back in me this time, onto a planet that I think is thus doomed? Well, you don't regret having children do you? That's what everyone keeps saying. They are tiring and hard work and blame you for everything, but for some reason you love them anyway and will on the whole be glad you have had them. I know there are exceptions to every rule, but it's fair to say this is pretty much the norm. And I can offer the child all the love in the world and an open mind and a sense of adventure...

I don't really agree with IVF and wrote articles against it when it first came about, against the 'Death Doctors' who created it, deeming them as trying to play the role of Mother Nature in a world that already had too many people on it. I would much rather adopt and do still intend to. My cousins were put into a home by my uncle. This has haunted me all my life and made me feel that I owe karma one in the adoption stakes. My Husband wants to have biological children though. And my body wants me to have my own. And the NHS is still able to help us to have them. In another few years the NHS will probably no longer exist. If we ever want to do it then we need to do it now. This is such a complicated situation. Life gets more complicated the older you get doesn't it?

It was the perceived wisdom when we were growing up, from our mothers, that we ought to go out and get an education and get on with our careers and have adventures before we have children. I actually think they were wrong. It goes against millions of years of evolution. We should have babies young. Our bodies are made for it, our energy levels can cope with it, and we are healthier.

At 35, not having had kids, I just carried on acting like a teenager... Trashing my body, having no money, thinking I am the centre of the universe. All my friends who I pitied at school, because they got pregnant and made the cardinal sin of deciding to keep the baby (Oh my god, what the hell does she think she's doing? She's ruining her life) now have teenagers and are free to do whatever they want again. Being 35 is not old anymore and they tend to have their own cars, their own houses and are still young enough to enjoy their regained freedom. I'll be in my mid-fifties the next time I'm free if this round of IVF works.

Sorry Jess, this is all a bit gloomy isn't it? This last seven years have been pretty rubbish, hey? I would love to be writing you an inspiring powerful letter about how I finished drama school and went on to become a huge dazzling superstar and had a string of gorgeous intelligent famous lovers and acquired plenty of personal wealth and an army of natural and adopted babies in a multitude of colours and how I'm now an ambassador for the UN and about to receive an honorary Damehood. But I'm not, and I didn't. Life kind of turned out to be pretty shit. I didn't take over the world. The world took over me.

I've often wondered why there isn't a manual for life. Why is it that so many people have come before us and have been through the same shit and learnt the same lessons, but for some reason decided not to warn us little upstarts about the pitfalls? Then I realised that old people are the manual and they're always trying to warn us... We just don't listen.

Anyway, that's enough from me. I hope you don't mind such a thorough answer to your question, I felt compelled to be honest and open with you after you shared with me so eloquently all that you had learnt from your experience in prison. I'm glad it hasn't made you bitter. You're a strong and wonderful woman, old friend, and I'm proud of you for standing up for what you believe in. Fuck the system. They sure as hell are fucking us.

I love you,

Esmeralda

'OH, YOU GREAT HAIRY TOE OF A CITY'

Esmeralda was parched. She peeled her eyelids back, like rind from an orange, and peered into the high ceiling of the gloomy room. She loved the smell of Berlin. A faint hint of dark wood, doner kebabs and European drains danced at the back of her nasal passages and triggered the many endorphins that loved swimming to that good old Bavarian beat. This great ugly toe of a city was Esmeralda's spiritual home.

Your roads are wide and your pavements shitty.

She had been frequenting the place since the early nineties, back when it had still looked like the set from a *Mad Max* film. The buildings had been

19

pocked with scars of bullet holes, which the communists had never seen fit to fill in, though more than likely they could never have afforded to fill them all in, as it would have required re-surfacing every building in East Berlin. The bullet holes had been everywhere. Those that were human height and along the sides of buildings showed where the Nazis had carried out their systematic murders, and those that were around the windows and up the sides of buildings showed where the Russian army had shot the shit out of the city during its liberation. You could not help but wonder at the story behind each and every hole. Had that one marked the death of a Jew? Did they finally get the soldier holding out in that torched mausoleum? And overall, they left the uncanny feeling that the war had ended only yesterday.

Herr Franz pottered around his apartment, laying down his daily collection of newspapers.

One of each paper, every single day. Already, he had leafed through the pages and highlighted the idiosyncrasies, comparing the same stories, noting the differences. Each paper was like a child to Herr Franz. He had been there at their birth, each fresh with individual personality. He had watched them grow, mature, flourish or flounder. He knew what they were going to say on a matter before they had even said it and his impartial love was served out to each of his children with equal attention. He just wanted to observe. There was no judgement.

His dark wooden walls had been lost behind the towers of yellowing paper many moons ago. Fluttering columns enclosed upon Herr Franz as he shuffled his way amongst the tight corridors of headlines, announcing events that had occurred out there, in the world, over the last decade. Outside had been communist once. It wasn't anymore. Frau Schlösser no longer lived upstairs. She had gone, along with all the rest. Youngsters had moved in, with metal through their eyebrows and dogs on ropes. They played noise they called music and cursed loudly on the stairs. But they let Herr Franz alone. That was all he wanted.

It hadn't occurred to them yet that the rats were coming from his apartment...

After the wall came down, everyone had fled and emptied the city and squatters from all over Europe moved in. They set about covering East Berlin from head to toe in graffiti. Where graffiti had been once used as an act of defiance against the infamous Berlin Wall, now it had become a defence against the flood of capitalism pouring in. McDonalds opened up but the punks kept pissing on it until it closed down and moved on. It closed and moved three times before its roots were able to take hold. Spray paint marked out where the punks had set up shop and it shouted their opinions into the faces of all nervous visitors. Although Esmeralda presumed that the aim of the graffiti had been far from aesthetically-based, it had sure as hell gone a long way to cheering the place up a bit. Esmeralda loved the way spray paint vibrated, that every movement of the artist was captured in the strokes of the paint, which meant that the city had become a toxic vibrating mess of colours, dancing over the acne-pitted scars bearing the weight of the dark memories that lay beneath. Like thick make-up on a fucked-up drag queen.

'What's that?' asked Timmy, pointing at the great space age erection.

'Communist cities always seem to have one of these,' replied Esmeralda, 'It's the TV Tower.' Shaped like a cherry on a toothpick, the landmark towered way above the rooftops of the city.

'Looks like something out of a James Bond film' he noted.

'It's nicknamed the Pope's Revenge,' informed Esmeralda, climbing onto her tour guide soapbox.

'Normally, when you shine light onto a ball it will reflect off of the ball as a spot of light but for some reason the light reflects off of the TV Tower as a golden cross. Now the Communists weren't too into crucifixes, in fact they were banned, so they weren't happy about a great golden crucifix towering over the whole of East Berlin.'

'How come it happens?' asked Kash, as she snapped away with her camera.

'No one knows,' replied Esmeralda, 'but they spent a fortune hammering out all of the panels trying to stop it from happening. As you can see, it didn't work.'

When Esmeralda had first arrived in Berlin during the nineties, the streets had still been lined with dog shit and pissed-off punks. It had terrified Esmeralda, but it had also set her heart lurching around inside its rib cage, because she loved anything from the realm of the 'other'. Esmeralda had always felt like she belonged to the 'other'. Berlin, throughout history, has been a sanctuary for such people; from its gay heyday in Isherwood's time, through the persecution of the Jews, to the great walled enclosure of the East, its history is as pocked with 'others' as its face has been pocked with bullet holes. But the bullet holes are all but gone now, as are nearly all of the punks and squats.

Esmeralda had been deeply disturbed to discover the day before, upon arriving at her old squat on *Rigaer Strasse*, that a fire had occurred a few months earlier, presumably started by the new 'owner' of the building, which had destroyed the entire squat and all of its contents. Luckily, no one had been hurt, but the large number of punks and dog shit in the area had been greatly diminished. When Esmeralda had lived there it had been with 46 punks, 16 dogs, 1 baby, and with only one bathroom for them all to share. She had spent six months over winter in a freezing cold room with a window that didn't shut properly because the house had begun subsiding. She'd had a skinhead then, with a tiny diagonal tuft of a Mohican along one side of her head, which meant that during the cold winter she had to wear a woollen hat 24/7 to stop her head from freezing. This left a ring of bright red spots around the circumference of her head where she never had the chance to either wash or to take her hat off. And my God, she'd stunk.

Whilst Esmeralda had stood on the pavement peering up at the empty shell of a building, tears welled up in her eyes and she mourned at its still formidable expanse. Then, stepping backwards, she planted her foot firmly into a great big pile of dog shit. She had been forced to laugh. There was still life in the old dog yet.

Esmeralda scooped around at the air beside her bed until her hand bounced upon the bottle of water she had filled up and left there the night before. After painfully gulping down half a bottle of *aqua vita* she flopped back on the bed and tried to come to terms with the fact that she simply had to go to the toilet. They had sunk a fair few *Berliner Biers* at the theatre last night, accidentally of course, and once again she was waking to a world of pain. The theatre had been amazing. Through a heavy metal sliding door at the back of squalid little remaining squat bar, quivering in candlelight, you picked your way around an unlit courtyard and down some slippery brick steps, until you found yourself entering into an enormous space, onto a balcony that over looked the auditorium and a wide beautifully lit stage. The walls were painted a deep rich red and the ceiling writhed with a wonderful array of archetypal portraits. A great statue of Helene hung from the wall. It was the perfect environment for her boss to perform in.

Her boss was a fool. No, really. He had spent the last 36 years developing a performance technique that he called 'Fooling' and which vaguely resembled the court jesters of old. But in his work the audience was king, and as The Fool, he held a mirror up before their eyes, revealing ridiculous reflections on the absurdity of life. It meant that working for the fellow was a rollercoaster ride, in which every job was made difficult as he couldn't help but in some way subvert it; even the role of producer was under a constant foolish scrutiny. It had been two years since she had devoted her life to his work and she had been fed up of the job on more than one occasion; but his path was her path, and at this particular moment in time she and The Fool were awash with love for each other... Mainly because the Germans had gone crazy for him. Esmeralda loved the way that folks in Berlin would say, 'We make a party' or 'We make a show'. It meant that it had been a breeze getting the tour off the ground, even across the Channel and through the language barrier, because the Berliners were happy to 'make' it happen. Every night the show had been presented in a similarly magical space and each show had sold out. For the first time in all the years she had known him Esmeralda could describe her boss as what one might call happy.

But now Esmeralda was paying for the evening's great success. She climbed out of the very comfortable sofa bed in which she had taken up residence for the week and pulled back the curtains, first of all to let the rather pathetic morning light trickle in (it had been grey and bleak for days) but also to inform her travelling companions that she was awake. She put some socks on and wandered into the kitchen in her warm red tartan pyjamas, and set about making her morning tonic: Half a lemon squeezed (she had brought the lemon juicer with her from her flat) a thumb of sliced ginger, a spoonful of molasses (also brought over from England... She had no idea what the word for "molasses" would be in German) a good dollop of honey, and the secret ingredient - only necessary on a day such as this - the wonderful pick me up of an effervescent vitamin C tablet. Whilst the concoction bubbled and fizzed away like a proper witches' potion, Esmeralda sat down and tried to complete another clue from the

Guardian crossword that had perplexed her all week. She heard her friend Timmy shuffle into the room behind her and mumble in her general direction...

'Fancy a brew?'

'No cheers, I'm having a honey and lemon.'

'Urgh!' grunted the morning beast disapprovingly.

He set about the ritual of making builders' tea whilst Esmeralda flicked through the old newspaper.

'I wonder if the Germans are continually blasted with regular and tedious updates on the lives of Posh and Becks?' Esmeralda mused, as she realised with the greatest relish that she hadn't seen their insipid faces for a whole week.

'Of course not,' replied Timmy, 'they don't mean anything to anybody here.'

'How fabulous.' exclaimed Esmeralda 'It must be simply divine to live in a world without Posh Spice in it.'

'Have you ever played the newspaper game?' he asked her, over the pouring of milk.

'No. How do you play it?'

'You go through the paper from the front page to the back and the further into it you get before there's any mention of Princess Diana, the better quality the newspaper.'

Esmeralda turned back to the cover and began scanning through the lurid headlines.

'How far did you get?' he asked her.

'Page two.'

With a huge sigh Esmeralda threw back the paper and rubbed her hands over her tired face.

'Do you feel like shit too?' she asked him.

'Oh yes,' he replied gruffly in his Worcestershire accent.

'What shall we do today?' she asked - but then continued before he had a chance to reply, 'I was thinking that we should go to the film museum today. It looks like it's going to rain so all of the animals will be hiding away at the zoo any way. What do reckon?'

'Sounds good to me.'

Timmy's girlfriend Kash staggered into the room and flopped onto a chair at the table beside Esmeralda. Timmy set a brew down before her and patted her comfortingly on the shoulder.

'What do you reckon, Kash?' Esmeralda asked her cheerily, 'You up for the Film Museum today?'

Kash was far from ready to engage in morning conversation, but soon enough all of them were fed, showered, and winding their way to *Potsdam Platz* on the fabulously efficient U-bahn.

Esmeralda loved the film museum. The last time she had been there was with The Sicilian. He had taken her there on a date. He had long flowing black hair, a beautiful bronzed Mediterranean face, and a cool bright blue leather biker jacket. After the date she had taken him back to her freezing cold room in the *Rigaer Strasse* squat and had embarked upon fairly uneventful sex on the floor, in amongst the soot of her feeble coal oven. He had been yet another example of the European man's obsession with wearing bright blue pants. She couldn't understand this fashion. The only conclusion she had come to is that they were easy to find again after love-making, seeing as they were exactly the same shade of blue as catering plasters, which had been designed so that they were easy to locate in food, should one fall off during cooking...

Pants
There is nothing more disconcerting,
Than after a good night's flirting,
Suddenly observing,
Not boxer shorts
But pants.
These funny little packets,
That wrap around the maggot,
Their little cheesy faggot.
And why are they always blue?

29

Upon returning a second time to the Film Museum, it did not disappoint.

'That is well cool...' Timmy and Kash cooed in unison, suitably impressed with the infinity room.

Mirrors lined the walls on all sides, with a thin knee-height walkway through the centre, which left the impression that the three of them were floating on a walkway in midair.

'Excellent...' exclaimed Kash, 'It looks like we're on the *Death Star*.'

One of the things Esmeralda loved most about her friends was that they had all maintained an ability to play. One of the main reasons for this, Esmeralda felt, was because they had all enjoyed positive and inspired relationships with hallucinogens over the years, keeping a window of childlike wonder and awe open their minds. It also meant that they were fully aware of, and, indeed, celebratory of, their own and each other's dark sides. Timmy, for example, was a miserable old git who you couldn't talk into doing anything he didn't want to do. But everyone loved him for it. And Kash... Actually Kash was nothing but lovely, but if she had ever taken the opportunity to throw a paddy about anything, Timmy's utter dogmatisms for example, then none of the group would flutter an eyelid. If anything, they were surprised it hadn't happened already. Esmeralda herself was a revolting little worm with a potty mouth and a view on life so liberal it almost dragged humanity back into the primordial soup, which she thought, all things considered, would be no bad thing. But for all the dark that they acknowledged in each other, it was equalled by the acknowledgement of each other's spectacular beauty. There wasn't an ounce of insipidness between them and they were all talented. Timmy made music out of bleep bleep noises, Kash was a photographer and Esmeralda made a fool of herself. They were all clever, talented, attractive, sexy, funny, and very, very, noisy. She loved them all so much. Even though fate had led to Esmeralda going on holiday with a couple, she had never for a moment worried about feeling like a gooseberry, because there was an equality, respect, and love between all of them that was stronger than the social structures that govern most human interactions. And the week had been nothing but fun. As they strolled their way through the museum they switched endlessly between furrowed brow and chin scratching, to rolling on the floor with laughter, as each room inspired and excited them in turn.

There were a few exhibits that once more caught Esmeralda's eye. The first had been two short pieces of black and white footage, *Le Charmeur* and *La Peine Du Talion*, illustrating some of the earliest attempts at making colour films, by hand painting each individual cell of the film. Esmeralda thought that the effect was delightful. The colour bustled around the screen with the similar vibrations of graffiti, in that every brushstroke of the artist could be seen. Ever since she had first watched these snippets of footage with The Sicilian years ago, Esmeralda had been determined to make a film in a similar style one day. Possibly a porno.

The second exhibit to capture her imagination had been a display of set designs, storyboards, clips, and advertisements for an old German black & white film called *The Cabinet of Dr. Caligari*.

'If Tim Burton hasn't seen this film then I'll eat my hat' commented Timmy.

Full of disjointed angles and abstract silhouettes, the film had a wonderfully grotesque gothic style that would look cool in any era. This film was special to Esmeralda. It had become one of those beacons of inspiration that throbs through an artist's life, surrounding itself in a fantastical mist of serendipity.

After her last visit to the museum, Esmeralda had managed to locate a copy of the film over the internet. Upon returning to England, Esmeralda had also returned to the arms of her then boyfriend. She had introduced him to the film and it had gone on to influence his degree show. He had been doing a printmaking course at Brighton University, but it was sometimes difficult to figure out exactly what his work had to do with printmaking. It was much further into the realm of live-art. His work hung on three main concepts; disposable art, artist participation, and audience created narratives. Inspired by these concepts his pieces were created with sets built out of black and white painted cardboard and using live performers, such as Esmeralda, to make the pieces come to life. The 'prints' were photos taken on colour film but looked black and white, as the palette of colours used in the scene were black and white, very much in keeping with the twisted style of *The Cabinet of Dr. Caligari*. The meaning of the pieces was always left open to interpretation, presenting the audience with a barrage of possible narratives for them to choose from. Esmeralda loved working with him on his projects. He had been a useless boyfriend, but a very talented artist. And he had taught her to call herself an artist. Everyone comes into your life for a reason.

The film had also cast its shadow over another moment of serendipity in Esmeralda's life. She had found it on the shelf at the house of her last significant liaison. It had been one of the many bells of coincidence that had rung in favour of the gentleman, all of which had turned out to be completely wrong. But never mind.

The early hand-painted footage and the designs for *The Cabinet of Dr Caligari* once more stuck their claws of inspiration into Esmeralda's imagination, and she made plans on her return to commence with a hotpot of ideas.

The three of them reached the end of the exhibition and dragged their tired feet back to the flat. There was always one flight too many stairs up to any apartment in Berlin. The buildings all have at least four floors and none of them have lifts. When she had lived in the squat on *Rigaer Strasse* she had been up on the top floor. The coal for the ovens was kept in the basement and as much coal as she could physically carry up the stairs lasted no longer than three days, which meant that every few days Esmeralda traipsed nine flights of stairs with as heavy a load as she could cope with, in an attempt to stop herself from freezing to death. And as much coal as the little oven in her room could take only just lasted the night, so no matter how much she wanted to stay in bed, be it with a hangover, a lover, an illness, or that time of the month, there was no way she could put up with the cold for long and this was doubled by the creeping anxiety that it would take twice as long to warm the room up again the longer she waited to sort out the fire. For a time, she cursed her little oven but it got her nowhere. So then she tried loving her little oven instead, even writing it an Ode...

Ode to a Coal Oven…

Oh little oven so small and snug,
The perfect size and warmth to hug.
Nasty brown tiles do not detract,
From the love and devotion you attract.
Nine flights of stairs I carry for thee,
The coal that you gobble up instantly.
A healthy portion of each of my days,
Is spent tending to your funny ways.
But without a grumble, or a moan,
I tend to you when I get home.
And I work each day for the endless goal,
To supply you with a steady stream of coal.

When she lost the will to live and really couldn't be bothered to carry any more coal up the one-flight-too-many flights of stairs, she would simply stay up for days on end in the bar that she ran on the ground floor of the next-door squat. The oven there was person-height and once filled with coal it would last all day or all night. And there was only one flight of stairs to carry it up from the basement. So it really did make much more sense to stay in the bar 24/7, as far as Esmeralda was concerned.

'What the hell is that?' Timmy yelped with indignation, confronted with the great grey metallic obelisk that is the Jewish Museum.

'Wow,' Esmeralda reacted 'I like it.'

'Do you?'

'It looks ominous and fortified. It makes you think of a concentration camp.'

Kash was snapping away already with her powerful digital camera.

They clanked across the metal faces that screamed with cold glass splinters of sound.

Esmeralda had visited Sachsenhausen Concentration Camp twice over her years of visiting Berlin and felt it was an important landmark in her life. Until her first visit, the First and Second World Wars had just been boring history to her. Kind of a brown-coloured, tobacco-stained history, like the Industrial Revolution was all black and grey and cold and miserable. Beyond history was colourful and vibrant. But after going to the camp she became aware for the first time of the magnitude of the horror. The reality of what humanity can be capable of. It was shocking, but vital.

On the plane back from Berlin Esmeralda saw a great March hare bouncing alongside the runway. It was the second time she had seen a mad March hare in October, hopping along beside a runway, and last time, it had been an omen marking the beginning of a magical year.

Esmeralda flicked through her passport and looked at her stamps: China, Turkey, Egypt, Georgia, Romania, Slovakia, Czech Republic, and Bulgaria. There was no way she was getting into America with that assortment.

'The invasion across Europe must have been so scary.' Kash considered.

'What's your nationality?' asked Timmy.

'I'm a drunkard.' answered Esmeralda.

The text read: *We need someone to perform our lyrics on the stage naked and painted pink doing some sort of performance art. And we thought of you. Can you do it?*

Of course, replied Esmeralda.

Never Worn

AURORA NOVA

Esmeralda woke up in the bright, airy room of her flat. Sunlight poured generously in from the south-facing window, where seagulls cawed across the rooftops, making life feel like a constant summer holiday. The flat was always cosy and warm, a snug safe hideaway from the world. Esmeralda slid out from her white satin sheets and slipped into her red cosy slippers and white fluffy dressing gown. She switched on the FM radio, which was tuned to FIP, a French radio station that was available in certain lucky areas of the town, thanks to a sneaky booster. Lilting Parisian music trickled into the room whilst Esmeralda went to shower. Her bathroom was clean and covered in products. There was always loo roll and the seat was always down. After her morning wee, Esmeralda removed her white satin slip, decorated with black floral detail, and hung it behind the door. Then she turned on, and climbed into, the shower, which, thankfully, had a powerful

39

blast. Her products were bought from the Trevor Sorbie hair salon, where she also got her hair cut. It cost £140 for them to bleach and cut her hair. The shampoo was bright blue to help keep up the brilliant whiteness of her hair tone. Because her hair was so heavily bleached she needed to use a decent conditioner and Esmeralda liked the one from the Aussie collection because it smelt of Hubba Bubba bubble gum.

Esmeralda didn't use any of these products a year ago and she swore that she had more fine lines around her eyes now, since she started using all these expensive things. But she couldn't stop using them now that she'd started, as she was terrified that this would only make things worse.

There's always Botox....

Never.

'I can't work under the pressure of worrying about getting an agent or getting published. I have to just work because I can't stop myself from making the art, and if at some point someone acknowledges me for this, then so be it.'

'Well that's true of all artists I think. When you find that you're working with the sold product in mind then the work becomes contrived,' he agreed.

Esmeralda noticed that she had started writing again.

Then she also noticed it had been exactly seven years since the last book she'd written.

Saturn returns... She thought to herself.

The news report said that a huge percentage of Post Offices were going to be closed down all over the country. Yea, because they're not exactly necessary are they?

'It's all about Eastern Europe in the world of theatre,' the director friend explained to her.

'What do the pages keep in and what do they keep out though?' asked Esmeralda.

'Maybe you're growing up sweetie,' the director laughed.

'When men get together with women,' piped up the youngest of the gang, a vibrant intelligent creature with a delightfully endearing belly full of fire, 'They never want them to change, whereas when women get together with men they normally do it with the intention of changing them in some way.'

'Yes. And when they split up it is normally because the woman has changed or because the man wouldn't,' laughed the director.

'What neurosis would you develop if you were kept isolated from the outside world?' they mused.

'Nothing worth possessing can ever be truly possessed,' her friend decided.

'I watched *Casablanca* today, and it's actually really rather good isn't it?' exclaimed Esmeralda.

'Really Esmeralda, that's hardly a newsflash now, is it?' her friend retorted.

'I know but I didn't expect it to be as good as it was. It was like watching a game of chess. I was absolutely glued to all their moves and how the story unfolded. It's just a shame so many lines from it have been bastardised. It couldn't help sounding like a spoof.'

Maja of Dah Teatre leapt around the stage on the edge of balance, her body twisting in double directions. Esmeralda was captivated by her beauty and composure. The inspiration this woman commanded intimidated Esmeralda down to her guts and filled her full of aspiration.

These Aurora Nova workshops always sent the universe into a swirl. They shoved Esmeralda off the precipice of reason and into the terrifying realm of possibility. And magic always followed. Last year, the love of her life had suddenly reappeared, after a decade of separation. This year, she had been presented with the perfect opportunity to metaphorically slam the door shut on a particularly disastrous relationship. Both were acts of unforeseen miracles. She wished the universe were a great big-breasted woman, so that she could bury her face in her vast cleavage and give her an enormous hug.

'It's amazing... You've always known your path,' said her father over a cup of coffee. 'I remember the first time we were called into school about your behaviour. Your teacher was worried that instead of doing the task you were meant to be doing you were to be found at the back of the classroom, getting all your classmates to be in a play.'

'Really?' smiled Esmeralda. She loved being told stuff about her past that helped cement her cause.

'Oh yes,' continued her father enthusiastically, 'and I remember saying to your teacher that this didn't seem to be a problem to me as it was obvious this was what you were meant to be doing with your life and hopefully what you will find yourself doing when you grow up.'

The first performance Esmeralda ever remembered being in was with her ballet group when she was about five years old. She was dressed in a little turquoise training tutu and had little black slip-on ballet shoes. Esmeralda could remember the dance clearly, though it wasn't really a dance, more a series of events. Clutching a fake rose she danced around with it lovingly before taking a great big sniff. Then she dropped the flower suddenly and clutched her nose as if she had just been stung by a bee, and ran to the back of the dance floor crying.

'You've always used money to...'

'...To buy things. I've always used money to buy things.'

Esmeralda was poor. Many of her friends were Trustafarians – pseudo-hippies with great big trust funds and not a care in the world. But Esmeralda had no back-up plan. She originated from a council house, debts, and her father going out to the car to head-butt the horn on the steering wheel after working out his accounts at the end of the tax year. Her brother had gone for money and power, like a wild dog on the hunt for meat. And, fair dos. He was going to create a different life for himself, where as Esmeralda had nothing to her name: no pension, no savings, debt collectors after her, and had been on benefits for six years. No inheritance was ever coming their way and Esmeralda couldn't imagine how she could ever afford to own a house, or have a car, or any of those things. It hadn't stopped her travelling the world and having a good time though...

'You know if I hadn't been very rich, I might have been a really great man.' - Citizen Kane

Esmeralda had made a commitment to herself not to judge or worry about, either her work, how well she was doing, or how successful she was being. Instead she agreed to be content to pour forth her creative juices by focusing her energies on creating a practice and a discipline.

His text read:

If I could, then I'd make you Prime Minister.

It was the best compliment she had received in a long time.

If Esmeralda absolutely had to pinpoint her political stance then she would have to say that she was an Anarchist, believing that we are all individually responsible for the world that we create, and our choices in life should be based on our own integrity and not forced by a law designed to fit all. She didn't hang out at the local Anarchist Club however, because most of the Anarchists she knew were angry activists and Esmeralda didn't believe that banging one's head against a brick wall helped to do anything other than to acknowledge the existence of the brick wall. Instead, Esmeralda focused her energies on imagining the wall away. This was where her work with The Fool came in. The Fool can see no walls and gaily skips through boundaries, tickling under the chins of the elite, making merry with the ostracised, and dancing with his trousers down upon the seat of power. She believed that the government would continue to become increasingly irrelevant and powerless over time, that capitalism would eat itself, and that millions of years from now, it will all just have been a bunch of stuff that happened.

To write a book one must pick one's way along a series of threads, like a musical score. Some people can write symphonies and some people are only capable of nursery rhymes. Both are worth creating though. The world would be a humdrum place if it was only littered with great cacophonies and there were no simple ditties to sing children to sleep with or to hum to oneself when in a good mood. Born out of dance culture, Esmeralda found that her own writing was probably more akin to the musical score of Gabba.

The morning was beautiful and misty. It had been a rubbish summer and it had also been a turbulent time for Esmeralda. She knew this winter was going to get her good and proper on the S.A.D. scale. Nonetheless she was looking forward to hibernation and stillness.

Esmeralda sat in the theatre surrounded by strait-laced folk. The saying 'strait-laced' comes from the days when women wore bodices. Crossed-lacing was much easier to undo than strait-lacing, which was, by definition, very narrow (the clue was in the word) and difficult to unpick, so women who wore their bodices cross-laced were presumed to be loose. Well-behaved women kept their lacing firmly straight. Esmeralda hated strait-laced women.

'Could you help spray me?' Esmeralda asked the lesbian roadie.

'What? And make my day?' She replied.

Esmeralda was naked, except for a pink glittery thong. Using purple hairspray, the lesbian coated Esmeralda's skin in a thin layer of purple paint.

'You might want to bend over so I can spray between your legs,' commanded the lesbian, much to the merriment of them both. "Spread your bum cheeks."

Once it was covered in purple paint, they applied sliver slashes across Esmeralda's body and sprayed her face silver. Then, after a few applications of silver glitter, Esmeralda was ready to perform.

I do not like change,
I do not like change,
I always walk this way,
I do not like change. - Prinzhorn Dance School

'Do you ever get scared that you've made the wrong decisions?' asked her sixteen-year-old best mate.

'All the time,' answered Esmeralda.

They were on the train on their way to the theatre. Esmeralda was taking her friend to see a physical theatre production called *Fuerzabruta* at the newly re-opened Roundhouse Theatre. It was the young lassie's first night out in London.

'But, you know, all you can really do is get on with what you enjoy and what you're good at. Hopefully, at some point, someone will recognise that what you are doing is good, but you can't just live for that or it will drive you mad.'

'I'm scared,' her friend admitted, flicking the ring pull on her can of Stella. 'It's so hard choosing what to do at college.'

'Whatever you do is whatever you do,' sighed Esmeralda 'there's no right or wrong unfortunately. Or fortunately... Depends on how you look at it.'

She really enjoyed how wearing a nun's habit made her feel. Esmeralda fancied the idea of being a nun. The feeling of her being absolved of sin and people treating her like she was pure again. It was a type of respect that Esmeralda had not experienced in a long time. She was respected, but not for her purity. And she respected herself. But not for her purity.

"I'm a virgin... Every time."

Actually that wasn't quite true. There was a part of Esmeralda that was still pure and it was her inner beauty; that bit of her of which there is no whicher. The thing that you see in babies, before the world has left any impression upon them, a pure personality without doubts or fears or any comprehension of what the word 'career' means. To parent a baby is to live as a buffer zone around the seedling, allowing it the space to breathe and grow, until it is strong enough to face the world on its own. It is the parent's responsibility, and the responsibility of oneself, to allow that pure seed of personality to express itself as fully and celebratory as can possibly be achieved amongst the great noisy forest of the world. And Esmeralda had done a very good job of keeping the essence of her seed unimpeded, thanks very much to her incredible parents, and thanks also to her own courage to express the unique bolt of life which she had been blessed with at birth, allowing it to course through her life and influence its way up from her twisted roots, up through to the wrinkling bark of the little old tree she was becoming. That was the purity she felt had remained. There was still a clear pure uninterrupted line connecting her back to the main frame of life.

The great hulk of a building fulfilled on all the criteria befalling a prison; dark, grey, ugly, and uninviting. It looked like a movie set, it fitted the stereotype so perfectly. Her friend had lost weight, but was still in his usual marvellous spirits. But there was a slight whitewash over his vibrancy. She truly hoped they wouldn't keep him there for long.

'I miss... the girls. I miss the girls.'

Esmeralda ran a hot bath and lit a joss stick to cover the stench of the vile roll-ups she had been smoking all night. Esmeralda was, and always would be, a smoker. But she had not smoked for longer than she had smoked over the last ten years, so that was all right. Her body was black and blue with bruises. She had been learning to do free running with some of the original French guys who had come up with Parkall. But she had been rubbish at it. There was no real excuse for how rubbish she had been. She had better coordination than over half of the others in the group and in many ways she was a very physical person, but she had screwed up each time because she thought before she acted, mainly because she was afraid of not being able to do it and looking bad. Her ego had got in the way. It always got in the way.

The absolution of ego... The holy grail of my world, she thought. *And just as mythical...*

The bed was amazingly comfortable. It had been one of the most mammoth sleeps Esmeralda had indulged in for a long time. 9.30am, what a treat. It was a grey pale day. The world had been bleached. Luckily it suited Wales, especially the grey stonework of the tiny village they had escaped to, out in the middle of nowhere. The troupe had vacated to a hideaway in the countryside to pen plays. But the lure of fine ales, the joy of singing fine folk songs, and the job of cooking fine foods, meant that the odds were firmly stacked against them achieving anything literary. Nonetheless, they had blocked the outline of seven plays over breakfast, one for each of the Seven Deadly Sins. And now the call of rolling hills and ferocious seas was leading them to adventures unknown. With guitar in hand and a watchful eye for magic mushrooms, they departed the cottage, leaving a stew slowly cooking on the great warm Aga.

As they reached the top of the mountain Esmeralda decided to cast her runes in the hope that they might guide her in the right direction of the medicine plants. She took out a bundle of stones and threw them onto a flat boulder. The answer made no sense at all.

'Sorry guys,' Esmeralda announced 'I can't get any signal up here.'

Brotherhood is life
Lack of brotherhood is death
In hell there is no brotherhood
Only the cry of every man for himself - John Ball

'You're an incredible woman. The question is… do *you* think you are?' he asked her.

'Good old ancestors,' said Esmeralda as she popped more slimy fungi into the carrier bag.

They had eventually found some of the little fellas. A small splattering of Liberty Caps grew through the thick spongy grass all around an ancient burial site. They'd probably grown up out of the very belly of the ancestors. They harvested enough to send them all silly then went back to the cottage, gobbled them all down, and penned a pile of songs and plays.

The sound emitting from Esmeralda's brother sounded like a whale giving birth and it went on for eternity. Everyone froze as they tried to figure out what he had done? By the way he was clutching himself it appeared that he had ripped the flesh off his back on the barbed wire fence they had all just jumped over. When it was finally revealed that he had only sprained his ankle Esmeralda's reaction was typically elder sibling... 'For God's sake.' she shouted, 'I thought you'd actually hurt yourself.'

He had though. Their dad and step-mum had to come to their rescue. It was rather embarrassing. Out of five grown adults only one of them could drive, and he'd just done his ankle in, so their poor parents had been called out all the way from Essex to drive them back from Wales. Esmeralda felt pathetic.

'If you told me this morning I'd be in watching a Russian choir in a church in Wales, I'd have thought you were mad,' announced her dad.

'I've written a film for you...' Her special friend, who was a film director, had got in touch with her.

She loved the attention.

He had decided the first time he met her that he was never going to sleep with her and had told her so a few minutes into the encounter. This decision of his had always kept her on the back foot, so to speak. It's not that she wanted to sleep with him, he reminded her a bit too much of her dad, but the fact that he had taken away her choice in the matter had never ceased to grate with her. He kept waltzing in and out of her life and whenever he did show up she was guaranteed an adventure. He had got her to drink ayahuasca, got her into squatting, got her to move to Berlin, gently nodded his head in the direction of S&M and now he had written a film for her.

'Do you want to see my attic?'

Esmeralda's day had been full of highly successful meetings. The first meeting had been with an old friend who wanted to work with Esmeralda as an actress on a film he had written especially for her. It was going to be a tool for getting producers on side to fund a feature film he wanted to make next year. He also wanted it to help launch

Esmeralda's career as a film actress, which was very nice of him, in Esmeralda's opinion. The next gentleman she called upon was interested in working with Esmeralda as an artistic director on erotic fetish films. He had an amazing attic filled with chains and whips, hanging from heavy wooden beams, against the raw brickwork of the walls. Esmeralda could see it really working. She wondered how often he thought about tying her up and whipping her? She knew that he knew she was a sub. And she knew that he knew that she knew he was a Dom.

Esmeralda started keeping the cotton wool she used to wipe off her make-up at the end of a night out. She only removed her make-up before bed if she had failed to get laid. It had always seemed to her a very sad and lonely act. So she thought she'd make a piece of artwork out of it called *All dressed up with nowhere to go*. Might as well get something out of it hey? So far she had one green glittery lump entitled *Halloween 31/10/07* and a deep red one entitled *Pelirocco Hotel 1/11/07*. It hadn't been a good week for getting laid.

The cherry on the cake was that she now sat on a train winding her way across the countryside to oversee a weekend workshop she had produced for her Fool. The workshop was in the middle of nowhere and just down the road from where her ex-lover lived. Apparently his new girlfriend was down visiting for the weekend though. This would be the first time they'd hung out properly since splitting up. *Brilliant,* thought Esmeralda. She didn't want to be with him at all. But she did want someone to love her now. She'd had enough of being on her own.

'Why doesn't anyone love me?' she asked the stars.

I wish you'd hold my hand, when I was upset,
I wish you'd never forget, the look on my face, when we first met.
And basically...
I wish that you loved me.
I wish that you needed me.
I wish you knew that when I said two sugars
That actually I meant three. - Kate Nash

Never Worn

PANTO SEASON

It was all right in the end. The girlfriend wasn't there. It was 100% the right thing that they weren't together anymore and that he had a girlfriend his own age and was doing all the things a guy of nineteen should be doing, but it was just nice for both of them to know that they still loved each other to death and that they thought the other one was awesome. That was all she needed from him nowadays. That was enough.

No one around the table listened to a word the other one was saying. It was just one big competition to see who could talk the loudest.

Most of Esmeralda's friends were like that.

She found one of the fools asleep on the floor in the bathroom.

Esmeralda woke up to the intrusive alarm of a mobile phone. She was in bed with her ex-lover's sister. Nothing dodgy had happened; it was just where she had slept. The sister woke up too and put the alarm on snooze, then they both went back to sleep. The evening before had consisted of pink cava, larger, and the ever-effective king of all spirits… Tequila. And, as always, the effects were still in full force the morning after. Esmeralda's head was pounding. The alarm went off again and they both moaned in unison. It was early, and they had things they had to get up to do. The sister was off to baby sit and Esmeralda had a tour to run for her Fool.

'We like doing it on the hoof,' her Fool announced at the start of the proceedings.

Tranquilly seated at the dining table, surrounded on all sides by walls covered in fairy lights and sarongs, Esmeralda waited for the workshop to draw to an end. She was tired. It was time for a bit of a detox she reckoned, before she made herself ill again. Esmeralda wasn't very good at taking things easy. Even though life was one long languid river of pleasure, she somehow still managed to make it seem pretty stressful. All the individual components were fun and full of freedom, it was just the sheer number of components that wore her out. Esmeralda was not the kind of girl who found it easy to say 'no'. But the day had been kind. She had walked through the fields of Norfolk with her boss's partner and their beautiful little boy, who was only just over a year old but already a fully-fledged bundle of personality. Esmeralda was head-over-heels in love with the little fella. She'd managed to sneak in a morning nap and spent the rest of the day eating delicious vegan food. Where the stress was in all that is beyond me, but it had taken it out of Esmeralda for some reason. Light weight.

The postcard on the fridge read: *I want to be what I was when I wanted to be what I am now.*

Harry the dog was scared of the fireworks.

The house was full of life affirming messages, political warnings, and lumps of crystals. The shocks of bright green in her auburn hair made her look like a witch, but she was the whitest of witches. Nothing in her life damaged a single hair on the head of anyone or anything in the whole wide world. Her every touch was blessed with kindness and generosity, wishing good fortune on everyone's street.

Her boss's partner practiced playing her banjo on the sofa whilst Esmeralda sat at the table writing on her laptop.

'I think I need to detox before Christmas,' she announced absentmindedly.

Walking with her was very nourishing. She had a completely different tempo to Esmeralda, but they were similar creatures in many ways. They were both pretty feral at heart. Talking with her had the same settling effects on Esmeralda as she experienced from talking with her Mother, or with her best friend.

'I'm pissed off, fucked off, sad, and lonely. But it's alright. It's just where I'm at, at the moment.'

Esmeralda rushed home so that she had time to dress up as Grace Kelly before going to meet her Film Director. He wanted her to be elegant and glamorous. She gave herself smouldering eyes, gold lip-gloss, a gold bangle, and hung pearls around her neck, over a flattering black sweater. She pulled on some natural stockings, wriggled into a black pencil skirt, and slipped on some black and white polka dot stilettos. Although Esmeralda loved dressing in glamorous clothing she still felt like a young girl putting on her mother's clothes. She had a natural theatrical flair that gave her a certain style, but she couldn't quite pull off that effortless elegance which delicate, well-bred women found natural. Click-clacking up the steps to the Directors house, she found a renewed confidence as the taxi driver who had dropped her off told her that she looked like the kind of woman who was driven everywhere, which was true after all, because she had never got her licence. But the confidence slowly ebbed away as she saw the amusement bobbing around on the Director's face as he watched her trying to be lady like.

'I want you to try slowing everything down,' he told her, 'talk slowly, but don't try and sound posh. I want your real accent but I want you to slow down. Your natural speed is too fast for the camera.'

It always came back to this for Esmeralda. Slow down. Talk less. Be serious. It made her feel like she was falling apart at the seams. If she slowed down then people would notice the cracks. But of course, that is exactly what the camera wants to see.

'I didn't manage to write down much of what you said,' the Director apologised at the end of the improvisation, 'You were talking too quickly.'

'What, you even have secrets from me?' he asked her incredulously.

'Yes,' said Esmeralda with certainty, though she couldn't actually think of anything that she had never told him, but she had a hunch it would be a good thing to pretend.

'I like that,' he replied, 'It means there is more to you then I already think there is.'

Esmeralda went to post her Christmas cards but found to her dismay that the city's main post office had been closed down, right before Christmas, and the nearest one was now to be found at the other end of town. Not only was this hugely inconvenient, but it also meant that she would have to start frequenting the Babylon that is otherwise known as Churchill Square Shopping Centre. This place was hell on earth. She didn't have the slightest inclination to go there ever, so she decided to wait until she got back to Essex to post her cards.

You're Late, texted Esmeralda to the Erotica Director.

She knew it would wind him up, seeing as he was used to playing the role of Master. It certainly flustered him and on arrival at the bar he commented on how he wasn't sure what to do with that. The model arrived soon after and they went about the ceremony of putting her at ease, passionately but nonchalantly describing their artistic vision. She was a lovely person, bubbly and open, so within no time at all they were all heading back to his place to introduce her to the attic/dungeon. It soon became apparent to Esmeralda that her role as Artistic Director seemed to have been forgotten about as it became clear which side of the camera she was expected to be on. Faced with the choice, she went with it. It excited her, playing out a fantasy scenario that didn't include sex, but was all about sex. The model was attractive. They got on really well and it seemed like work. Fun, sexy, work.

And no one else knew about it.

'Hanging out with you I can see how the witch burnings got started.' he declared.

Esmeralda's heart felt as if it was turning inside out, just from slowing down her tempo.

My first kiss was with my next-door neighbour. I was eight years old. It felt mechanical and it tasted of slimy bad breath. The oddest detail I remember about it was that he told me to flick my tongue left and right rapidly.

They went and watched *Knots* by Cois Ceim at the theatre. It was amazing. There were but two moments in the whole hour and a half show where their frantic furious dance moves went slightly out of time. Esmeralda wanted to be that fit and agile.

'Those were the days my friend, we thought they'd never end. We'd sing and dance forever and a day. We'd live the life we choose, we'd fight and never lose, for we were young and sure to have our way.' - Mary Hopkin

'I'm allergic to hippies,' said her brother 'They bring me out in dreads. I had them when I lived in Brighton, but they've cleared up since I moved to London.'

'I don't think I'll ever understand men,' she mused to her friend.

Tell me, she texted him, *exactly which part of the no-strings-attached-filthy-sex-on-tap was it that you have a problem with?*

The rope was long, white, and made of satin. An umbilical cord. Sometimes the window, now the coffin, it weaves its magic across the dance floor. Four creatures entwined in its hypnotic snares. The creatures are women, are generations. Blood relations. The faint smell of the father, where only smells and old clothes linger. We will have our day. Behind every great woman is a man who tried to stop her. Or is that unfair? Patterns, habits, karma. Spinning owls. Cakes. A mother who chops off toes. Here comes your mother to put you to bed. Let's hope she doesn't chop off your head. We are not dead, just stuck. And alone. Jewels. And yet it makes us feel safe. Knowing everything and choosing to forget, who we are and what is expected of us. Ashes.

The *Cinderella* improvisation they were working on was coming along well.

'Mankind has always created this idea of someone watching us all the time, making sure we are behaving ourselves. There has always been a Big Brother. It just used to be God.'

Esmeralda clutched, arms outstretched, the rusty iron hoops that hung from the attic ceiling. Her full-length black leather gloves and wrist restraints creaked against the metal that bound her. With legs outstretched in thigh-high PVC boots the weight of her body kept swinging her back and forth on the axis of her six-inch heels. A whip was selected; a cat-o'-nine-tails and the loose tendrils began to rotate against the bare flesh of her back and buttocks.

Thwack. The whip cracked against her thighs and her knees collapsed. *Thwack.* Gasping at the air like a dying fish. *Thwack.* A bead of sweat rolled down her forehead and into her eye. It watered. *Thwack.* Tears. *Thwack.* Tears. *Thwack.* Tears... Then the world becomes a blur.

Esmeralda was miserable. Her seasonal affective disorder had kicked in and she felt lonely and fed up. All she wanted was a cuddle; someone to love her and keep her warm in the long winter months. But there was no one, just a few insignificant fucks.

Esmeralda felt sorry for herself. She sat in the pub on her own and drank a gin and tonic. She wanted to cry. She wanted to go home for an early night, but she had tickets for a show. Sinking the drink she dragged her feet to the theatre and sat on her own in the bar waiting for it to begin. Some people she knew turned up, said a few words, then they entered the theatre together as if they'd all arrived as a group for a jolly night out. As Esmeralda took her seat she realised that she was sitting right in front of her recent ex-boyfriend's new girlfriend. Esmeralda didn't know if the new girlfriend knew who she was, but she spent the whole performance feeling like she was being watched. She found that she couldn't breathe.

The performance was incredible. *Quetzal* by Duruevo...

Six skinny shaved heads,
On naked bodies with tight skin, writhing.
Androgynous, childlike, tasting of mental illness.
Devoid of narrative...
Hell into madness.
Rituals of dying fish and sex origins.
The nightmare of childhood.
I keep feeling sick.
They flooded the dance floor,
Flung water all over where I sat in the front row.
Anonymous.
Yet feeling watched.

As Esmeralda left the theatre, the world became a film set. Couples walked past her feeding snippets of conversation about people she knew. Someone walked by discussing how the Erotica Director she knew had said she could 'do whatever she wanted'. Then a director she had once worked with sat outside a bar smoking. He said something about contraception. Esmeralda's head was swimming.

This town was becoming too small for her.

She crawled home.

Alone.

According to Alistair Darling the public are entitled to trust their government.

Doh, and there I was thinking the government was EXPECTED to be trustworthy.

The theatre company worked their way down the streets, working on counter directions, playing with the light and dark patches created by the street lighting, and playing with characters represented on the street in paintings and statues. The night before had been a mess, but tonight they were working as an ensemble, albeit at the last minute. Afterwards they went back to the theatre to discuss what parts of the experiment had worked and what they had discovered as performers. When they entered the room, they found that the shutters were closed and a circle of candles sat on the floor, glistening through several bottles of bubbling pink cava. Mightily cheered by such a presentation, the performers set about planting themselves around the circle and opening the bottles. Sitting in the dark, sipping their cava, they gave their feedback. Esmeralda had worked very hard during this series of workshops. Not only at developing her work as an artist, but also struggling with her feelings of not really being welcome there, as she had weaselled her way back onto the training programme after not initially being invited back. Seeing as the workshops were all about revealing oneself and stepping into the void, it had been made twice as hard for her, having this sense of being judged hanging over her. But she had pulled through and created some really superb work. Yet as they gave their feedback she sensed the response to what she said was being misinterpreted and misunderstood. Tears welled up in Esmeralda's eyes. Her defences were down and her emotions heightened, so she could do nothing to hide her tears but grit her teeth together hard and not blink, to stop the tears rolling down her cheeks. The darkness saved her. No one noticed, they were all too busy trying to shine to notice another part of someone else's flame having just been pissed on.

'I've got to hit the bottom before I can start coming back up again,' she revealed to her friend.

The darkness opens up before her, empty and meaningless. All she has to do is step into it. Something will happen. Something unimaginable will occur and she knows that whatever it is, it will be exciting. But she can't bring herself to do it. Not this time. She has stepped off a thousand times in her life, and it's always been incredible. But today she is scared. Esmeralda is terrified. She sinks down onto the precipice and cries into her arms, her sobs echoing into the nothingness, all alone with her fears. She wants her old courage back and the magic to return to her life.

Have you ever been in love? Horrible isn't it? It makes you so vulnerable. It opens your chest and it opens up your heart and it means that someone can get inside you and mess you up. You build up all these defences, you build up a whole suit of armour, so that nothing can hurt you, then one stupid person, no different from any other stupid person, wanders into your stupid life...You give them a piece of you. They didn't ask for it. They did something dumb one day, like smile at you, and then your life isn't your own anymore. Love takes hostages. It gets inside you. It eats you out and leaves you crying in the darkness, so a simple phrase like 'maybe we should just be friends' turns into a glass splinter working its way into your heart. It hurts. Not just in the imagination. Not just in the mind. It's a soul-hurt, a real gets-inside-you-and-rips-you-apart pain. I hate love. - Neil Gaiman

It was an icy cold, full-on, biting winter. The short film night was in a freezing dirty cellar bar, with low lighting, and walls covered in graffiti. It could have been a bar in Berlin, had there been candles on the tables, and if the bar had been full of people. As it was, only a handful turned up. Oh the joys of being an artist in England.

I really don't know why anyone bothers.

Esmeralda felt out of sorts. She wasn't sure what had set her off this time. Perhaps it was because she had necked three pills at the weekend and then drunk like a bastard until nine in the morning? That always screwed up her week; Moody Monday, Terrible Tuesday, followed by Weird Wednesday. She was certainly having a Weird Wednesday. It may have been the memory left over from the night before, being reunited with a lover who had disappeared without calling her for months, only to reappear, having briefly had a girlfriend in between. It wasn't the coming and going that had bothered Esmeralda, it was the fact he had told her didn't want a girlfriend. What he had really meant to say was 'I don't want *you* as a girlfriend'. Even that wasn't really the problem, as, although Esmeralda would probably go out with him if he pushed it, she could tell he was yet another 'project'. A man who had not yet given up his fight against the concept of commitment; whom she would train up until he was ready to commit and who she would then ship off, because too many wounds would have been administered during the whole process, into the arms of a lucky new girlfriend who he would then commit to properly, because finally he was ready to. She was sick to death of always being the second from last girlfriend. Surely it was her turn to be the permanent one? Speaking of which, her misery may have stemmed from when she suddenly found herself being shown 'how to do it properly' by her recent ex-boyfriend's new lady in a clown workshop earlier that day. It seemed as if this woman was better than Esmeralda at everything, even at clowning. Whatever it was that had set her off Esmeralda felt empty inside. As stone cold and empty as the bar they were hunched up in.

What cruel joke is this that has been played on man, that he should be given the courage to love and the folly to love again? - Shakespeare

Raising her arms above her head, Esmeralda slipped her pale hands into the rusty iron rings that hung on chains from the rafters. She faced a bare brick wall with a split chimney running up and out through the roof. She looked up at the shadows of the swinging chains, then down into the big brown eyes of her friend, the model. She heard him selecting his weapon and she could see in her friend's eyes that she was about to get a good thrashing. The wind cracked and Esmeralda's knees collapsed under a series of sharp pains across her back, wrapping around her tender sides. He had selected the cane. Even through the white shirt and school pinny, the leather-bound bamboo smarted. *Thwack.* He came down hard on the back of her legs, which were exposed between the bottom of her navy blue skirt and the tops of her knee high white socks. Esmeralda screamed out in pain.

'What do you say?'

'Thank you Master...'

'Look how red your bum is,' the model cooed

'Yeah, I bruise really easily,' replied Esmeralda.

'I always get jealous of girls whose bums go red,' explained her friend as they both inspected their bottoms in the mirror, 'it takes ages for mine to change colour.'

'I'm going to whip you until you cry.' The Master announced.

The young man came over to her place for the evening and Esmeralda instantly handed him a spliff. She had been smoking all evening and was completely spaced out, but he began nuzzling immediately, so she didn't have to struggle with small talk for long. She really enjoyed having sex with him. He had the right level of authoritative control, eager-beaverness, open exploration, and childlike fun. It was the kind of sex that used to trick her into wanting to go out with the man, back when she thought a chemical connection was enough to see you through. She had no idea what was enough to see her through anymore. She couldn't even remember what it was she was meant to be seeing.

'I really need a weekend with my mum.'

What if Esmeralda wasn't an actress, what would she be? Who is Esmeralda, without the actress? She is a strong woman, a fighter. She is up-tempo and her default setting is at happy. She is naughty and disobedient. She respects people who are brave and who have the courage to be real. She loves honesty. She loves being in the present. Which is why she likes being on the stage. She likes drama and good stories. She likes things to be colourful and ever-changing. She likes looking for the good in people. She enjoys learning and discovering. She likes pushing herself. It makes her happy when she finds her groove and in doing so feels invincible. She likes getting fucked, both mentally and physically, because she likes relinquishing control. She likes the fantasy of being a sex slave, but in real life she likes it more for the outfits. She likes dressing up and trying on other people's souls. She likes her own soul. Her soul is full of fire and earth. She likes being near the water. She likes horizons. Figuring out the messages hidden in the past is one of her favourite pastimes, along with listing all of her past lover's names. She loves falling in love. She loves the memories of romance and magical tender moments. She doesn't think about them enough though. She really enjoys all the people in her life and the differences they make in it and she likes knowing the differences that she makes in other people's lives. She likes making a difference in people's lives and she likes making a difference in the world. When she was young she said she was going to change the world, but I think she might have forgotten that. Now it's all about her trying to be an actress, or some sort of eccentric vaudeville caricature. Once, acting was a medium through which she intended to create change. Now it has become the goal rather than the tool. At the moment Esmeralda is stuck in a cycle of ego. Struggling between wanting to be something and a fear of being it. Until she accepts that everything just is and gets on with the matter in hand, which is changing the world, then this ridiculous navel-gazing will never cease. Acting isn't an aim for Esmeralda, it's just something she does, and is part of her make-up. But sometimes she tricks herself into believing that if she doesn't do it 'well' then she is nothing. But in doing so her work becomes nothing, because all the audience is watching is a big ball of fear and ego. She's been through this cycle a million times and will do so all of her life no doubt, but she is well and truly stuck in the middle of one of these cycles at the moment. Eventually Esmeralda will emerge on the other side, with some powerful choices and a fist full of points to prove, but until then we just have to sit back and wait whilst she chases her tail. Popcorn anyone?

'You are a fucking lunatic.'

Esmeralda was finding this particular 'Saturn returns' quite uncomfortable. She had just developed a deep wrinkle on one of the sides of her mouth. It only appeared when she was dehydrated, which was most of the time, but luckily it looked like a dimple. Esmeralda knew what it really was though. She was getting old. Old. And she wasn't even famous yet. And she didn't earn any money. And she was single, couldn't drive, was being chased by debt collectors, and had started working in the frigging sex industry. This really wasn't where she'd expected herself to be at age thirty. She could remember her parents turning thirty. She was nine years old. She could remember being freaked out by the idea that they were turning middle-aged and just how old she thought that was. Now here she was, having achieved very little in terms of material accumulation, or any real responsibility, since the time of her first thinking that. A bunch of qualifications, some wild stories to tell, and a graciously tolerant body was all that she had to show for it. And a bunch of performance and life skills that she's too scared to use half the time in case anyone might think that she's not very good at it.

I thought I might give Esmeralda a hard time today. I'm bored of her sulking. I have to write this shit down, and it's tedious.

'I wish I'd stop smoking,' moaned Esmeralda, rolling another cigarette.

'Yes but, I have slept with a *lot* of people.' Esmeralda admitted to her new friend.

'People?'

'Well, yes, I mean... men and women. All different ages, shapes, and sizes.'

'How many is a lot?'

'Erm... Less than a hundred... But definitely getting close to pension drawing age.'

'Well, there's not much you can do about that now is there?'

'Not really… No…'

10:52pm Nov 23rd
Hey you
11:51pm Nov 23rd
Hey trouble… So you're in NY?
12:32am Nov 27th
Is that all you going to say?
1:38am Nov 27th
Just came back from the gym.
Getting more and more comfortable in this place.
Getting married on Wednesday and am really anxious.

Found an acting guru here his name is john and his method of method acting is fucking altering all of my previous perceptions concerning acting and merging them into a wholesome one with the rest of my now ever more manifesting ideas about communication and authenticity.

Have you ever done method acting?
How about you?

Her Israeli was getting married.
Yippee.

10:46am Nov 27th

Yes, my school was based on method acting, mainly the ideas of Chekhov.

My best friend is training at David Mamet's school in New York. Mamet is an interesting chap. You should check out his book True and False: Heresy and Common Sense for the Actor. *It is completely different to anything I've read about theatre before. I don't agree with all of it but it is certainly refreshing.*

I certainly enjoy method acting in a self indulgent way, for example last year I played Mary Mooney in Once a Catholic *and I spent a year going to church on a Sunday and doing confession and even went to Rome to visit the Vatican. By the time I went on stage I knew the Angelus back to front and knew what the procedure was for becoming a nun. I think for this play it really helped as the traditions of Catholicism are very exact movements and recitals that enough people in the audience will know themselves for you as an actor to need to be doing exactly right. And it was fun spying into the world of Catholicism.*

But I like to cherry-pick between different styles of theatre. Today I have woken up happy for the first time in a very long time because I was training with an amazing company from Milan who are directing me in a show this weekend and are a physical theatre company. The work we were doing last night has wrung me out like a piece of material, so all of the bottled up angst and toxins stored up around my body have been released and I feel great. I find physical theatre puts me back in my body and gives me more definition, presence, and accuracy on the stage, but I need that because I'm a cerebral person and so it helps me to silence my inner dialogue. I don't find method acting helps with that at all, but it does make the experience of being an actor more fun as you get to have a nose into other people's worlds and I love doing that.

So how were you taught and what style of acting have you been using all these years?

I knew you were going to marry your lady for some reason, congratulations. I saw your photos of her on Facebook, she looks like a very beautiful person. You're obviously already happy but I wish you both many years of happiness.

I've had a tough and strange year. I'm feeling really low and have found myself in a completely different world to the one I was in a year ago. Creatively this has been brilliant. I've written a novel and a children's book and I'm getting loads of acting work. On the outside life is amazing. But inside I'm lonely. I just want a partner in crime now. But I know it will happen when it is meant to and at the moment I'm meant to be getting my life together after finishing school, which is what is happening and to great effect.

Good luck with the wedding. Don't be nervous, you're telling everyone in your life how much you love your woman. Brilliant.

3:18am Dec 10th
Hey honey,

You deserve so much love I can feel it building inside of me at the thought of you.

Hey I just finished reading David Mamet's book. Really fucking interesting and with a well timed recommendation.

What I study or in a way un-study currently is just to follow my impulses and judge nothing as irrelevant on stage very much like what David says.

So basically each session is intensely therapeutic and it has managed to completely alter my approach to acting it has become effortless and endless.

Just been cast for the part if Cassius in a local production of Othello. Started rehearsing last Friday and am really excited towards it.

Am fortunately very much in love as we seem to stretch our communication envelope further and further.

Tell me more.

12:03pm Dec 10th

I now feel more single than I have ever felt. After my last relationship I cast the spell that I would be single for two years and I met a man exactly two years later. It all seemed so perfect. But now I am single and for the first time in my life I don't have a plan. I hadn't manifested this. I don't want to be on my own anymore, but I have a feeling I will be for quite a while yet. It was a real blow and has taken the wind out of my sails, but I have grown from the whole experience. This year has been full of gold and once my heart settles and opens up again I will be drawing on this experience for many years to come. I now eat differently, dress differently, I am producing work at a rate of knots, and I fuck differently. I feel like I've become a woman in the last year. But it has brought with it a lot of pain and I still haven't worked my way through all of it yet. The light is at the end of the tunnel though.

I'm doing a lot of film acting at the moment and am finding it really hard as I'm feeling so self conscious that I can't relax in front of the camera. I've done some good film work in my time, but at the moment I feel like I'm falling apart at the seams and I can't bare invasive eyes watching me fall apart. But that is why I'm getting so much film work I guess, that is exactly what they want to see. A tortured soul trying to keep it together, with the excitement that maybe she won't. It's very uncomfortable, but it is helping me to work through all of these difficult feelings.

So how was your wedding? Did all your family and friends come over, or was it a quite affair? Tell me about it. And how is New York? I'm fascinated by the place...

3:37pm Dec 14th

The wedding was anti-climatic as it took about a minute and a half and we had another couple in front of us and another couple in line right after us.

So this was mostly paperwork wedding and the real thing is yet to come. We have very different real wedding plans. Something in the line of a week-long gathering in the desert, with a copious amount of drugs and live music, so we will see when we will be able to do the real thing.

Right now I am working hard. Just got a new bartending job where we make about 1200 dollars a week! So this will sooth our painful fiscal status in this great expensive metropolis and also I was cast for an off Broadway production of Othello that will be on next month. I am playing Cassius and am loving it. So good to relieve oneself from the need to be good and replace it with a want to be truthful. The director and I are really working well with each other so far and brainstorming a lot of crazy suggestions for the scenes. He is also the one who plays Iago and he is wonderful at it. New York is fucking great. Surprisingly for such a large city the people are really warm and friendly whereever you go. So unlike the cold, violent, and alienated London. Art of all sorts everywhere and a plenty. After a long and agonising couple of months here things are really working out and we are both settling in very comfortably here. You should definitely give this city a try at some point. Has so much to offer and it's relatively easy to get a chance and audition for numerous parts (just sign your resume on backstage web site)

What are you playing in?
What films?

6:14pm Dec 14th

I'm making a feature next year with a local director. I'm playing a cool hard bitch who never smiles but who is fighting on the side of the goodies. It's the lead. Will be a good experience and I'm happy to work in low profile stuff whilst I really get the hang of things. I'm still not fully in control of my face. Then two of my best friends are up-and-coming directors who are beginning to make a name for themselves and one of them has written a short for me because he knows how to push my buttons and wants a powerful performance out of me. It's great because I feel safe with him and can shine. The other friend was over today taking photos of me, learning how to play with light and allowing me to play with the camera. He's texting me now about it, apparently the shots are great. I just want to be in front of the camera as much as possible. I grew up on the stage, you can't get me off the damn thing if you let me near one, but the camera is not quite second nature yet. It's getting there though.

This Friday I'm performing in a burlesque cabaret. I will be sauntering around the place, scantily clad, dressed as a demon. Doing some naked fairy wrestling at some point I think. Then Saturday night I'm trawling the pubs with a band of players performing a traditional folk play with plenty of diddley-diddley music and ridiculous masks. Then in January I'm working on a piece of physical theatre loosely based on the story of Cinderella, *but more about female relationships. The performance emerges out of our interaction with a long piece of white rope, which kind of represents the umbilical cord.*

It's funny you talking about going to the desert to take drugs. I remember when you'd never even got drunk. How things have changed hey? But a celebration wedding would be good. It's what it's all about really isn't it?

I'm moving to London in the summer, but am already thinking of moving out of the country soon after. I might move back to Berlin, which is my spiritual home and unbelievable magic happens whenever I go over there. But I'm looking forward to going to New York next New Year to see what happens there as one of my best mates has moved there too and keeps telling me how much I would love it. I'm so excited for you. You're going to go far there, I know you are.

Tell me more, what do you think of the people? Friendly, annoying, accessible?

Esmeralda woke up happy for the first time in six months. Although her outside world was exciting at the moment and the focus was very much on her creative self, her inner world was in turmoil. She was miserable and lonely. But today she woke up happy. It's all about the small victories.

'So I'm hot. So what? I go out looking hot, and I find myself at the end of the night dragging my sorry arse back home, on my own, in painful shoes. It's called losing your mojo. But it's not really. I could have asked someone to come home with me. There were options. But I don't want to ask. I'm sick of asking. I want to be pursued. I want someone to come up to me with the raging horn and tell me that

I am everything they have ever been looking for in a woman, and I want to be able to turn to them and look them in the eye and like the projection they're seeing of me. To feel like they may actually have almost hit the nail on the head with whatever assumptions they have made about me. I can lean over and say 'I fancy you' any time, any place. But those days are over for me. I'm sick of instigating. I WANT TO BE WOOED....'

Create it.

Esmeralda had not been ebullient for a rather tedious amount of time.

'What has happened to your life force?' he asked her.

She didn't look at him. He was trying to make her cry and she just didn't have the energy. If she cried now then she would never stop.

'You know James Dean?' he persisted, 'You know how he has this presence? How your eyes are drawn to him when he is on the screen? Well you have that. You have that presence. But at the moment you aren't living into it. It's like you've settled for something. Something much less than what you are.'

'I'm being still,' sighed Esmeralda, dragging her hands over her tired face, 'it's time to be still. I'm packed up in ice for the winter. Spring is on its way, but right now I have nothing left in me to give. I'm hibernating, that's all.'

'As long as it is temporary,' he warned, 'You're so much more than this.'

She went and met her now seventeen-year-old best mate, who had wanted to introduce Esmeralda to her new girlfriend. Esmeralda was very excited.

I always knew you were a wrong'un. Esmeralda congratulated her little friend over a text.

Not that being a lesbian made you a wrong'un, but for her friend to have taken a stand so early in her life, standing up to the world and saying 'This is me. This is who I am,' was an impressive gesture. It takes most people years to muster up the confidence to do that. And by making a stand so early in her life, she now had many years ahead of her to figure out exactly what she wanted out of it all.

Her girlfriend was ace and a good few years older, which was perfect as she could teach her little friend a thing or two and it wasn't going to just be some teenage fling. They were proper lesbians. Walked around town holding hands and everything. In Essex, as well.

Good for you, thought Esmeralda.

'I don't believe in myself anymore. It sucks.' She moaned.

The town she grew up in was so ridiculously Essex. She was only home for a few days over Christmas, but a fight kicked off in the pub she was in every evening she went out. They were never too nasty, more a scuffle than a proper scrap, born out of boredom rather than hatred. It really made her laugh though. *This is what the rest of the country is like,* she reminded herself... *The world of alcohol rather than the world of drugs.*

'Aren't I the faithful one, the unswervingly loyal one, practical, honest, dutiful: the list of my supposed virtues reads like the 'Boy Scout Handbook'. So how have I come to be dressing in the woods after fornicating with a faun?'
- Cloven Hooves

It was the New Year, and Esmeralda didn't know what she wanted to do with it. She was out of inspiration. She thought that maybe she could do something really radical, like change her life completely. Esmeralda had been planning to move London, but it didn't really inspire her. She was tempted to move back to Berlin, but the language barrier would set her back. She had wanted to move to New York, but her true love had just got married and was living there. And she had always wanted to learn midwifery and to go to South America to learn about the medicine plants and how they do midwifery over there. But she couldn't speak a word of Spanish or Portuguese. Everything was a dead end.

For New Year Esmeralda decided to go on a little trip to Hell and back again

She wondered if she was having a nervous breakdown, and how one knows when one is. It seemed as if her life was falling apart at the seams. Esmeralda had gone through tough times before, when unforeseen incidents, out of her control, had occurred in the world around her and had made her miserable. But this was the first time she had fallen out with her loved ones.

Esmeralda had gone to bed on Christmas Day and wept into her pillow for most of the night and well into Boxing Day, after a ridiculous row with her brother had led to the worst atmosphere she had ever known in the house. It had been so horrible it had also affected their mother, who normally kept well out of their bickering. It had all been over a lost wire. The worst thing was that after things had settled, her brother and mother began talking again, but neither of them were talking to her. Esmeralda went to bed on Christmas Day completely alone. No one said good night to her.

And now here she was, back in Berlin, her spiritual home, which she had returned to with fifteen of her closest friends, who had all come to see in the New Year and to celebrate Esmeralda's birthday. And on the day that could have marked a new start for Esmeralda and an escape from her misery, she had fallen out with one of her best friends. They had been left alone together in the street on the way to a house party when her friend had turned to Esmeralda and told her that she thought it was good that she had been going through a miserable time as 'people' had been saying that Esmeralda had been getting too 'cocky' and no one likes a cocky person. She then also had a go at Esmeralda for not being there at her birthday the week before Christmas, which Esmeralda had missed because she had been performing in a show.

It was now the 4th of January and Esmeralda didn't want to be alive anymore. There was not a single drop of happiness left anywhere in her life. She didn't want to see anyone, she couldn't talk to anyone, she didn't want to do anything, and she didn't want to go anywhere. It was 1pm and she was lying face down on the bed in her apartment in the middle of her favourite city, which was also filled with loads of her favourite people, and every possible choice of what to do next felt like a cold concrete wall in her face. Esmeralda had never felt like this before.

She could understand that her friend was hurt. No one had gone to her birthday party and she had made it mean that no one liked her, and then she had arrived in Berlin with all these people who had travelled all this way to celebrate Esmeralda's birthday, and she was pissed off. It was understandable. But they wouldn't have gone all that way unless it was New Year's Eve, and Esmeralda wouldn't have had the audacity to ask them to go anywhere special just to celebrate her birthday. She only organised these kinds of trips away for her birthday because it took the pressure off of everyone else trying to find ways to have a better night than they normally do, just because it was New Year's Eve. It inevitably meant that the night ended up being crap because of the stress. But trips away made the evening a bit different and it being her birthday gave it all a slightly different focus. Took the pressure off. Sometimes she hated having her birthday on New Year's Eve. It made her feel out of control and forced to do things she didn't really want to do. She started every new year of her life with the worst hangover of the year.

And she had also agreed with her friend that she probably had been too cocky. But anyone who really knew her had known it was a façade, hadn't they? Had people really not understood her THAT much? She had been single for the first time in ten years, she'd slept with far too many men to make up for it, and was struggling her way through drama school, terrified that at some point someone would decide that she didn't actually have any talent... The bravado had been a smoke screen. One that had now cleared to reveal... Surprise, surprise... A person who didn't really like herself and who at the moment it felt that no one else liked either. She had been binned off by the man she was falling in love with because he had got to know her better and changed his mind about falling in love with her. She had left school six months ago and was one of the few in her year who didn't have an agent. She had lost her mojo. And now she was also finding herself completely alone, that even her friends and family didn't like her or understand her. Then to top it all off, all she could think about in her every waking moment was her own self-obsessed misery, and she was sick to death of herself. Esmeralda did not want to be Esmeralda anymore. She wanted to change her name, go somewhere else, and leave her whole stinking life behind. She was sick of all the stories that defined her as a person. She wanted to shed them like an old layer of skin. To re-invent herself and start all over again. It was the only thought that inspired her. But she had responsibilities. She couldn't just walk out on them.

She caught the *S-bahn*. It was a dream. She never waited more than 10 minutes for a train to arrive, and normally she only had to wait a couple. They ran all night. They didn't have many escalators, favouring stairs instead, which helped to keep everyone fit. When there were escalators they only moved when someone stepped onto them. The rest of the time they didn't move, because it saved on energy. There were no ticket barriers. You have to go out of your way to buy a ticket, and then even further out of your way to stamp and validate it, but everyone does it. The ticket inspectors are civilians who have volunteered to check tickets. There weren't many ticket inspectors about but everyone bought tickets, because they are cheap and the service is brilliant. There are hardly any adverts, instead the billboards are covered in artwork by local artists, and inside, the trains are bare, so your brain is not endlessly reading the same pointless fucking slogan over and over again. And most importantly there is no tannoy. Nothing tells you to 'Mind the Gap', 'You are now approaching Worthing', 'This train calls at...', 'You guard today is called Nigel', 'Please do not leave luggage unattended...', and the new one they've decided to inflict upon us over the festive period, presumably because some git somewhere has sued the train services for some stupid accident, 'Please walk slowly along the platform, as surfaces may be wet and slippery.' How many years have English passengers survived wet weather in train stations? Why do we now need to be protected from it? Do they have to shout the warning in our frigging ears... Again, and again, and again, and again? One of the main reasons why Esmeralda loved Berlin and found it an incredibly peaceful place to inhabit was because it's so quiet, even though it is a huge city. It isn't continuously blasting you with pointless noise like England is. Tannoys and sirens... *Do* piss off...

Esmeralda took a sunflower head with her into the forest. A thin layer of snow clung to the evergreen trees and lightly sheeted the forest floor. Cold enough for the lakes to be frozen over and hard enough to walk on, but warm enough for the forest to snugly encase Esmeralda with the light dripping of melted snow from the branches of dark leafless trees. Esmeralda felt happiness again. It was thawing through her heart as the snow thawed through the forest. Her depression had been beaten out of her. The holiday had been too long really. There were things she needed to be getting on with. Work to do and stuff to organise. But Berlin had gripped Esmeralda tightly, like a doting Mother, refusing to let go, until Esmeralda had finally stopped squirming and relinquished her misery into the city's arms, which had chewed it all up and spat it out like the greasy wrapper of a doner kebab. She wasn't going anywhere until she had turned that frown upside down and had turned her pain into something creative and beautiful. That's the Berlin way. Esmeralda bent down, clearing a patch in the snow, and dug into the frozen earth with her nails. It yielded easily under her scratching hands. It wanted her to enter it. In the little hole Esmeralda buried the flower head, full of seeds and promises for the new year. Stepping back, she breathed in deeply and smelt the scents of the forest… The sticky sap of the evergreen trees, the crunchy smell of the snow, and the smell of clean air. She hadn't smelt for a long time, her head had been jammed too firmly up her own arse for her to be able to smell anything other than her own shit. But her head was back out again and into the world. She was present. And her heart had found its voice once more. It was singing.

Esmeralda smiled and smelt the warm wet air as she climbed the ramps from the *S-bahn*, up towards the bright lights of Shoenfeld Airport. She could smell and feel again. It had been a good four months of feeling numb at best or, at worst, excruciating pain, confusion, and utter helplessness. She had almost disappeared completely but thankfully her quest to re-find herself had eventually turned out to be successful. She felt battered and bruised; Ill and worn flat. But she could feel. She could smell. She was present. And it felt like gold.

Touching down in the airport two weeks earlier Esmeralda had been in the thick of getting by through surviving. Surface conversations with her friends filled with the notion that they were going to 'get fucked' for New Year's Eve, but behind it all Esmeralda had been filled with foreboding. She knew the shit was about to hit the fan. She had been straining under her own weight ever since her emotions had begun to thaw in the run up to Christmas.

But good old Berlin had done it again. She bounced down the street, present to the feeling of happiness, for the first time in weeks. Why? Because she had gone and met with a friend and fellow artist with whom she had enjoyed a wonderfully uplifting conversation with about theatre, and about writing, and their plans for future collaborative work. As soon as she returned to her friends she suddenly found she had nothing to talk about, she was bored and depressed again almost instantly and it occurred to Esmeralda that it really was time for her to move on. She loved all of the gang so much. They were the best friends a girl could have, but she had nothing to offer them anymore. In her current role in her current life Esmeralda had been bled dry. It was absolutely time to move on to new pastures and new people. Then whenever she saw the gang again after that she would have plenty to talk about with them. As she left her favourite city and boarded the plane she knew what needed to be done and plans were afoot…

It was time to re-fill the well.

Esmeralda made her first decisions of the year. She was moving to London and she was going to learn German. That way she could also lead a double life in Berlin. Fantastic. Esmeralda felt alive again.

'It is amazing how much faster it is to find one's way out of the forest of depression than it was to find one's way in.'

Her friend, the Director, did not trust how fast she had sprung back.

'You're looking amazing,' he told her, 'but how can you feel better so quickly? Can I trust this? Are you not going to flip back to how you were before?'

'It will be a long time before I feel like that again,' replied Esmeralda, 'and it will be for completely different reasons. The events that sent me into the woods this time have been resolved. They won't affect me again.'

'How have they been resolved?' he asked her, searching her face for traces of misery.

'By just being with it all,' she replied, 'misery is like a huge, tangled-up piece of string that the more you mess with the tighter it gets. The only thing you can really do with misery is to sit it out. It's painful and uncomfortable, but you're only going to get yourself in a bigger mess if you refuse to leave it alone, like a spot or a cold sore. If you sit it out then eventually the whole mess will collapse in on itself and reveal the end of the string. It will show you the way out of the misery. It can take forever to find your way to the centre of your heartache. It can take years and years. But the second you find the middle, when you hit rock bottom so to speak, it takes merely moments to find your way back out of the mess again. Then once you're out, you're out.'

'It's crazy. You look completely different.'

'I *feel* different. I'm glad I went through it. I understand what my friend meant by the cockiness comment. I was bigging myself up the whole time, in a wild frenzy, sowing seeds left right and centre in a desperate attempt to make things happen. But it was all born out of not trusting myself, not believing in myself. People see it as being egotistical, but it is actually fear. I was so scared of not succeeding I spent my energy on trying to convince people that I was. So I came across as arrogant. But it was fear. Then I got knocked down so hard that I gave up the fear. It felt like I had lost anyway. And now I feel calm, like I have nothing left to prove. The seeds have been sown. I'm just going to sit back and see what pops up.'

He looked at her, flabbergasted. Only a few weeks before she had slumped around his flat in a crumpled mess, completely lacking in energy and uninspired by everything. But now she was glowing. Not too brightly, not in a burning the candle at both ends kind of a way, but in a calm and confident way. Glowing peacefully like steady embers in the hearth.

They rolled around his flat capturing gestures and expressions for each of the shots.

'You're giving me more than I was expecting,' he told her, 'this is really good stuff.'

'It's all in the thoughts,' she explained, 'we just have to find the right thought for the expression you want.'

They sat together in the snugness of his flat with the rain beating hard against the windows, writing down the train of thoughts like a script, trying out different sentences and discussing the different effects it had on the muscles in her face.

He smiled at her maternally.

'What?' she asked him.

'Nothing,' he replied, 'I just love watching you work.'

I told the camera guy and the producer today that you had nailed it. They were very excited. I'm proud of you.

'That wasn't the next day. I shall punish you when I see you.'

'I'm sorry, I temporarily lost my phone. How are you?'

'Great. I've finished editing the school girl video…'

'Have you?' she squealed, 'What's it like?'

'I want you to come over and see it. When are you free?'

'Next Tuesday?'

'That's perfect. Be at mine for eight.'

She had cancelled her subscription to desire. It had enslaved her for long enough. She imagined desire as Neil Gaiman had described it, personified as an androgynous creature, attractive to all, and residing in a great eye the size of a cathedral. The eye of the beholder. For the last year, desire had coursed through Esmeralda's veins, like fire, weighing up every man and woman, searching their eyes and the way they held themselves for the possibility of sexual gratification or even the possibility of love. She had felt like a wild animal with an insatiable appetite for blood. The fire having cooled, she had cancelled her subscription to her insatiable lust. There were no longer any lovers on the go. She no longer weighed up all the people she met. And she had stopped frittering away her thought-space on fantasies. When she caught herself fantasising, making secret circles in her seat, she imagined the creature in its eyeball and she thought to herself *No More*.

From now on, she was free from desire.

'Love belongs to desire. And desire is always cruel.'

- Sandman

She finally settled on her resolution for the new year. There was only one this year, and it was that she would train herself to use the words 'I' and 'Me' a lot less.

The funny thing was that there was no way for her to be able to tell anyone her resolution without using those words, so the resolution had to also be a secret.

Esmeralda checked into the Stan Laurel Inn. She had just been to see her boss, The Fool, perform in the tiny Cumbrian town of Broughton-in-Furness, and it had been excellent. There had been fifteen locals in the audience, all in their autumnal years, and he had blown their *status quo* out of the water. He had got in amongst the equilibrium of their community and given it all a bit of a wiggle, just to see what happened. Just because... Why not? They loved it and it was brilliant. They were really excited about the idea of The Fool returning next year and causing more trouble in their lives. It was moments like this that made Esmeralda so proud to be involved in his work. It really does touch people's lives and open their minds to the infinite possibilities of the moment. After the show, they headed back to Ulverston and dropped Esmeralda off opposite the Lantern House creation centre, the amazing residential space that the fools had set up camp in for the next ten days, training with The Fool in his technique. And she was staying at the Inn opposite the centre. Ulverston was the perfect setting for a creative week. The town was built with wet grey stone and held together by mud flats and moss. Esmeralda loved it. And it was the first time Esmeralda had ever checked into a room on her own. She unpacked her bag, turning her room into a little nest, placing her Sandman comics, diary, and asthma inhaler on the bed side table. Then clothes in the wardrobe, toiletries in the bathroom. She sliced up a piece of lemon and made herself a hot drink, swallowed a clove of raw garlic, and curled up in bed with the TV remote control. The most amazing programme was on telly called *Virgin School*, where a guy was learning to get over his fears concerning sex by getting him to train with sex therapists until he had been coaxed into the headspace where he felt comfortable with the idea of losing his virginity. Esmeralda mildly toyed with the idea of becoming a sex therapist, but she batted the thought away. It was only desire trying to stick her claws in again. Esmeralda liked being in a room on her own in the pouring rain, in an inn hidden far away in the middle of nowhere, deep in the darkness of Cumbria. She felt safely on her own.

'They require an audience with you...' came his answer, with a twinge of sarcasm.

Esmeralda had travelled to Cumbria to spend time with the fools. She had sensed that they had sensed that things had broken down a little bit on the admin side of the fence. The way they were running things had shifted, owing to unforeseen events and this had ruffled things up a wee bit. The fools were panicking because they could feel that everything had gone a bit out of control. Walking through the rain-drenched night, Esmeralda calmly marched towards her reckoning. The fools were stressed and unhappy and she could tell she was set to get an ear-bashing for the breakdown in the administration. But, as is ever the way, the mountain became a molehill the second they all got into communication with each other. The meeting had felt like it was all set to be a general attack, but soon enough people were talking about solutions and, when she finally left to head back to the Stan Laurel Inn, the air hung lightly with a twinkle of inspiration.

'When your integrity is out, get in communication.'

'Your hand is shaking.'

Esmeralda sat on the edge of her bed and wept. She was so tired and felt unappreciated. She had returned after spending weeks away from home and her own bed, working hard for no money, to find that her Housing Benefit had been suspended because she hadn't returned an evaluation form, because they had sent it to her just before Christmas, after she'd already left. It meant all the cheques she had sent last week to pay bills would bounce. Just this tiny little hiccup, one that would be resolved in a mere nine days, completely destroyed what little self-control she had. The amount that she was putting out into the world was not being reciprocated. It was all out of balance. She desperately needed some acknowledgment. Some

TLC. She needed a hug, goddamn it. There was no food in her fridge, no man in her bed, no money in her bank. Mascara-laden tears fell and stained her favourite cream trousers, She felt like she was falling. Saying goodbye to the world she thought she knew. She had been powerful once, and the universe had been almost tangible with possibilities. But her magic had left her. No longer feeling like the architect of her world, all she could do was stand by and watch as it dissolved before her. Everything she believed in, melting into a puddle of self-pity.

Esmeralda wept harder than she had wept in years. She begged the universe for some magic. Just something, anything, just to keep her going. But this made her cry even harder.

'I don't deserve your pity,' she wailed, doubling over in pain as the sun set over the Brighton rooftops outside of her kitchen window, 'I'm so lucky. I'm so fucking lucky.'

She was lucky. Esmeralda led a blessed life and was a beautiful and intelligent woman. But despair doesn't deal in details. She deals out her attention without bias.

Esmeralda had slipped out of her slavery to desire and slipped into the slavery of desire's twin sister, despair. She knew her new mistress watched her through the mirror at the foot of her bed, as she rolled around in agony with internal pain. It made her feel a little less lonely.

One always thinks great poetry and art often comes from misery, but really, when you're in the thick of it, it actually is very dull. It's a scratched record that wears one down to madness. There is nothing interesting about misery other than the shared human experience of it. We've all felt it. We all spend our lives trying to create structures that will protect us from it, and all of us will get shot in the foot by it from time to time and when we are least expecting it.

A bit like love.

She felt a bit better after a really good cry.

The prison was much more pleasant than the last one. There was a community centre feel to it, with a focus that seemed more directed towards rehabilitating than punishing. It was a prison filled with drug offenders. Four of Esmeralda's friends had been in prison for drug offences, and she had been to visit three of them. One of them had been a bit of a toe-rag, the sort that you'd expect to get in trouble for something, but the rest were really lovely guys minding their own business. Yes they had been dealing, but they only dealt to their friends, pottering along in a social group who had all forgotten it was illegal to monkey around on drugs. Who had forgotten that there were sometimes consequences. They forgot because initially it seemed a ridiculous concept anyway. Every one of them had done millions of things they deeply regretted whilst on booze, but hardly any of them had fucked up on drugs. Most drug dealers could be heralded as purveyors of party time, not banged up longer than low-life thieves who take from people who've worked their arses off. How can you possibly justify giving dealers longer than burglars? Or violent offenders? It is more ok in the eyes of the law to smash someone's face in then it is to provide you and your mates with a bunch of pills for Glastonbury festival, which is what one of Esmeralda's friends had got four years for. He'd been searched and caught in the festival. How shit was that? The law on drugs is an aging kind of madness that really needs looking at. The prison was full to the brim with cases of downright injustice.

When Adam dug and Eve span,
Who was then the Gentleman? – John Ball

GEORGIA

The huge great hare bounds heavily beside the roaring engines of the plane,

'A Mad March Hare in October,' my vibrant Mentor does exclaim.

'Compared against the other omens we have seen along the way.

It seems the gods are watching over us... And look. There's a bird of prey.'

Warm hearts welcome us the moment we touch down.

A flood of big brown eyes, into which we happily drown.

Driven to our apartments, loaded with cigarettes and booze.

Then songs upon the piano, just to get us in the mood.

The next day, in drunken haze, the magical story doth unfold,

One that is peppered heavily with pain, but is rich with hearts and souls.

We have dinner with a soldier, but now a hunter he's been left,

And on his hand you'll see no blood, only the tattoo of a double cleft.

We meet with Mother Georgia, who led the White Scarf Revolution,

Who helped bring an end to the war with a multitude of women.

A visit to the Opera House with its majestic chandelier,

The chorus children welcome us with a royal cheer.

We visit a disabled children's home, that's, thankfully, quite pleasant,

And a song from one disabled girl is the greatest thank-you present.

The dancing movement of deaf young people was truly magical to see,

As my Mentor led an inspiring workshop in sign language poetry.

Her bright orange flashing eyes and wild peroxide hair,

Always astounding those she meets with just how much she cares.

Stopping the cars at the sight of ribbons blowing in the breeze,

Making wishes as we tie our strips of cloth upon the trees.

The actors we watch rehearse and perform are like nothing I've ever seen,

They are so comfortable in their skin you surrender to their dream.

Language did not thwart the telling of their tale,

With movements and gestures so precise, the meaning could not fail.

Each day we eat a delicious feast with our new-found lifelong friends,

And a Tamada leading the way with toasts, so into drunkenness we descend.

But each toast tries to outdo the last with truer words never said,

And soon all around the table are in tears from the toasting of the dead.

We make our own toasts in the bathhouse, to the Arts Council and Tony Blair,

For getting us together, and then paying for our fare.

Another national obsession is the giving of meaningful presents.

Not the expensive variety, but priceless gestures of love and friendship.

I love giving and receiving presents with my gorgeous Georgians friends.

It always results in the pair of you declaring your love will never end.

LIGHTS, CAMERA, ACTION.

Esmeralda's days were spent going from meeting to meeting:

9am – Rise/shower/breakfast

10.30am – Leave house

11am – Meet Harlequin in a café and discuss creating a Guild of Fools

12.30pm – Marketing colleague joins them and they discuss branding the Guild

1.30pm – Go check out a possible space to turn into the Nomadic Academy of Fools for the Brighton Festival.

2pm – Back in a café making future plans with her marketing colleague

5pm – Go to a bar to meet scriptwriter to swap Esmeralda's novel for his new script, both agreeing to read the other's work and meet again soon to give feedback

8pm – Get on bus and go to a village outside of town to check out a new communal house her friends have recently moved into. It is beautiful and exactly the kind of set-up Esmeralda would love to move into in the near future

1am – Go to bed

8am – Rise/shower/pack

10am – Get on train to London

11am – Meeting with Producer at the Battersea Arts Centre

12.30pm – Chill in café, eat, and write

2pm – Meet Director friend with whom she will spend the next four days making a film…

…and so on.

Esmeralda was now in London for the next seven days. Four of these she would be making a film. One of them she would have to herself. One of them she would be going into a London school dressed as a Tudor woman. One of them she would spend visiting her friend in prison.

Esmeralda hadn't had time to do her laundry or clean her flat in over six weeks. She had spent two nights in her own bed in the last five weeks. Her life was a lot of fun and she loved her work, which is what she spent most of her time doing, but she was tired. She wondered how she could slow things down a bit. She thought that moving to London would probably help. It would result in a little less travelling.

'Action!'

Reaching her hand into the carrier bag full of bugs Esmeralda scooped up a handful of bright green grasshoppers and piled them into her mouth. Then she leant down towards the big reflective circle of silver and threw them up so they jumped out of her gaping mouth, but gently enough to allow a few of them to crawl up over her face. She hoped they had got the shot this time. Not because the bugs were bothering her, but because she was shivering from the cold. All she could think about was a hot bath and a good cup of tea.

Not that Esmeralda drank tea.

The guy coming at her with the Bedouin knife was really freaking her out. He was crazy-looking and his naked torso was covered in blood. She had suffered from nightmares of being stabbed for years.

But he was a very lovely man.

I saw your headshot on the Internet and would like to cast you for a short film I'm making. Can we meet for a cup of tea next week?

It was amazing how much work Esmeralda was getting, considering she wasn't applying to any casting calls and all she wanted to do was hide under her covers and weep all day.

'I think the reason why I'm going through all this pain at the moment is that it is a tool for forwarding my career,' she mused to her friend. 'All I can think about is how miserable I am, whilst my career seems to be getting on without me. I think if I was worrying about my career then I wouldn't be getting anywhere. It seems the trick is to not to go to auditions.'

'Stage acting is different to film acting. Film acting is all about you. The director will have chosen you because they can see in you the character they are imagining. You look and act like them. They want you to be you, doing the things the character does. Whereas with stage acting if you think the character you're playing is just like you then you aren't trying hard enough. I don't know which one I prefer really. Both are fun.'

Esmeralda arrived at the station at 5pm to discover that the train to Winchester was going to take four hours, rather than two, because it was a Sunday. She phoned her boss and checked that wasn't too late, and then got on a train to East Croydon, where she waited for her connecting train. And she waited. And she waited. Finally she realised she was going to miss her next connecting train, so she pressed the information button to find out what time she would arrive on the next train and it turned out that she wouldn't arrive until 10.30pm. So she got the train back to Brighton.

The Author had intended to avoid mentioning trains having badgered on about them quite a bit in her last book, aiming to point out how the 'shit hitting the fan' was currently explicit through the closure of post offices, but one just cannot ignore the ineptitude of the rail services or that the service you get represents so beautifully the decline of the country as a whole. As a writer, and therefore an observer, one cannot stand by and let the metaphor pass. It's just too good.

'Hello ladies and gentlemen, due to a technical difficulty, there are no toilets available on this train. I apologise for any inconvenience this may cause to your journey today.'

The teenager sat opposite typing texts into her phone with the key tones switched on. Esmeralda could see that everyone in the carriage was suffering from a case of teenage tinnitus, but no one had the guts to say anything, including Esmeralda. She used to. A couple of years ago she told a couple of teenagers at the back of a full bus to stop swearing. But people get killed for that kind of thing nowadays.

They had stopped doing direct trains to Winchester. She couldn't wait to move to London.

On the platform was a blind guy. He was young, a little overweight, with crazy curly hair, and a gentle disposition that stirred Esmeralda. There was something attractive about the idea of not being able to be seen, only listened to. A man that listened instead of looking. Wow, that really was an attractive idea.

Outside every young thin girl, is an old fat man trying to get in. - Katharine Whitehorn

In the sixteenth century, the law in the Isle of Man stipulated that, should 'any man take a woman by constraint, for force her against her will; if she be a maid or single woman, the deemster shall give her a rope, a sword, and a ring; and she shall have her choice either to hang him with rope, cut off his head with the sword, or marry him with the ring'. A report on how well the law operated said, every complaint has been lenient except one, who presented the rope; but relented on the prisoner being tucked up, and desired he might be let down. She then presented the ring; but the man replied that one punishment was enough for one crime: therefore he should keep the ring for some future occasion.
- The Amorous Antics of Old England

Moments of serendipity were beginning to creep back into Esmeralda's life, like the golden sun-rays that were also beginning to creep through the winter clouds. She had lost her phone three times in one week, before finally ridding herself of it all together, which led her to believe that her plans for a new start were being supported by the universe. She had sent out an email to all her friends asking them to send her their numbers again and she had put all of their replies in a folder until she had received her new phone from the insurance company. Once she had finally received it (after a couple of botched attempts on behalf of the insurance company) she sat down in front of her computer and began to enter all the details. To her horror, Esmeralda opened an email that revealed that the lover of her Mentor had died of lung cancer on the 2nd January. A world famous dancer, and the most hilarious eccentric, whom Esmeralda had greatly enjoyed getting drunk with around the campfire by his beloved gypsy wagon in the middle of the countryside on the outskirts of Brighton. Esmeralda had visited him with her Mentor and her own eccentric lover, a composer, and they had filled the night with the roar of their laughter, the two couples like a shadow of each other: Two fiery blondes with their two larger-than-life alcoholic lovers, overburdened by their own talent. All four of them dripping with something vibrant and magical. Something rarely found. Esmeralda felt a punch in her stomach as she read the email. Her Mentor had lost her man. He was cantankerous, in ill health, and pretty much impossible to live with, but he was always there, living in the forests at the sides of the mind, and the concept of him not being there any more made Esmeralda feel sick. She hurriedly wrote her Mentor a text, then immediately felt it had been inappropriate. Her Mentor was the sort of woman who gave out her energy all of the time and it felt almost impossible to give back to her, so Esmeralda desperately wanted to be there for her. But then the next morning she bumped into her in town, which never happened, and it provided Esmeralda with the perfect opportunity to give some time and energy to the amazing woman.

They went for coffee and her Mentor gave Esmeralda the full story of what had happened,

"I shall give you this while I get the coffees" she said, "It's his obituary, and it's..." she trails off, disappearing back up the illustrious path of his career, "…appropriate."

And appropriate it was, a whole page in the Guardian, listing his achievements, of which there were many. In fact there was hardly room for any sentimentality amongst the lists of prestigious achievements, which is exactly how he would have liked it.

Her Mentor returned with the coffees and Esmeralda settled back into her seat to be handed a series of photographs and to listen to the tale of his funeral, which was, of course, as rich and amazing as his life.

'He didn't want a "bloody limo with tinted windows" and insisted that Frank drove him there in the back of his van,' said her Mentor, handing Esmeralda a photo of a yellow transit, 'and that Frank didn't clear out his van, but leave it as it is. Frank's an artist, so his van was full of his paintings and equipment.'

Esmeralda was then passed another photo of the opened back of the transit. It is indeed filled with paintings and dustsheets. Sitting in the middle of the colourful mess was a cardboard box decorated with graffiti art. Esmeralda looked up at her Mentor quizzically.

'He insisted on the cardboard box,' she explained 'and his daughter decorated it. She's an artist too.'

Esmeralda chuckled.

'And here he is on Christmas Eve.'

He looked frail, but his mischievous grin was still splitting his face in two. There is this funny thing where you can see in babies what they will look like when they are old and you can look at someone on their deathbed and tell exactly what they looked like when they were a baby. Esmeralda had seen it in her Granddad, when he had died of cancer. She would never forget it. The flash of childlike innocence that lit up his face, when he came to and found Esmeralda standing by the side of his bed, with a grin that could have been from the face of a baby.

He had taken her hand and gripped it tightly before returning to sleep. It was a pure smile that flowed all the way back to his first ever smile.

'And this is what the sea looked like on the day that he died.'

Esmeralda looked at her Mentor. This was the reason why she loved her so. Because things like that mattered to her.

'There just isn't a duvet big enough to help you deal with life.'

'All that's important is what goes on up here,' said the coke dealer, tapping his finger on his head.

'Shut up.' shrieked Esmeralda, 'That's just a labyrinth of nonsense that's never gonna get any better. It's everything else...' she thought about it for a second, 'yea... *everything* else is more important then what goes on up there.'

He thought about it for a second '... I think you might be right actually.'

Esmeralda was in a council flat on the Isle of Dogs with her best mate, who she had fallen out with on New Year's Eve. They were cool again now, though, after hooking up at Esmeralda's ex-boyfriend's 30th birthday burlesque bash in a poncey bar in Shoreditch. It had been fancy dress and Esmeralda went dressed in a red curly haired wig, in a highway woman's red tricorn hat with white fluff trim, a red basque, black rah-rah skirt, stockings, and black satiny knee high boots. Her face was white, then rouged with red cheeks and red lips. She looked amazing, but it was all a little bit surreal finding herself dressed up this way now, as she presently sat in a flat full of inbred BNP supporters; whilst they scored from a dealer, in a bleak flat, in a bleak block of flats, on a bleak housing estate, on the Isle of Dogs. They were all coked up to their eyeballs. They'd brought a Bulgarian with them, who they'd bumped into at a Russian Disco, which they'd popped into on their way back to her mate's flat, located elsewhere on the Isle of Dogs estate. Esmeralda managed to navigate her friend, the Bulgarian, and a few of the inbred loons back to her mate's flat, after they'd picked up all the coke they needed. She'd genuinely been scared at the other flat, even though all the rednecks had loved her and her sexy costume.

The come down from the coke had put her on her arse again though, and, once back in Brighton, she'd gone for a drink with her chum to put her out of her misery. Whilst sinking a G&T he'd mentioned there was a new lad in town and that he'd been going on about how much he loved blonde sluts. They'd all said how he should meet Esmeralda. He'd responded 'Bring it on. I'll fuck her and marry her.'

This piqued Esmeralda's attention...

You don't know me, but last night your housemate was making promises that I want to find out if he intends to keep? Love the hot blonde chick he's going to 'marry' x

At pancake party last night he was proclaiming his love for a woman he's not yet met. Apparently I'm that woman and they told me to locate him...

Can I have his number so I can check out his intentions? Mine are filthy x

Ha. He better be. Afraid I've already paid my friends fees for pimping me out. If he likes the idea of getting tied up by a little blonde pervert, give him my number x

What's your name, stranger?

Hi. This is your new Husband. What have you been asking my housemate about?

Where shall we meet?

Can you send and receive photos?

I only just got up too... You look fucking sexy as hell x

Yes Ma'am, Monday it is then... Pity you're not about today though as I'm home alone till late afternoon and I'm standing bolt upright.

Yes. I'll be out of the shower in 20 minutes. I want the first place you touch me to be my cock. And don't say a word x

Esmeralda was in the mood for trouble. She took a long hot bath and shaved her body, buffed it, exfoliated and then covered it in yummy smelling moisturiser so she was silky smooth from head to toe. She donned a pair of silky sheer hold-ups, a pair of satin red knickers with a big black bow on the bum, a black slinky dress with big frilly eighties shoulders, a big white plastic bangle, and a pair of shimmery Lycra knee high boots. Her eyes were smoky black and lips rouged. Then out into the night she descended. First stop was to an older gentleman's house. He took photos of her as she swung around the pole in his living room wearing nothing but her pants and a T-shirt he had asked her to model that advertised his club night. Then he put a collar around her neck and made her jump around the living-room barking like a dog whilst he spanked her with leather clad gloves. She left the house with the T-shirt as a gift and went to another pub to meet another older gentleman to talk about some possible work, but whom she really knew fancied her and wanted to spend time with her. They went off to a party and pretended to be going out with each other. At the party was a load of first years from the course Esmeralda had been on the year before and she spent the evening chatting up the young lads, joking to them how she was going to fuck a fresher. They loved it. She didn't fancy any of them though. The next morning she got some texts from the guy she had never met before who her mate had met at a party and thought she'd adore, so she had tracked down his housemate's number and sent him a bunch of dirty texts. She initially tried to arrange to meet him at the weekend, but when he suggested she go around and spend the day fucking him that very morning, she decided she couldn't resist. It was a school day and she had loads of work to do, but the thought of throwing that all out the window for a day of filth fun was far too alluring. Chucking on the T-shirt she had been given the day before, some tracksuit bottoms, and trainers, she jumped on her bike and pegged it over to his place. He answered the door and she was greeted by a pretty faced, buff bodied, shaven-headed fella in just a pair of surfer shorts. He put his finger to his lips indicating not to speak, grabbed her hand and led her upstairs. He took off her clothes and she got down on her knees and started sucking his cock. Then he dragged her onto the bed and ate her out for an eternity before plunging his cock into her sopping wet pussy. Afterwards they lay about and got to know each other a little bit. He was a drug dealer. That's all. He took drugs and fucked. *Fair enough,* thought Esmeralda. She didn't give a fuck what he did with his life. After about half an hour he fucked her again. For longer this time, and at the edge of the bed. He really rammed it into her, just the way she loved it. Deep and hard and fast. After that they went downstairs and he cut up a load of wraps of MDMA ready for a guy who was coming over to pick up. They made plans to intimidate and weird out the fella, just because they agreed that dealers should weird their customers out. It was good for business, as it added to the experience of going to a dealer's house. When the guy arrived Esmeralda sat on the sofa looking just about decent in a dressing gown that stank of boy. She didn't say a word to the guy or even acknowledge his presence. The chap she had been fucking had put on some eyeliner, just for effect. He looked hot. He had very sexy eyes. After the guy had left another guy turned up, whom it turned out she knew. He had been the sound engineer for the piece of live art she had done the other day where she had been naked. He laughed that the dressing gown she was wearing was the most clothes he had ever seen her in. After he left, they fucked again. This time he licked her arsehole till she was screaming with pleasure then he fucked her hard and slow in the arse. After they finished they jumped in the shower and she put her clothes on and left. They said it was nice to meet each other and then he asked her how promptly she thought she'd be able to get to him if he texted her demanding sex.

'I'd get here as quickly as I can,' she replied, 'unless I really can't for some reason, then I'll apologise profusely and make it up to you some other time.'

'And what if you're in the middle of fucking someone who isn't as good as me. Will you ditch them and come to me?'

'Of course,' she confessed, 'seriously... I really would.'

Esmeralda left the young man and returned to her flat.

'Because you must remember I have a limited understanding of personal boundaries,' he said.

She had met up with her dear friend, the Film Director.

'You do have someone always with you' he said, 'And they're here...' he said, and placed his hand at the top of Esmeralda's belly, just under her heart. 'If you don't love that little you in there then no one else is going to. And you've got to love it, it's such a happy little thing.'

She felt a warmth come over her. There was so much she had forgotten. Stuff she had understood years ago, stuff she was even born understanding, but that she had presently forgotten. Love your silent you. It's very basic stuff.

They left the pub and walked out towards the seafront.

'My God, look at the stars,' he exclaimed, spinning around with his neck craned back, 'I bet you know all of these don't you?'

'Yes' answered Esmeralda, feeling rather smug and rural, 'Those three there, they're Orion's belt, and that strip of weaker stars coming down from it make up his sword. And those four marked out at the corners are his limbs, those are his arms, and those are his legs.' She stared around her, trying to catch hold of another nugget of factual information. 'There is the Big Dipper, and look, that cloud of stars there is the Milky Way. We are on one spiral arm at the edge of a galaxy. That there is the rest of the Milky Way. We're looking into the centre of our galaxy when we look into that cloud.'

'That's mental.' he exclaimed, 'doesn't it make you feel dizzy.'

'I know. It feels like your legs are only just clinging onto the surface of the Earth.'

'That is so beautiful. It's like being a child again. I live for stuff like this.'

'Me too.'

'It's perfect, almost scripted, that we should see stars after what we've just talked about, because that's exactly what I was trying to tell you. It's not that you're pretty, or sexy, or talented, or fun, or insightful, or clever or a good writer or any of that. That's all great, but it's not the real thing. The real thing is the beautiful infinite nameless little star child inside you. The life force of boundless pure love. And you don't have to do anything about it because it's already perfect. All you have to do is stop thinking about love enough to feel it. And the fact I couldn't say that right back there doesn't matter, because the stars say it perfectly.'

'Don't forget.'

'I won't.'

She didn't forget on the way home. She hung out with the stars and thought of how much she had enjoyed her time in Brighton. She reflected on all her favourite things about the place; the wind chiming sounds of the sail rigging that rang delicately against the masts of the small fishing boats along the seafront, the heavy smell of fish and chips at all hours of the day, the gangs of foreign teenagers who always spilled over the cycle path and got in your way, the sound of drag queens singing fabulously to an equally fabulous pop song in a bar with a rainbow flag flapping outside wildly in the wind. When she moved to Brighton, Esmeralda had walked the streets looking up at the buildings thinking to her: *There are all sorts of naughty things happening on the other side of these walls.* It was all so lurid and fascinating and she so wanted a piece of the action. And she had got it. With bells on. Then she had gone on to become one of the main instigators of it. She rode past George Street, with the infamous party house, all done out in original 70's decor, past the police station where her ex had feigned being mugged in an attempt to claim his mobile back on insurance, only to realise he had told them he was on the phone when it had been nicked and so had to ring his friend quickly to talk them into collaborating his story. She rode past the dodgy pub where her old housemate had kept their recording studio and made their last album, past the flats where her recent bastard ex-boyfriend had left her to fight off the attack of a bitchy-mouthed woman who was a total dick. Past the spot where they had all once gone to watch a particularly incredible sunset. Then up the hill she had climbed a thousand times. The hill her whole life had revolved around for the last seven years... Hanover. Muesli Mountain. She had lived on Bentham Road, Islingword Street, and now on Coleman Street. All a stone's throw away from each other. And at the bottom of the hill was her studio, on Grand Parade, next door to Hector's House Pub. It took no more than a twenty minute round trip on foot to visit all of them. 'Thighs of steel' her friend had said to her when they first moved up the ridiculously steep hill and Esmeralda had ventured to moan about it. It had certainly kept her fit. She'd notice the difference, not walking up it every day. The town, city, whatever you wanted to call it, was whitewashed with her memories. Most of them brilliant. Some of them quite dark.

As she rode past the various pubs and houses that people she knew had lived in over the years, she thought to herself, *I now know exactly what kind of lurid things go on beyond these walls*, and she laughed out loud to herself, and it rang brightly into the crisp darkness, and up into the stars.

When Esmeralda got home she logged onto her email and wrote him a message…

That was so perfect. And I love you so much. I love the beautiful star inside of you. I feel all tickly inside when you talk to me, because your star talks to my star, and you're one of the special people in my life who does that. Who reminds me about the silent me.

Thank you star child.

See you on the other side… xxx

He almost instantly replied…

I love you Esmeralda, I don't know why I never tell you face to face, maybe it scares me, but I do love you. Now I wish you were moving in with me.

No… I know you're better off in Brixton. See you on the other side…

Her adventure in Brighton was nearly complete. Just a few more weeks left before moving to the big smoke. Everything had been arranged and she couldn't wait…

SOUTHBANK

'The trouble is, if there is no one there to listen to you, then you start listening to yourself.' Moaned Esmeralda. 'I could have been a prophet if anyone would have listened.'

'You look so well' Esmeralda smiled at her dear friend, whose knee she was rubbing fervently.

She loved her friend. It was in a weird kind of future investment type way. It had been since they first met, as if it was clear that they would grow into each other, whereas at the moment their common grounds were like the different levels of ground in Sonic the Hedgehog, or some other platform game. Made from the same stuff, but floating in the air, separate from each other, not quite connecting, but with the distinct possibility that one-day they most certainly would.

Another friend had been similar. Everyone had told Esmeralda how she was just like this girl they knew and how much they'd get on when they met.

129

It got built up so much that when they finally did meet it was like being introduced to a long lost identical twin, which for an individualist is quite simply your worst nightmare, so they didn't really connect. They got on, and they 'respected' each other, but there was no love. No trust or enjoyment in each other's company. Quite simply, it had all been over-hyped. They lived together and everything, but no sparks flew. Then one day, after being abroad for ages, the lady in question rocks back onto the scene with a baby. She was the first equal of Esmeralda's to have a baby. Loads of her mates from back home had given birth before that, but they were on different songlines to Esmeralda. This was the first counterpart to give birth, and she had given birth to the most beautiful, inspiring, lock- up-your-sons, potty-mouthed, feral, force to be reckoned with, little girl the earth has ever seen. It blew Esmeralda out of the water. This child was the first baby that Esmeralda had ever held, and she fell asleep in her arms whilst Esmeralda was belly dancing around the living room, changing forever Esmeralda's view on maternity. And changing forever Esmeralda's view on the mother. Something clicked between the pair of them, and suddenly all the hype made sense.

Esmeralda was happy. For the first time in the best part of a year, Esmeralda was genuinely happy. She had two weeks left in Brighton and then she was moving to London. Everything was arranged. It was all sorted. All she had to do now was enjoy her remaining time with her gorgeous friends then pack up and leave. She was performing in a burlesque cabaret night the weekend before she left, which meant she'd be leaving with a bang, and would mean that she'd be heading to London feeling all toned and sexy. The quiet her was happy. The little dot of light in the centre of her chest was throbbing away merrily in a fluffy blanket of love. She loved herself once more. It was amazing for her to be feeling like this again. It had been awful being separated from her little soul, like having your demon sliced from you, it tears you down into the pit of your stomach. But they were together once more, lying in each other's arms, all warm, comfy and full of bliss.

She covered his cock in shit, but he was cool about it. It pissed her off that she couldn't work out when it would cover them in shit and when it wouldn't. She was certain there must be some technique. She suspected that maybe it was just lots of lube. Or compulsory enemas.

Esmeralda had met her A-man. He fucked her in the arse. That's what he did. And she fucking loved it. He wasn't boyfriend material. He was a 32-year-old drug dealer. All he did was fuck and take drugs. There was more to him than that though, obviously, or she wouldn't have been attracted to him.

Underneath all the bravado he was a charismatic guy and loving to his friends, even to Esmeralda most of the time, apart from the odd flash of being an arsehole that he dealt out to her occasionally as a reminder that this wasn't a love thing. Not that he had anything to worry about, he was far too inappropriate. But then he was in a funny old place. He had just been shafted by a wife who had spent half of their two year marriage having an affair, and now he was on the rampage against woman kind and was fucking everything that moved. But that suited Esmeralda down to the ground. All she wanted at the moment was to be rampaged. At the moment Esmeralda was only interested in filthy satisfying sex, and for her to be satisfied she needed someone with a whole lot of cock to give. She wasn't into the numbers game at the moment. He was obsessed with becoming a Centurion, and was already into the 80's. Esmeralda on the other hand just needed a constant supply of cock that she didn't have to make any effort for and that was dished out with style. And he defiantly knew how to dish it out. He had fucked her in the arse for five hours on Saturday night whilst on MDMA. It had been amazing. She hadn't covered him in shit this time, but she had bled a bit at first. It had stopped after a while though. She was a bit worried that she was internally damaged, but it had been worth it. He drove her crazy. Her A-man was up for anything and wanted to do everything. Most of it she had done already, but the one thing she hadn't done, that he was really into, was having group sex. It would really piss Esmeralda off if she got into another long term relationship without having had group sex, so this seemed like a perfect opportunity to get that one under her belt too. He was up for it. It was definitely going to happen…

I'm missing your cock now please…

Esmeralda sent A-Man a text that read *I fancy the fuck out of you.* When she next saw him he chastised her for sending, what he felt, was an inappropriate text, seen as they were only fuck buddies and nothing more. She told him to get over himself, she was only being flirty, and he was as far from boyfriend material as any man could possibly get.

Esmeralda spoke to her best friend on the phone for an hour. It was always great talking to her best friend. She was such a special woman. They were in completely different places in their lives at the moment, her friend was picking a village outside of Manchester, to move to with her lovely young man, with the intention to nest, marry, and have children; whereas Esmeralda was moving to London to try and further her career and social scene. But they still needed to be in each other's lives because they were both a standard for who the other one was in the world. They phoned each other up for reassurance.

They could always tell if the other was coming from the right place or not.

It occurred to Esmeralda that the people she knew who partied the hardest and took the most drugs were also some of the most successful people she knew. This meant that the people she knew who partied hard and took lots of drugs but also did nothing with their lives were just lazy. They could be doing everything they were currently doing *and* be successful. There really was no excuse.

Esmeralda called her A-man up onto the stage. She was dressed in a black and red basque, hooked up rah-rah skirt, and stockings in knee high boots. He was wearing eyeliner. She was also covered in a wedding veil and holding two suggestive black and red lilies. Then she dragged up his best friend, who was celebrating his birthday, and another old friend whom she had worked with for years in theatre. She pulled them onto the stage to test each of them out for becoming her future husband. First of all she snogged them all, then she rode them as ponies, then they all had to simulate sex with her. The theatre friend won. After the show they all bundled back to A-man's for a party, which ended up being completely rammed. Esmeralda spent the whole night trying to convince two of her best male friends to have a threesome with her. They weren't up for it, so she located her A-man and they began a 36 hour sex bender, dragging in anyone they could to get involved in the action. They started to have a threesome with a girl from Esmeralda's drama school, but she ended up projectile vomiting all over the room, so they got down and dirty on their own for a bit. As he was about to plunge into her arse he told her he wanted her to tell him she loved him. 'I do love you,' she gasped. And she did. The sex was so good and he was so rich in personality, it was kind of impossible not to fall in love with him. He gave her everything she wanted in her inner world. The outer world didn't fit at all though. But she was leaving town in a week. She could afford to let her heart run riot for seven days. And so as he plunged deep and hard into her tight arsehole, her tight and aching heart opened up like a flower to accommodate him. Then for the next 48 hours they were a tag team. Dragging people into their fold to fuck, or fuck in front of, like an unstoppable train. He pumped her full of drugs. 2CB's, mandy, weed, booze, then sex, sex, and more sex. He spent days wandering around in nothing but her black frilly burlesque knickers with eyeliner smudged all under his eyes and he looked so goddamn hot. They ended up having a threesome with a lesbian who wouldn't let him touch her but loved Esmeralda and loved touching her all over. Esmeralda sandwiched herself between the two, licking the girl's gorgeous pussy whilst he fucked her hard from behind. It had now been five days since she had been home. They had spent several days making outfits out of tin foil, covering a hilarious young lad they had made friends with in inspired costumes and sending him off to the shop in character to demand yet more tin foil to play with. Then they built things out of Fimo. Then they tried to climb around the room without touching the floor. A girl came in at one point and tried to seduce A-Man. It looked like he was up for it for a while, until Esmeralda heard her name being called,

'What?' she asked.

'Aren't you the best fuck in the world?' he asked her.

'Yep,' she grinned.

'See,' he said turning back to the girl, 'why would I fuck anyone other than her?'

She overflowed with pride.

In the end she was too sore to fuck anymore, so instead he stuck strawberries up her bum and made her squeeze them into his open mouth. At one point he pissed on her in the shower. Whilst pissing he started to cum. He was pissing cum. Then he started pissing again, then cumming again. They both laughed with glee. By the time she got back to her flat it was Thursday. She had been on a 6-day sex and drugs bender with people she had only just met and she had her whole life to pack up and everyone in her life to see before she left off to London on

Saturday. She felt great, though, and managed to catch most of her friends over many cups of coffee. There was no comedown. Life was too good. She had fallen in love and was blooming again. She had re-found her wrong and felt colourful once more. On Friday, she went to see him one last time and they talked for ages about past relationships, how they dealt with life's blows, and what made them tick. He said if she asked him to marry her he would have to seriously think about. He gave her his cock ring, they said their goodbyes and she left him. They would fuck again. But it was good that she was leaving. It had been a perfect affair. And it was perfect that it was now complete.

Her little brother rang her up at 1.30am on her last night in Brighton...

'Hello!' He announced triumphantly, and then proceeded to begin tittering down the phone 'Tee hee hee.'

'Are you drunk?' Esmeralda asked condescendingly, though she didn't mean it. She loved talking to her brother when he was drunk. He was a very funny drunk.

'Yes. I've drunk two bottles of wine to myself and my housemate has just gone to bed'

'So you needed someone to talk to?'

'We're going to America,' he suddenly yelped.

'We are, it's true...'

'You can't be a lightweight there. You've got to come out with me.'

There was a long-running gripe between the siblings over their family holidays, which they'd only started going on in the last few years, since their mother's wage had begun to produce a little surplus cash. They used to go camping with their mum and dad when they were little, to places like Hastings and Robin Hood's Bay, but that stopped when their parents broke up. Three people living on a teacher's salary and negative equity had not allowed for many treats over their teenage years, but now they could all cover their own spending money and mother was a school advisor rather than a teacher they could afford all sorts of exotic climes. And they got on so well with each other and there wasn't anyone else they'd rather go with.

'I can't wait to go to America with my favourite girl and I can't wait for you to move to London.'

Esmeralda went all squidgy. Her brother had a girlfriend he was deeply in love with, so she wasn't really his favourite girl anymore, but it was nice to be reminded how much she meant to him once in a while. They hadn't been very close over the last year. He had fallen in love just as her heart had been broken. He'd gone off on a spoork and Esmeralda didn't want to be around it. But they were the closest brother and sister on the planet and she was so pleased they were going to America. The pair of them were going to wipe the floor with the yanks, switching on the charm and lapping up the attention. They were both very vain and very cocky. As well as witty, intelligent and sexy of course.

Esmeralda went to see her best friend's baby. He was the first man out of their inner gang to have a baby. The little baby girl was beautiful and her friend was being so adorable cooing over her. Esmeralda loved him so much and it made her heart sing to see him this happy. She looked forward to her new life in London. She was looking forward to a more settled time.

One of her best friends came to help her pack. Ever since they had bonded in Berlin she had been such a support to Esmeralda. She loved her very much. She was a generous woman.

Another friend of her best friend came to meet her at the pub. She had brought Esmeralda one of her beautiful ceramic pots as a leaving present. She had come up with the foil costumes idea the other night and was so much fun to hang out with.

She met one of her best friends for lunch and they walked through the streets of Brighton arm in arm cackling into the sunshine…

A bunch of best friends came and met her for dinner. He had just got out of a negative relationship and was flowering beautifully. It was a pleasure to see. One of them remembered Esmeralda's first day in Brighton and was chuffed to be there for her last too. Esmeralda was touched her friends were being so adorable.

'I'm having a baby' one of her best friends confided in Esmeralda, before he started to cry. It was scary. And it was brilliant.

'Wow,' mused Esmeralda, 'Life is really moving on…'

HOW TO MOVE HOUSE (NOT)

It is claimed that moving house is the second most stressful ordeal one can go through, after organising your wedding day. There are many key elements that will reduce this stress level though. Forward planning helps to smooth the way; for example, spending a few months prior to moving house sending out replies to all correspondence, informing them of your change of address. A thorough and merciless reduction of pointless personal possessions is also a grand idea, as this means that you'll need to transport less in the move. A thorough and organised system of packing will make life a thousand times easier at the other end when you desperately need a cup of tea and don't want to unpack several boxes to find all the components. Then, on the actual days leading up to the move, it works to have a schedule planned so that you are able to juggle all of the final details, like having some time set aside after everything has been removed from the flat for you to go around and give the place one final scrub and, with inventory in hand, make sure that all is as it was, so that the deposit will be returned without delay. Also being on top of what feels like a never ending list of requirements from both sets of landlords. The ones you are leaving and the ones you are heading to. Last but not least, make sure you spend some quality time reminiscing with the home you are leaving, the area you have been hanging out in, and the beautiful people you were hanging out with for all these years. If you do all these things, then the stress level will be minimized greatly.

Or you just can do what Esmeralda did. Leave your house on the Friday week before moving out, all dressed up in a Basque, stockings, and a wig, then not return to your house till the following Thursday, covered in bruises, with significantly fewer brain cells and significantly more STD's, after spending 6 days boshing down hallucinogens with a bunch of people you've never met before. Then proceed to pack up a year and a half's worth of crap, thanks to the help of dear Kash, who came and saved Esmeralda from the partying and made her sort her life out, otherwise she would never have left the party, shoving all Esmeralda's belongings into carrier bags (seemed like a great idea at the time) and then pathetically attempting to clean the place in some 'teenager sent to their bedroom' type way, before going back out again to drink one's body weight in coffee, desperately trying to catch up with all the people one loves and cares about and haven't seen to say goodbye to yet.

When one chooses *this* approach, one can expect the following experience...

She woke up hung-over and began to thoroughly clean the flat, to the standard one needs to get a deposit back, and like a series of Russian Dolls, the task opened up to reveal more tasks underneath. She forgot about the cooker. She never cooked anything, so never thought of it as dirty, but of course after a year and a half it was and at this stage she had nothing to clean it with but a worn out sponge scourer and a dribble of washing up liquid. Therefore armed with a butter knife and a scrap of good will the cooker is cleaned, the kitchen cupboards wiped down (which is now tricky, after using the sponge to clean all of the grease off of the cooker), and the bathroom gleams. All she has to do now is clean the floor once all the stuff is out of the way, which will happen as soon as the dad turns up with the Luton.

Which he doesn't.

He turns up at 10am with what looks like a Tonka Toy Transit. He also has a mate in tow who is a proper Essex geezer with a bright red gin face. She leads them upstairs to experience the pile of plastic bags resembling a city sized landfill and their heart sinks. It's definitely going to take two trips, if they're lucky. They heave-ho the heavy stuff down and stuff the bags around them. Turns out that although the bags are good little pieces for the game of Tetris they have found themselves embroiled in, it also means millions more trips up and down the stairs to bring them all down. And because they're full of books they keep splitting. They finally get the first load in and make their way up to her new hood. The hangover is in full swing by now and she falls into a deep sleep...

...Through a distorted maze of books and carrier bags she somehow stumbles into a post office and joins the end of a queue. The queue is not moving and she's agitated. She can't remember what she's waiting for, but she know it's important and she's not going to leave the queue because she knows as soon as she does she'll remember why she was there and will have lost her place. But the queue begins to move and she's slowly edging closer to the check out, towards a woman who looks like Mrs Merton, only sterner and less forgiving. She will show no mercy. She has to remember what she's doing there. What was it she needed to sort out...

...Leaping up with a snort from slumber she blurts out to the startled van mates 'The contract!' She'd forgotten that the landlady was sending her the contracts so she could get the guarantor signed before moving in. Vague recollections of stumbling in from the 6 day bender to find a missed delivery slip on the floor float into her frontal lobes and she slaps herself on the forehead. At the same moment jolting another sudden realisation. 'Did anyone pack my black rucksack?' A round of head shaking ensues. She's now heading to her new flat without the contracts to move in or her cheque book to pay the rent and deposit. Luckily the Landlady is her boss's partner. It should be cool.

'I'm sorry but I can't let you move in.'

Esmeralda looks at her dad and back at the van that has couscous pouring onto the street out of the opened side door, all in disarray after a last ditch attempt to discover the black rucksack, and the steady rain is making the granules fluff up quite nicely.

'But I can't move back into my flat. I have to give them the keys today and my dad won't be able to come up during the week to help me again with moving,' she cries in despair.

Her boss looks at her over his partner's shoulder with utter resignation. This is yet another black mark against her already blotted record in administrative organisation. She's about to cry and throw herself onto the floor in the vain hope that it will swallow her up, when her infinitely wise and organised little brother, who has turned up to help with the move, points out that they can go to an internet café to do a money transfer and probably download some temporary tenancy agreements. Thank heavens above, the bitch goes for it and Esmeralda almost pisses her pants with glee. They go find an internet café, transfer the cash, print out some forms and head over to the flat. It all finally feels like it's coming together when they discover the bedroom is covered in glass as the window frame had flapped viciously in the stormy winds and has shattered the pane.

'But I'm sure I shut this,' insists the Landlady.

'Well I hope you *didn't* shut it' Esmeralda replies, 'or that means someone has broken in.'

They creep up the stairs nervously, expecting to walk in on a crack den in the living room, but all is well. The rest of the house is intact and they are now on a more equal footing in the fuck-up stakes.

By the time they've moved everything in from the first van load it is 6pm. They decide to go for a pint and, joy of all joys, the local pub is brilliant. It's a big friendly place with good music, free WiFi, amazing cheap food, an old fashioned dumb waiter, and a huge garden area with BBQ for the summer. It is her new second home. Freshly lubricated and well fed they attempt the last leg of the journey and head back to Brighton. By the time they have loaded the van, which they only just manage to fit with the last of the stuff, and by the time they've finally finished cleaning the flat so it gleams ready for inspection, it is 10pm. They have been moving things now for 12 hours and are all beginning to hallucinate from exhaustion. They get back to the flat to unpack and the heavens decide to open up, which means by the time she finally collapse on her bed at 2am the mattress and bedding are still soaking wet and the rain is banging hard against the plaster board, gaffer-taped to the window, next to her bed.

When she wakes up she's startled by some strange sensation. She can't quite work out what it is, but it slowly dawns on her that all she can hear is the delicate twittering of garden birds. She pulls up the blind and comprehends for the first time that her whole flat faces onto nothing but overgrown gardens filled with huge old trees. She can see branches filled with chaffinches from her bed and can hear nothing but their little chirrups. She realises how she'd grown used to the scream of the seagulls every morning and the holler of students at night. What with the open red brick work of the huge fireplace in her living room, and the regular dark wooden features around the flat, it feels more like she's moved to the countryside, rather than into the big smoke. Within spitting distance there is a brilliant local pub, Tulse Hill train station, a Somerfield supermarket, and an excellent organic shop selling all Infinity Foods products and organic meat. It's like a little village, and everyone knows each other and seems really friendly. She spends the next few days pottering around, filling up the flat with an endless stream of pointless crap, and begins settling in for what seems like a very relaxed and slow paced existence. Her heart had been in the mood for moving to the country, but she'd gone to London for work reasons. It seemed now, though, like she'd found the best of both worlds. Perfect.

And considering just HOW MUCH FUN she had enjoyed in her last two weeks in Brighton, she thought that all things considered she'd got away with it all fairly lightly. Though her father probably didn't agree. She hadn't moved house in an organised fashion. She did have to unpack everything in the flat just to make a cup of tea, but she had experienced her first ever threesome, so... you know, swings and roundabouts.

Esmeralda sat bathed and finally relaxed in her newly-made bed in her newly-acquired bedroom of her newly-moved-into flat. Her gorgeous London friends had rung her drunkenly to welcome her into the fold, which had been just what the doctor had ordered. It was hard to sit in a new home at 2am on a Saturday morning, after a particularly arduous day, and know exactly how much fun the world you had left behind would be having without you right this second. But she was glad to be where she was now, because it wasn't the same old nonsense with the same old people in the same old environment. She was on her own, in a flat of her own, in a whole new city of lights, that was ready and eager to play with her.

Life had slowed right down. She spent the day in her local pub using the WiFi to catch up on work and get her life back in order. It was great to feel on top of things again. She liked being clear in the head and organised. And without all the hoo-hah of Brighton she suddenly had loads of time on her hands. She had time to work. To cook. To think. To breathe. And already she had already lined up a ton of work. Life was grand. Grand and settled.

Ok, um, I'm getting withdrawal symptoms already. Are you free of an evening any time this week?

I will be in town on Tuesday for a meeting. Afterwards I'm going to devour your cock.

That's the best news I've had since you said 'yes let's try that' x x x

It was the last time she'd be able to see him for 3 weeks. She couldn't help herself.

Esmeralda spent the day getting to know her local area by trailing the local STD clinics and chemists trying to get the morning after pill for free. She wondered idly, whilst strolling down the dripping grey streets around Camberwell Green, why she had let him cum inside her. Overwhelmingly, it was because she had fallen in love with him and wanted to feel him fill her belly with his seeds. Physically, her body was of an age where it was crying out for the game of Russian roulette that might possibly lead to its impregnation. But intrinsically the roots were in the realm of self-respect. Her relationship with him was not born out of a space of self-respect. It was born out of her filthy murky wrongness. Her wrongness wasn't the problem mind you: one can be wrong with self-respect in the same way that one can be a hedonist with success. To not manage both is simply a case of not trying hard enough. Doing it all without integrity. She had spoken to her best friend on the phone that morning, wishing her a happy birthday, when Esmeralda had mentioned her need for the morning after pill.

'When are you going to stop seeing him then?' she enquired, 'if you know he isn't what you are looking for and that he's not really good for you... When is it going to end?'

'Erm…' stammered Esmeralda.

Her best friend was training to be a counsellor and she was becoming very good at her job.

'...First week in May? I will be back in Brighton for the week and it will be fun to hang out with him then...' she answered feebly.

But as the day wore on and he didn't text to see if she had located the pill, and as she kicked herself for screwing with her hormones this way yet again, after managing successfully not doing so for ages, she began to think that she had got what she needed from this affair and it was time to move on. Meeting him had kicked her back in the right direction. Reconnecting her with her daring dark side, her sexual capacity, and her confidence. Her ego had taken such a kicking from her last affair, it was marvellous to be fancied the pants off again by a very fit and sexy slag. He had been around the block and this meant he really got how fabulous Esmeralda was, both for her competence in the bedroom, as well as her ability to entertain him and his friends once out of it. He got her greatness, and she got his too. He was a wrong'un, but was emotionally in touch and intelligent in a way that her ex could have only dreamed of. Her A-Man knew how to love and he loved passionately. But he wasn't what she was looking for and nor was she what he really wanted. They'd made life choices that just didn't compute and she had learnt enough from previous relationships over the years to know that, without dispute: those choices will matter, they can never be reconciled, and they will eat their way through the relationship like woodworm. Anything more committal than what they had would end in tears. But what they had...

It was sexy and passionate and funny and dark and fun and twisted and beautiful and dangerous and magical and disturbing. It was hard to walk away from it. She was wearing his knob ring, which he had given her as a leaving present, dangling from a silver bracelet around her wrist. And she wore it with pride. She'd earned it. But she knew that it would also be a wise idea to tie up the end of this fabulous affair into a big beautiful bow and to walk away from it satisfied with a job well done.

It would end whenever and however it ends though. There was no point worrying about it. Like giving up smoking. We all know we should do it, that it's damaging us in the long run, but we won't give up until we give up. There is no point beating yourself up in the meantime. Same with eating too much and putting on weight. Same with all the things we love to do but wish we didn't. Fuck it. Enjoy it whilst you're doing it, safe in the knowledge that you'll stop as soon as feeling healthy and good about yourself becomes more important to you than the cheap kicks you're getting from the poisons. It all goes in cycles.

It really was like living in the countryside, though. Whilst pottering around her kitchen, making smoked salmon and scrambled eggs on toast, Esmeralda's attention was elevated above the noise of Radio 4 to a strange twittering in the bare branches of the tree outside of the window. On closer inspection she discovered two greenfinches courting amongst the branches, displaying proudly their fantastic plumage of bright yellowy-green feathers. As she watched, Esmeralda also noticed a pair of magpies nesting amongst some overgrown ivy that was strangling a poor old tree at the other end of the garden. And then, as if out of a Disney film, a pair of squirrels began to chase each other about the neighbours garden, slithering their way up and down the tree trunks and around a shed; like one of those furry worms you could buy from the joke shops, which you dragged through your fingers on a thin piece of fishing wire, making it look alive. The flat was completely organised now. She had even found the lost DVDs she had on hire from Love Film. Everything had completely slowed down. It was simply marvellous. Last night she had discovered, much to her surprise and delight, that all of her old friends whom she had hung out with many years ago when she lived in Blackheath no longer lived in Hackney, where they had temporarily migrated to, but had all recently returned to South London and were living a short cycle ride away from her flat. She couldn't believe it. What a fluke.

Her attention was called back to the garden. Three crows had surrounded the magpie's nest and were squawking murderously at the terrified pair. The couple stood their ground though and saw the attackers off. She was enjoying the light sprinkling of garden bird twitters after seven years of pigeon coos and seagull strangulations. She didn't much savour the idea of a murder of crows at her casement window though. Although she loved it when crows set to the sky, in an ominous black foreboding cloud at dusk. They were however incredibly noisy and she didn't quite fancy them squawking at her every evening.

Her totem animal was the crow. She had asked to be shown her totem animal when she had drunk ayahuasca and she had received a vision of a whirlpool pulling down into a point, and at the point a black bird's head had appeared. It was either a crow or a raven. This had made sense to Esmeralda as she had a natural affiliation to Odin, in that she had learnt to read and write runes fluently when she was only eight years old. At the time she had been far too young to know anything about the divinatory meaning. She'd just found the alphabet on the back of the Jorvik Centre guidebook after a visit there with her family on a day out whilst camping in Robin Hood's Bay. She had learnt to write in runes so that she could use them in her diary when she didn't want anyone else to know what it said. It was only later on that she found out that she could cast them too. She had made her own set, out of chopped-up branches from the conifer trees at the bottom of her garden. The branches had been perfectly round and exactly the right size, so once chopped up, all the runes were smooth round circles of wood. She had burnt the symbols on with a pyrography kit she'd been given for Christmas. Over the years some of these were lost and so Esmeralda had made a new set out of pebbles from the beach in Brighton, which she painted with the bright yellow acrylic paint. Then some of these had also disappeared. The next set she created, which was the set she still used today, had been made out of stones from the Ardèche Gorges, where she'd camped with the fools many moons ago, and the site of the Chauvet cave which housed some of the oldest cave paintings in world. The stones were chalky white and before she painted them she'd dipped each one into her vagina. Not for any particular reason, just seemed like a good idea. Then using blood red paint she'd inscribed the runes upon each one of them. She loved her runes. They helped her call through to the silent part of her that hid away in its own dark cave located deep within her chest, the part of her that could only communicate in movement and images too, like the ancestors with their cave paintings, bypassing the noisy old beast of words and language who sat on the throne of her mind.

Esmeralda met her brother and his girlfriend then they headed off to the countryside in Suffolk. They arrived at the stunning Tudor manor house at 9am and set about switching off their brains ready for the day ahead. It was the induction day for the Tudor re-creation that they would all be participating in later that summer. Esmeralda had been working at the manor since she was ten years old and her participation in it had changed her life. She'd entered the hall as a townie who wanted a perm so that she could look like Kylie Minogue from *Neighbours*, but she left there a Levellers fan who wore tie-dye and sported long straight henna'd hair. The induction days were a bit of a chore though. Most of it was spent either queuing or listening to long speeches about how the number of school parties coming to visit the re-creation had diminished due to coaches costing too much to hire and because parents nowadays would sue the schools at the drop of a hat if anything went wrong on a trip, so visits back to the Tudor times weren't worth the risk. It was a shame, but it had been the same speech for twenty-five years and it was hard not to switch off whilst sitting freezing to death in an overcroft listening to the lengthy lecture. In reality though it did mean that the re-creation could not go on forever and that was a total bummer as

Esmeralda wanted her children to grow up playing there too.

It was the best place in the world for children, what with there being no cars, and a whole estate filled with muck and animals to play with. She had taken her little cousins there the last few years and they had ridden horses, learnt sword fighting and had earned a feather in their caps shooting arrows at the archery butts. When Esmeralda had started working there she had spent her first three years in the dairy and had learnt how to make cheese and butter. It was all very inspiring. And the whole place was a feast for the senses. It was visually spectacular... A beautiful E-shaped red brick manor house, a style popular at the time in honour of Queen Elizabeth I, and surrounded by a pea-green moat. The grounds were full of cedar trees and gnarly old out-house buildings all littered with the remains of Tudor artefacts left over from many years of re-creations. During the re-creation weeks that ran from the end of June through to the start of July the air hung heavy with the smell of wood smoke and drying herbs. The ears would be continually bombarded with the sounds of hurdy-gurdies, bagpipes and the desperate cry of peacocks. And the month was spent using your hands to do things they wouldn't normally do; like carving spoons, chopping wood, swigging large clay flagons of ale and scratching dirty, matted hair. It was awesome and Esmeralda wanted her children to be part of it.

A tiny chestnut-coloured stoat bobbed across their path.

'I'm not sure if I'll ever be a mother,' she said to her mother, as they sat and ate a delicately delicious lunch in a health spa in Essex, 'I think there's a good chance I might just end up being the mad old aunt to all my friend's babies.'

'I was saying to a friend of mine,' replied her mother, 'that it's difficult for you to find someone you want to settle down with, because you attract men who are as passionate about their futures as you are, but then they often end up expecting you to give up your future to support them in theirs. And when you're not willing to it ends up being irreconcilable.'

'I know,' agreed Esmeralda, 'that's the problem with going out with artists. Maybe I should go out with someone who doesn't have any ambition?'

I fancy the fuck out of you xxxxxx read the text from her A-Man.

She didn't think she wanted to go out with A-Man. But she had fallen in love with him nonetheless.

She wondered if it mattered too much that she was feeling completely embittered toward the male race. She didn't mean to be. Her intelligent self understood that all men were not bastards and that women were part way responsible for turning men into gits. She had just spent the last month shagging one of the biggest gits she had met in a long time, but it wasn't really his fault. As a natural geek, he had learnt how to 'treat' women so that he got them into bed, and what he had learned was simply to be a shit. Why, oh why, do our fairer sex insist on men being shits before we fancy them? She had seen it happen with her own brother. Naturally born a loving and caring man, he only did well with the ladies when he behaved like a bastard towards them. He didn't enjoy doing it, and it took a good twenty-odd years for him to figure it out, but he suddenly realised the old 'treat them mean, keep them keen' motto worked, after a massive broken heart incident. And it worked. He got a lot of pussy for a bit. Luckily for him he met someone wonderful who loved the pants off him, so he didn't have to be a git for very long, and now he got to dote on the young lady and she felt like the luckiest princess on the planet, which she was. But she wouldn't have thought he was such a catch or that it had been so much of a successful conquest, if he hadn't been acting like a git when she had met him. It sucks, but we women are suckers for monsters, and we create them without rhyme nor reason.

She was wondering why he'd send her that text? The next time she saw him, he behaved terribly towards her. The romance had been devoid of respect right from the start. She wasn't impressed by the lifestyle he led, it did matter to her that he wasn't doing anything with his life and that she wasn't intending to be a wreck head anymore (or so she was trying to convince herself). Esmeralda took full responsibility for his lack of respect though. She had not treated herself with any respect throughout their brief time together. Not using condoms, it's always a bad move. By putting yourself in such a dangerous situation, it gives off all the signals of someone who does not value themselves. And, to top it off, A-man didn't respect himself either. He was fun, gorgeous, and a twisted prankster. He *could* have been amazing. But he thought it was funny to throw it all away just because he could. She had a couple of friends like that. They were fun to get wrecked with, but it soon became tedious, as they had nothing to talk about other than getting wrecked. His sex drive had been amazing and he had boosted her ego just as it had really needed boosting. It was greatly appreciated. But she was worth more than this to herself, and it was time to treat herself as precious.

London was awesome. Her friends came up to stay from the commune in Norfolk. One of them was celebrating his eighteenth birthday. They spent three days chomping down magic mushrooms and bowling around town. They went to a house party where they met lots of lovely people, who they fed mushrooms to. Soon the whole party was rolling around the floor in fits of giggles. Everyone decided to go to a gay club at 5am. The club was a heaving mass of bare sweating muscles. Totally surreal.

One of the girls she met was going off to Sweden to develop a practice with a theatre company she had formed. It was an inspiration. It was really that easy. Esmeralda knew it was time to pull her socks up. She had been the fittest and healthiest she had ever been eight months ago when she had just finished drama school. Going off the rails for a bit was completely justified, especially as she had been broken-hearted, but it was time to take the reins and get her shit together again. Create or be created. Time to start creating again. She just wasn't quite sure what it was she wanted to create...

'You were really rude to me the last time I saw you.'

'Was I?'

'Yes,' she replied, 'It's because you sent me that text. You were scared of how you were feeling.'

'You might be right...' he agreed.

'I'd never go out with you, but I'd run away to Vegas with you and get married. That would suit us more than being in a relationship.'

'Let's do it then,' he replied eagerly.

They spent the next two days together before her trip to America pretending they were going to get married. And whilst on MDMA they had both really believed it. There was no reason why they couldn't do it. They were the kind of people who did that sort of thing. And they'd have so much fun if they did. Both of them were proper little troublemakers with a belly full of spunk. If she was going to go off and do something as reckless as marry a waster then he was the one she'd pick. And at the moment, an adventure on the road with him was so much more appealing than the hill she was climbing up that she chose to call her 'life'. There was absolutely nothing on the path that was doing it for her at the moment, whereas *he* was doing it for her big time. Even though he was capable of being a complete git when he wanted to be. But this visit had been totally different and unexpected. She had turned up at his house resolute that she was going to tell him to sling his hook the second he was rude to her, after the ghastly way he had treated her last time she had been down. It was a good time to call it a day, with a fabulous holiday looming, and the reality that she couldn't keep coming down to Brighton all the time. There was a whole new city filled with men with her name written all over them to be getting on with. She had nothing to lose. But guys can always smell when their luck has changed within a woman's emotions, and he was adorable to her from the second she arrived. It also might have been because an old friend of his was there who was also into theatre. She became embroiled in a thoroughly inspiring conversation with him, in which Esmeralda was able to reveal a part of her soul that she had never had the opportunity or reason to expose to A-man before. When she came downstairs from the loo she caught them talking about how great she was. With A-Man feeling proud of his catch, they embarked upon a magical 48 hours in which he gave himself to her completely. They simulated love and it was beautiful. Proper partners in crime. He really knew how to lay it on when he went for it. But as the drugs wore off, reality sunk back in and he started being a shit again and the games were back on. Esmeralda couldn't be bothered. She wasn't looking for a project. At this moment in time she was enough of a project herself to have the energy for anyone else's bullshit. She could love him, *did* love him, but she wasn't going to fix him.

'Have you fallen in love with me?'

'No... yes... no... I don't know. Yes... a bit. It's hard not to, the sex is so fucking good.'

'And we're both so fascinating.'

'You're fascinating. I'm simple.'

'You are not simple.'

'I've fallen in love with you a little bit too.'

'Don't say that... I was about to say something really dark.'

Thank God she had moved to London.

The scar in his belly button had formed into a star that was exactly the same as the star tattoo at the small of her back. He'd noticed it and pointed it out. They both realised how cosmic that seemed and quickly acted cool and brushed it off as stupid.

He smelt just like her Granddad. The best man she had ever known.

Is it really better to have loved and lost than to have never loved at all? Is love not like a concentrate? That with each new vessel this intoxicating liquor is poured into its power dilutes and the effects grow weaker? If only it were true.

She needed saving. And mainly from herself.

You've got to love summer rain. It's so goddamn luxurious.

Esmeralda swam languidly in the small lukewarm pool at the hotel as the heavy rain plopped onto the surface all around her head. Her metallic blue nails glinted through the breaks like phosphorescence as she parted the water. *Divine decadence darling.* The cool water soothed her sunburnt skin. They'd been out searching for alligators in the Mississippi swamps, just outside of New Orleans. They'd seen loads. Big one, little ones, some as big as your head. They'd come up to the edge of their hovercraft, one that looked like it was straight out of the old TV series *Gentle Ben*, and snapped raw chicken from the hands of the hick who was their tour guide. Then he'd got out his own baby alligator, a tiny little specimen called Nemo. He'd handed it to Esmeralda and it had made little duck-like quacks as she stroked her shimmering blue thumbnail across its scaly neck. Then it fell asleep in her hands. Esmeralda was a sucker for things falling asleep in her arms. It was so goddamn cute. On the way out to the swamps it had suddenly down-poured, as the guy drove the hovercraft full pelt through the wider stretches of river. They had all been soaked to the bone, but then the sun had beat hard, without any shade, and their clothes dried out almost as soon as the rain had stopped. It was the perfect time of year to visit New Orleans... Humid, but in a sexy way. It left you glowing rather than dripping with sweat. Felt like you were under a cosy duvet. Today was the first day it had rained, and it had been perfect, like a *Coca Cola* advert. The whole place felt like you were in a movie. Esmeralda had known she would love America, but she hadn't realised she would love it this much. Everyone talked to each other, without it being a big deal. You didn't have to ask each other your names or what you did for a living. You didn't even have to say goodbye. You just plopped into conversation like the raindrops plopped into the pool. People were characters, like in films, singing blues into the night, or telling everyone how they were off to Cincinnati tomorrow, or preaching at cars. Actually... that was the same as Brixton.

Thunder began to roll across the sky and Esmeralda trudged her wet bikini butt into the bedroom and curled up on the huge dark wooden bed. The hotel had character. The whole French Quarter had character. Balconies made from ironwork, dripping in Mardi Gras beads, with jazz music bowling out into the heavily scented streets, filled with jasmine and Cajun spices. Esmeralda wanted to stay here forever. Or rather, Esmeralda wanted an adventure.

No matter how great the problem, bureaucracy will always make it worse...

Graffiti on a toilet wall in New Orleans

She had failed to ignore the A-man since arriving on her holiday, continually texting him lewd photos and raunchy messages. But she had been trying to unpick the reasoning behind it all, and she had come to the conclusion that she really needed a change. Not a 'move to Brixton' kind of a change, but a total life overhaul. The movie of her world was in need of an unexpected twist. A-man was an exciting character and this was the thing that had been gripping her attention these last few months. He made life feel like it was all a film again, albeit in a

Trainspotting kind of a way. And now it was becoming clear to Esmeralda that she just wasn't in the right place for de-toxing and knuckling down. Responsibilities and success were not making her moist. All she wanted to do right now was draw out a load of cash, chuck some things in a rucksack, and run off into the night, hitching-hiking her way across the States, on an adventure into the unknown. Her ambitions were no longer interesting her. Even if she made it as an actress, all it was ever going to amount to would be a life plastered all over *Hello* magazine. It wasn't really what she was after. She wanted to make true, beautiful, inspiring theatre. But you could do that anywhere. The one thing you needed to achieve doing that was inspiration, and that was exactly what she was craving. Inspiration. Even after the move, and even though the depression had finally lifted, she still felt her well of ideas was empty. She had nothing left to give and it was time to do some taking. The A-Man affair had jazzed things up, with sex that really suited being witnessed by an outside party because it was just so fucking good, but it wasn't enough. She wanted to run away to Las Vegas with him and get married. Go on a road trip for their honeymoon and hold up some banks when they ran out of cash. Some truly off-the-wall excitement. Anything other than the humdrum of everyday life. She was single, childless, and nearly thirty. Now was the time to go off the rails, before life walled her in and made it feel impossible. Not that it was ever going to. But at the moment there wouldn't be too much consequence if she suddenly lurched her life off at a right angle. And now the floodgates had been opened upon this way of thinking, there was no chance of being able to stop the desire to smash it all up and start again.

Lightning suddenly split the sky with cracks of brilliance and the heavens opened up with a heavy plume of thunder. Rain poured down into the neon-lit streets and Esmeralda went into the bathroom to take a shower.

Ok, that's it, you're the one. Do everything you want to do without me before next we meet, because after that I will be there for every scrap of your beautiful filth. Kiss.

She guessed that was his way of asking her to be his girlfriend.

It was partly the challenge that was driving her forward, but there was indisputably more than simply an urge for her to conquer him. The attraction was because he was good fun and a great fuck. And there was a lot going on in him too. He was super emotional. And he felt like home. It felt dangerous, but familiar. And he was totally loyal to those he had committed to...

A week after returning to England Esmeralda found herself engaged to A-Man. What a strange twist of fate that was. The strangest thing about it was that she meant it 100%. It turned out that he wanted everything that she wanted. A partner in crime, a lifelong soul mate, to commit wholeheartedly first and foremost, then figure out the logistics of how things were going to work out after that. He had decided that she was the 'one' and the most amazing woman he had ever met, and he meant it. The whole thing was spinning Esmeralda's head. After a year of depression and feeling decidedly unacknowledged, he was now acknowledging her left right and centre. He hadn't dived straight in with these affections as he hadn't been looking for a partner. His wife had just cheated on him for a year. Women were not currently on his Christmas card list. But he'd admitted that he thought she was a thousand times better in bed than the second best girl he'd ever bedded, he thought she was the sexiest woman he had ever met, he said he'd still love her and marry her even if she was mangled tomorrow and could never have sex again, he thought she was the kindest person he'd ever met, an intellectual equal (he wished) he said she rocked his world, she made him feel like he was getting a second chance, and whenever they went out and met people he'd turn to her when they left to tell her that he thought she was ace. He'd given himself to her completely. Now, normally, when this had happened to Esmeralda in the past it, had meant that the fellow was a bit insipid and needy.

A-Man was pretty needy, in a high-maintenance kind of way, but he was far from insipid. And she was hardly an easy ride herself, except of course when she was single. No, he was certainly a fiery hot pot of masculinity, and someone who knew how to stick his cock in her better than anyone else she had ever met. As well as being an absolute lunatic with whom there was never a dull moment. Esmeralda was struggling with the acknowledgements. She wasn't used to all this. But he loved her. And he saw her in the same way that she saw herself, which was also a highly original situation. There was a damn good chance they were actually going to get married by the looks of things.

I turn you on, like electric company - Lovage

DISINTEGRATION

Never confuse a single defeat with a final defeat.

- F Scott Fitzgerald

Esmeralda woke up to the alarm on her husband's phone. For a few years now they had plumped for Nina Simone's *My Baby Just Cares for Me* as their wake up melody and thus far, the song hadn't grown to annoy them. He quickly put it on snooze, though. He needed to snooze four or five times before he could get up, whereas Esmeralda had always been a morning person. Once sleep had slipped from her mind, like mercury slipping from a bowl, no trace was left behind. She stretched out in their large queen-sized bed. They had one of the least cuddly sleeping relationships she'd ever been in, because they were both hot-blooded people, especially if toxins were involved. They would burn like radiators if they'd enjoyed a drink or two the night before. It had been a while though since they had burned that brightly, but they still found it difficult to cuddle up all night without overheating. Instead, Esmeralda usually awoke with one of her cats pressed up tight against her, as the cats had no qualms about making the most of her hot-water-bottle constitution. She lay there for a while giving the soft fur a stroke and adjusting to the day. It was dark winter and the light blue promise of dawn had only just begun to nudge the thin white curtains. Esmeralda needed to absorb as much light as she could, as the darkness brought with it Seasonal Affective Disorder. For a long time now she had been in the habit of painting her whole house bright white as soon as she moved in, to reflect as much light as possible. It also complemented her huge array of brightly-coloured clutter.

The house was still, but already disturbed, as their lodger had departed for work an hour earlier. Before they had even got married, her husband had suggested to Esmeralda that they take on a lodger, his reasoning being that then they could rent larger accommodation for less money than they would have been paying for a dingy little studio or damp one-bedroom basement flat. And on the whole, it had worked out well. They had lived in three brilliant houses since moving back to Brighton. One had been an extraordinary space they had named Wonderland and had been built by an artist in his garden to use as a studio, and mainly consisted of an eight-metre-squared living room with a two-metre-squared skylight in the middle that slid open. The second house had boasted a sauna and a roll-top bath. The third house, and the one they still lived in today, had a large garden, by Brighton standards, and Esmeralda loved it. She had never grown her own garden before and she had taken a great shine to the new hobby. The house was shabby compared to the previous abodes, but the landlord was private and the rent was cheap, which was a blessing and a half since the banking crisis. They had taken lodgers in all three houses and had seen six or seven come and go over the years. It did get a bit tiresome that they didn't have full privacy, but it had helped to some extent to stop them from arguing as often or as loudly as they would have done had they been on their own, and on the whole, their lodgers had either kept themselves to themselves or had been friends. Their current lodger was a friendly chap who kept himself to himself. They had lived together for two years and were in a good routine with each other's habits. He left for work much earlier than they did, which meant they all got the house to themselves in the morning, which was preferable.

Esmeralda wrapped herself tightly in a soft white dressing gown, donned her fluffy white slipper boots and trotted to the toilet. Having had a quick wee she took herself downstairs to the freezing cold kitchen to feed the two mewing cats, who circled the floor with slinky twists of the tail imploring her to hurry up. She flicked on the radio, always tuned to Radio 4, and let the tragedies of the day begin to fill the otherwise peaceful room. Once the piles of stinky meat had been administered, she put the kettle on and made two strong cups of coffee, both with milk, one with a heaped teaspoon of brown sugar- for him. Carefully carrying them back up the stairs to the bedroom, she placed his drink on the bedside table on his side of the bed, with a kiss on the forehead, and climbed back into her side of the bed, wriggling up close to his hot naked body for some much needed warmth and the hope of a spot of morning sex.

'I can't believe I'm thirty-five. How extraordinary is that? I know it's terribly dull to say but time really does pass ever so quickly once the veil of childhood has lifted and the death slide of adulthood has revealed itself. I'd hoped to be so much and had planned to do so many exciting things with my life,' she lamented to her mum. 'My lists were endless. Far too much for me to attempt in several lifetimes, let alone one. But here I am, aged thirty-five years old, and somehow I have found myself frozen in fear, unable to do anything, let alone everything.'

'Perhaps you put too much pressure on yourself,' suggested her loving mother. 'And it's not like you've had a huge amount of choice over the situation. This is all down to circumstance. But you'll get back on track again, you always do, and this will just seem like a bad dream.'

Esmeralda sat and ate carrot batons, dipping them into hummus, alone, in the starkly-lit dressing room of the Stanwix Theatre in Carlisle. Her fellow company members, who were the cast of the show, got ready next door in the dressing room that was actually being used for getting dressed in. Esmeralda's dressing room, in contrast, was being used to fall apart in. She had spent over an hour walking in circles practising shrilly on her pink violin, as she selfishly wept over her ineptitude. There was a burning desire inside of her to talk to someone about the struggle she was going through, but she also felt like it was all she banged on about in some ways and that professionally it wasn't a good idea to break down to her colleagues. And for Christ's sake, they were there to do a show. This is what really bugged her about misery. It was so fucking self-obsessed. The doctrine of suicide being one of the greatest sins made perfect sense to her now. It was on her mind all the time, but to do it would be the ultimate selfish act and the only thing stopping her was knowing how much it would hurt the people she loved.

If only the train would stop.

Seven seemed to be an important number to Esmeralda. She didn't really know anything about sacred geometry, but she knew it was meant to mean something in all that. Most cells die and are replaced in seven years, so she was pretty much a different person now than the woman she'd been when aged 28. Then every four lots of seven years is meant to be your Saturn Returns, whatever that means... There's the seven year itch. Seven days of the week. Seven virtues and seven deadly sins. Even seven stages to fooling...

Like The Fool, much of her last seven years had been spent stepping off of a cliff into the great abyss. It had not been a particularly easy Saturn Returns. Her hardest yet, in fact...

If only she could get back to the start. If only she could go back and make things different. Perhaps if she had stuck at something, then she might have found that things would have turned out differently?

'I should have stuck with stand-up comedy,' she mused, staring out of the window on the moving train. The signals had failed and they'd been stuck at East Croydon for ages. Some things never change.

'All the stand-up comedians who had got through to the semi-finals of the competition I was in during my twenties are now on TV every day; propping up dreadfully dull panel shows.'

'I hate those fucking things, with their stupid fucking token woman,' bitched her friend. 'Farting around trying to prove how smart and witty they are whilst successfully failing to acknowledge any of the awful shit that is actually going on the world.'

'Yep,' agreed Esmeralda, 'The world is turning upside down and they are talking bollocks about some celebrities and useless politicians whose heads will be on pikes, come the revolution.'

Her hopes had been so high. And her belief in her abilities. But alas, Esmeralda had discovered that she was nowhere near as intelligent, witty, talented or beautiful as she had thought she was. Her mother had lied, and she could see why. Mothers often tell their children the same lie. They ought to. The trouble is, she had really thought that she was rather unusual. 'Bespoke,' as a friend referred to her once. This singularity had tricked her into thinking herself much greater, brighter and better than she really was. But she was not a genius. She was just an oddball.

Perhaps, also, it didn't help that she'd been born into a family with very little money. She suspected her natural blessings would have gone a lot further with a bit of extra cash behind them. But that was an awful thing to think.

It pissed her off that she thought about things like that. Her family were the best. Their love was so deep and precious... Absolutely precious. She wanted money to fuck the hell off. She hated money.

The beautiful sleek black cat leapt onto the sofa and forced its soft head into Esmeralda's loving hands. *This is real* she thought to herself, *The present... There's nothing to fear here in the present. It's only in my head.* And she lost herself in the fur of her loved one.

Fractions of fear.

If you're anxious, then you are worrying about the future. If you are fearful, then you are thinking about the past. And if you are content, then you are in the present. At different points throughout the day, Esmeralda was all three of these things.

'I'M HAVING A FUCKING CRISIS...!!!!' she screamed into the night. She hated it when she overused the exclamation mark.

Bad habits.

Tacky.

Esmeralda was drowning in a sea of bad habits.

Nothing. I've absolutely nothing to say. My forehead is throbbing against my skull and I long for a release from the pressure in my head. I saw a programme on trepanning when I was a young teenager. Saw some crazy rich hippie couple that lived in a castle who shaved back their hair, cut open their skin by slicing a cross through to the skull and peeling back the flesh, away from the head like orange peel. Then with a surgical drill they bored through the castle wall, until it popped into the cavity beneath. I feel that if I were to drill through my skull right now then a jet of steam would burst out. I long for release from all this bullshit in my head.

I've been here many times. In this state of reality breakdown. 'Confusion is your greatest teacher,' my friend once told me. But confusion isn't providing any answers at the moment, it's presenting far too many choices. I find this happens most when the heart and mind are at odds. When the connection between the two are for some reason severed, then the brain is left in a state of distress. Wondering what the hell is going on...

Nothing seems to stick in my mind at the moment. I need to sleep. I must sleep. All I can do is hope and pray that my wits will return and my guts stop wrenching. They won't though, will they? Not until I admit the truth.

How to admit that which one is not yet privy to? Well, that is the conundrum. When the world has changed before your eyes and you don't know up from down, how to stop spinning and discovering once more... It all moves too fast. A melodramatic pain in the backside, who wants to feel comfortable with all that? Nothing has to change other than my level of acceptance. How to be nothing and be it with ease?

I know exactly what you're going through my dearest friend and I want to hug you tight until all the pain has gone away. I believe it will work next time. I have a feeling... Stay strong. Can't wait to see you...

Headaches smell of metal.

'Come on, what's going on?'

She hadn't seen her friend since August and the second failed IVF attempt. They were talking about her husband and how things had been going.

'Where the fuck do I start? Well... Okay, so I learnt to call myself an artist, but now I feel that I am growing further and further away from my art. I've always been about keeping it real, but I've never felt further from my real. I've lost confidence in my acting abilities and my writing abilities. The theatre world is a small world and I'm scared of fucking anything up, because I won't be able to get away from it if I do. At the moment, I feel like I'm in the middle of a slow car crash.'

'What's causing this, though?' asked her lovely friend as she lifted a few hot steaming chips from the bowl, blew on them, and popped them into her perfect mouth.

'Since the second round of IVF,' continued Esmeralda. They were sitting at a hipster cafe on a cold grey afternoon on the sides of the South Bank in London, where they'd managed to snatch a few hours together.

'They had to abort the procedure because I over-stimulated and I've been completely screwed up ever since, because the drugs they gave me made my ovaries swell up to the size of tennis balls. I'm an absolute hormonal mess and I can't think straight. I feel like I'm slightly coming up on acid the whole time. And it's made me so fat. I'm puffed up like a balloon.'

'Oh no you're not,' reassured her friend, squeezing her hand. But she was. She had put on two stones.

'And I'm so freakin' poor. Poorer than I ever wanted to be and I can't see how to get out of the debt I'm in or how to make money in a way I enjoy. I don't believe in myself anymore. And I think the world is going to fall to pieces in the next twenty years anyway. The environment's fucked and governments are evil, and general chaos is growing. I don't think there's any point having a pension or a career. I think you need to be learning how to be happy on the move and how to grow your own food. And possibly looking into getting hold of a gun...'

She dropped her head into her hands and sighed from deep within her soul.

'I feel like I'm having a nervous breakdown.'

'How does He feel about all this?'

'He tries to be supportive... We've been through so much together and it hasn't been easy for him either. He blames himself.'

Esmeralda felt like she was unravelling. And if she didn't do something about it all soon, she knew she was going to snap.

'AHHHHHHHHHHHHHHHHHHHHHHHHHH
HHHHHHHHHHHHHHHHHHHHHHHHHHHHH
HHHHHHHHHHHHHHHHHHHHHHHHHHHHH
HHHHHHHHHHHHHHHHHHHHHHHHHHHHH
HHHHHHHHHHHHHHHHHHHHHHHHHHHHH
HHHHHHHHHHHHHHHHHHHHHHHHHHHHH
HHHHHHHHHHHHHHHHHHHHHHHHHHHHH
HHH!'

She missed him terribly...

'I love you so much.'

'I love you too. I miss you. The cats miss you.'

'I miss you all.'

Her mum also gave her all the love she needed down the phone and reassured her that she ought to chill out and do less. Esmeralda always took on too much and was overloading herself at a time when her body couldn't take it. Her Mum asked if she needed any help with money. Even at 35, Esmeralda always needed help with money.

She came on her period. Earlier that day an old friend she hadn't seen for years, who knew she had been trying to conceive through IVF, asked her if the belly she had was because it had worked.

'No, that's just fat,' she quipped. She was getting very good at brushing off emotions.

Later that day, she started to bleed. On the one hand this was a relief as it explained why she had been going quite so insane and also why she was quite so fat. On the other hand it was rubbish because she was on the pill and hadn't left a gap, so shouldn't be having a period. Even though they were trying to conceive she had gone on the pill anyway to give her and her husband a much needed break from the hormones that had been making her life a misery. Ever since the overstimulation, she had been suffering from the most horrendous PMT. She felt like she was losing the plot and it was affecting all areas of her life. Taking the pill again had been an attempt to help, to try and give her a break from the periods, but her periods appeared to be stronger than the pill even, and she was bleeding anyway. And she had lost her mind for the last week regardless. No respite had been offered this month.

The fucking joys of being a woman.

'Having a baby is the most important thing I've ever done,' slurred the pissed 45-year-old blonde, dolled up with false eyelashes and fake tan. They were at a social club in Levenshulme, eating a curry after a performance in Manchester.

'I had my first at 16, my twins at 19 and my baby, who is now 20, my baby I had when I was 21. And even though it was so painful and you think there's no way you'd ever do it again - and I've been in some pain in my time, I can tell ya, I've been beaten up and - I used to live in Moss Side – still, there's no pain like it. But the second you see them and you hold them, you straight away want to do it again. It's the most important thing I've ever done. Being a mother.'

She went on and on and on. Esmeralda tried to enjoy her curry but was feeling increasingly sick. Everyone around the table knew that about the IVF.

'The most important thing I've ever done. I'm a grandma too now. Me eldest has just had a little boy...'

A bleary-eyed little girl, no older than seven years old, appeared behind the bar in her pyjamas. She obviously lived upstairs above the pub and looked grubby, and like she had been crying. The hardest thing about not being able to have kids, is seeing people who shouldn't be having kids breeding like fucking rabbits.

'When are they having the Christening again? Is it in the summer?'

'I don't know,' she replied. She didn't know anything about any Christening.

'They've asked me to be the Godfather.'

Was that why she didn't know about the Christening then? She hadn't been asked to be the Godmother? The emotions immediately rose up, but she brushed them off for now. It wasn't the time or the place for getting upset.

Freezing cold and aching from an uncomfortable night's sleep on the sofa was *precisely* the time for it, though, and she sobbed uncontrollably. If it was a family member who her best friend had asked to be Godmother then that would be understandable. Fine, she could handle that. But if she had asked her other friend, the one with the nice house in Spain, then Esmeralda would never be able to forgive her.

The last laugh of a dying hag, on the cold slab of existence.

I FUCKING HATE THIS WORLD. I hate the lies and hypocrisy. We are entangled in a web of bullshit that is dragging us all into the darkness and no one has the strength or the guts or the clarity to cut through and free us, without becoming entangled up themselves in their own bullshit before the job is done. Every direction I take my face smacks into limitations. I USED TO LIVE IN A WORLD OF INFINITE POSSIBILITIES. It is easier to do this when you are at the top of the ladder... White, westerner, educated. That was, is, the top of the ladder, compared to so many. But I was an artist who relied on support from the system, because to create you need time and space. You can only spare time and afford space if somehow you're being financially supported, by rich parents or the government (because the public sure as hell won't pay enough for your finished work to make up for all the time spent that's gone into it, no matter how much they love it). I spent years on the road creating beautiful, inspiring work that transported the audience into the *dream world and tickled their imaginations. Truly beautiful work. Everyone loved it, wanted to train in it. We ran workshops and started an academy. It grew and grew and grew and *Pop.*. It was gone. Benefits were pulled, rents had to be paid. Everyone was suddenly skint. We had worked on donations, as all good people should. First of all, when we were finding our way, folks used to throw copper coins into the hat. Have you any idea how that feels? You work all day, probably having hitch hiked across countries to get there, have been in 'process' all week, pulling yourself apart, without much sleep and all catching each other's colds, only to have some tosser chuck a handful of shrapnel into the hat in gratitude for the hours of performing you've just done for them. As we grew in confidence though, and the hours of work we had put in turned into days, then weeks, then years, I would not let anyone put anything into the hat that could not be folded. I felt proud to have reached the point where I knew my worth and was not scared to ask for it. But even then, it was never enough to cover anything. It didn't cover costs. It didn't cover the cost. At least we could work, though. We felt we were moving in the right direction, trying to be part of the solution. Awakening, opening, inspiring. It's funny, the whole time I was on the road I moaned constantly about the people I was with and how small the audiences were. Never realising how lucky I was to be living the dream, instead of eking out a meagre existence in a FUCKING CALL CENTRE... How the fuck did that happen?*

Her attempt at writing a suicide note was proving difficult. She kept going on about all sorts of random nonsense. She wasn't planning on actually committing suicide. Penning suicide notes had become one of her favourite past times.

I'm not dead yet. She thought to herself...

Who could we kill where it would actually make a difference? Those in power have done a very good job at hiding themselves. Let's all turn red and scream and rip our clothes off and run through the streets of London, Washington, Beijing, the Vatican, everywhere these creeps are loitering and rip them all to pieces. Let's be angry. Not try to stay calm and carry on. Let us be fucking angry and not stop the anger, because every day we see huge fucking cocks being shoved up our arses from evil selfish cunts who don't give a fuck about anyone other than themselves and their weird kleptomania for collecting cash. And yes, do give them a fucking gender. You fucking bastards. You've fucked our world up and we are coming for you. We're just working out how.

How do we get to them?

How do we make a difference?

How do we live without feeding the beast?

How does one keep calm and carry on?

How does one not keep calm and carry on?

I don't know what to do... I don't know nothing anymore.

Her friend rolled around on the blanket next to Esmeralda. The baking sun had dipped beneath the wonky backs of the block of regency houses, leaving the bountiful garden, tended but overgrown with age and full of fairy laughter, dappled in a gentle twilight. She hadn't realised he'd taken 'G' until he'd suddenly fallen backwards and started lolling around with his eyes in the back of his head. She'd just painted his nails bright red for the wedding day. Blots of polish were now splattered around the blankets and his clothes. It was quite annoying, they'd been having a rather pleasant conversation, but she was stuck in the garden with him now for the foreseeable future to make sure he stayed safe. Esmeralda didn't want to leave him alone in this state. A few minutes ago he'd grabbed the material scissors she was using to make a pair of sock puppets with, wedding gifts for the soon to be newlyweds, before wielding them around in a rather unhealthy manner, chopping a branch off a rose bush whilst laughing wickedly and ripping up part of the lawn fencing, before she managed to wrestle them off him. He was now fully dropped and twitching like a dying rabbit with Myxomatosis. She needed the toilet, but he wouldn't stay in the recovery position and she didn't want to leave him unguarded.

'Twas not the end of the world, the puppets needed making and the garden still hung heavily with the scents of baking summer. Esmeralda wove the luminous orange wool in and out of the sock puppet, cutting it at lengths and tying it into dangling strands to mimic the look of flames. This one would be a phoenix. She played FIP through the digital radio on her phone, enjoying the sporadic news reports which sang to her in French. Names she knew peppered the seductive sounds of the reporter's voice, as if a kinky teacher was whispering his deepest desires into her ears, whilst dropping in the odd fact or person she ought to be learning about. Esmeralda much preferred the news in French. It made everything far less terrifying.

About an hour or so later the birthday boy came out and relieved her of her duties. Her husband had called and required Esmeralda's presence back at home. They had to head off imminently to spend the night with the bride and groom, her brother-in-law and soon to be sister-in-law. It was only 24 hours until the wedding service after all...

'He won't stop going on about bum sex,' she answered.

'Okay,' she smirked, 'that wasn't what I was expecting.'

She explained, 'There are three reasons why we don't have bum sex anymore, well not as often as we used to anyway. Mainly, it's because we are trying for children. Secondly it's because he's said so many horrible things to me my bum holes has closed up. A fanny stays wet and open no matter what someone does to it, but your bum seizes up if it's not feeling loved and adored. Every name and nasty word he has said to me has made my bum hole less and less up for it. But finally, it just physically wouldn't be possible to keep having bum sex as much as we did when we met. I'd have the most dreadful piles and would need to wear a buttplug just for plumbing reasons.'

'A man of simple pleasures...' smiled her friend.

'He sure is,' she laughed.

The world is about to kick off. This has happened so many times before. Armageddon is always hanging over us. And here it is, once again. This time they say it's wearing a burka, but really it is wearing a dollar sign. Muslims. Islamists. Taliban. Terrorists. Fear. Lies. People set up against one another. Someone somewhere getting something out of it at the expense of everyone else. False enemies. Common people used as pawns. Again and again and again.

They drove from Brighton to Bromsgrove, Bromsgrove to Carlisle, Carlisle to Manchester, Manchester to Edinburgh, Edinburgh to Birmingham, Birmingham to Maidenhead and from Maidenhead back to Brighton, imparting their knowledge of special and general relativity as they went. Like pilgrims of science, they preached their way around the country spreading the miracles of nature's laws, both theoretical and empirical.

Never Worn

PURE HELL

At some point we had fallen off of the ride, Esmeralda thought.

Walls suddenly appeared around us that had not been visible before. Great crevices opened up between myself and those friends I had become accustomed to being equal to. Around us erupted the malignant and ever present realisation of a world lost in its own lie, an unsustainable bubble burst into a volcano of destruction around our ears, as the financial crisis reared its ugly head from beneath the parapet of sleeping ignorance and silent denial.

The numbers of homeless people living on the streets sharply increased and for the first time I realised how easy it was to suddenly find yourself on the wrong side of the fence. That one day you are in a walking dream, playing the game and believing in the path, the next you are shut out, cold and being told it is your own fault or just the way it is.

Friends with large inheritances became as distant to us as the hope of ever owning our own home. These friends looked increasingly tanned and relaxed, their teeth became whiter and their conversation more coke-fuelled and full of figures. At the same time those who moved in the same circles as us grew paler and dark circles formed beneath their bloodshot eyes, no longer dazzling with the promise of possibilities. Our voices became thin and transparent, our opinions treated like those of angst ridden teenagers, whilst in dark corners we began to whisper our words of revolution and hopes of change.

"You're an engineer, aren't you?" boomed an authoritative voice at an old and dear friend's wedding.

"No," replied her husband in a small embarrassed voice, trying to stifle his humiliation. 'I work in a call centre."

At which, everyone fell into awkward silence. They were in their thirties. It was simply not acceptable for them to be working in a call centre.

Aged thirty-three years old, the age by which one ought to be achieving the pinnacle of one's success, or ought to be getting nailed to a cross for the commotions you have caused, Esmeralda tumbled down from the path she'd always believed had been pre-ordained for her and found herself penniless, prospect-less and living in her own personal nightmare.

They had just been enjoying a right royal time. In the lead up to their wedding day, a bundle of good luck led them to complete freedom from the system with six fun years of working as a producer for The Fool, and three of these years spent actually training in his fooling technique, which lay the foundation for her style of work as an artist in her own right, and even her husband joined her, something she never thought would happen in a million years. That she'd meet someone who wanted to try out everything she did was a miracle. He was annoyingly brilliant at fooling as well. After the fools all went their separate ways, they were left with a stunningly-beautiful home in Brighton; a two-bedroom flat hidden behind an ordinary-looking garage door on a non-residential street, with an eight metre square living room, two metre square sunroof that opened up revealing a great expanse of sky, turning the white walls and pine floor into a courtyard that served perfectly as an art studio. Within it, they were able to, with the landlord's permission, open it up to the public as an ever-changing art gallery, residential space, rehearsal room and theatre. Every week, they held life drawing classes, barbeques, dance classes and elaborate parties. The furniture never remained in one place, the lighting changed ceaselessly from neon and UV, to sunlight, to sexy red. Someone likened the place to Andy Warhol's Factory and it certainly felt like an event, a happening in time that coined such terms as *Champagne Anarchists* and *Divine Decadent Dandies*. A time that would never again be equalled. The last 'Hurrah Henry!' before the reality of the world crashed in around their ears.

One week after the wedding, in the first week of their honeymoon and the first week of a whole month in which their home was open to the public as an art gallery 'Open House', their landlord told them they had to move out. His daughter was pregnant and coming home from South America. He chose to break the news whilst Esmeralda's husband's arm was up to his shoulder in shit helping the landlord to unblock a sewer pipe. They could not believe their ears. That Christmas they had wined and dined them, obtaining a gentleman's agreement that they could stay in the house indefinitely and that they would be able to use it as creative space. And yet here they were, five months later, utterly skint from the outlays of a hugely expensive wedding, without any income other than what they had achieved from running the space and were now faced with an unavoidable month ahead of them, where they had to continue opening their house up to the public, knowing they had to leave. The brochures had all gone out. Even if they had shut the doors the bell would have rung ceaselessly.

Luckily, crates of wine remained from the wedding day and they spent the month of May 2011 drowning their sorrows on an epic scale at the poor unsuspecting punters and neighbours who discovered them in their misery. Every day, people cooed over how gorgeous their home was, adding woe upon woe to their unavoidable defeat. One old man spent a whole day and night drinking with them. He had spent his life working as a nuclear physicist, safety checking power plants. Sitting in their home with them, drinking, he said he now felt he had wasted his whole life, that there had been all these other options for ways of living that he had been unaware of. He said that they made him feel young and carefree again. But they were not carefree. They had to work out what to do next. Esmeralda tried desperately to get a new job in theatre, but with all the Arts Council cuts happening at just the same time, suddenly hundreds of people were applying for the same jobs and plenty of them had many years' more experience in much more mainstream and understandable positions. Six years experience as a Director of Fooling didn't really mean anything.

Then Esmeralda's husband came home, having done the one thing she'd always dreaded... In the city of Brighton, there are only three options for employment other than self-employment. These three options are hospitality, social care or call centres. He had gone with the call centre. She'd feared this day happening, because it would mess up their benefits, now that they were married. But after three months of job applications, only a handful of interviews and absolutely no joy, Esmeralda was forced to follow suit too.

One and a half years. Precisely 547 days. Around 1641 hours. All these were lost to an awful, soulless, mind-numbing job. From 2pm until 9pm every day, in a cold, strip-light-lit, germ-infested, industrially-ugly, call centre. Four nights a week and Saturday mornings, every week. It still astounded Esmeralda that it happened. She didn't mean to sound like a snob, but it wasn't at all what she wanted to be doing with her life. Some people want security and money in their pockets. She had never cared about that. All she wanted was to create and earn enough to get by. But she also had ambition and dreamed bigger than that too. If you'd asked her when she was eighteen where she'd like to be when she was thirty-three, the year Christ was crucified, that Jimi Hendrix's died, Kurt Cobain shot himself... She'd have said that, by thirty-three, She'd like to have already starred in several great theatre productions, performed at the National, the Globe, and then gone on to perform in several art house films and at least one that had been a really big hit. By thirty-three, she would have liked to have already established herself as a financial and professional success and be now looking at moving into directing and forming her own theatre company. She'd be in a position to be able to take some time out to write a book, even, and expect to get it published, as she'd already be a name and likewise this would also allow her to have a voice on political matters.

She'd be an activist, working as an ambassador for several important issues dear to her heart, like taking the money out of politics; or fighting for our right to privacy and promoting the fair distribution of wealth. Possibly starting to think about having a family and certainly in a position that would comfortably allow her to do this.

Instead, at 33 years of age, Esmeralda found herself calling up skint old women wrapped in blankets, who couldn't afford their own heating bills, and struggling Mums with screaming children who, according to the Tory government, were no longer on the Autism spectrum so they'd had their benefits completely cut, and she was then asking these people to up their monthly direct debit contributions to the charity she was calling on behalf of from £3 a month to £12. She was phoning up penniless old women and asking them to give her their last precious pounds to feed starving children in countries where their governments were selling off what little food they had to buy tanks and missiles from countries like ours. It was complete insanity. Esmeralda was always amazed and touched by how often people said yes. She raised over £36,000 for charities in one year. She'd speak to around 160 people in three hours. Around 50 of them said yes to a small increase. Maybe eight would meet her halfway. Three an hour would say yes to the full amount. Which meant that almost a hundred people a shift didn't want to hear from her, didn't want to increase their monthly donations and occasionally took it upon themselves to tell her exactly what they thought of her for having phoned them up. This is not good for the soul. It was a hideous job. The money she was asking for would go to causes that were, to all intents and purposes 'good', but on the whole, lost causes. Black holes of hope within which the only change that would make a real difference needed to come from the governments and business practices that profiteered from the horrible mess trying to be sorted out. And of course they had no intention of altering their behaviour, because they were raking in the cash.

160 times a shift, she'd read the same script over and over again. This means she said those words around 87520 times.

She would never get those hours back.

Every single day, she cried in the toilets. Every day, she grew increasingly bitter and depressed. She blamed her husband for choosing to take the job. She blamed the woman who stole her role with the theatre company she had built up with my own bare hands. She blamed their landlord for evicting them. She blamed her family for not being wealthy. She

200

blamed the government and the bankers for driving the country into ruin. But all her blame and tears only wore one person down... And that was her. And her poor husband too. Together, they shrank into invisibility behind their own veils of depression and perceived failure. And on top of all of this, they discovered that they couldn't have children.

Never Worn

A SHORT ACCOUNT OF DEPRESSION...

The silent woman stands frozen to the kitchen floor, her weight on her left slippered foot, her right about to lift off towards a destination now long forgotten. With one hand she grips the work surface, whilst the other hand holds a kettle. Once boiled, now it has cooled.

Her dressing gown wraps tightly around her once plump figure. Now the flesh hangs sullenly about her gaunt frame. Black rings circle under her blank eyes. Her greasy hair lies lank about the crumpled face.

She does not move a muscle. Her eyes are unblinking. There is nowhere left to move to. No direction leads to relief. No delinquent idea can emerge, as no option is the right one. All choice is gone. Her brain has short circuited.

Life is meaningless.

Never Worn

BEFORE THE STORM

Esmeralda lay on a sofa bed with period pains. It was the day before she started her injections on her third and final round of IVF. After this they'd have to pay for it, and they didn't have a spare £8,000. Until now, she'd been on the pill and today was the first day she had been told not to take it. Therefore she was suffering period pains from a flow that should have come on a few days ago and had been spotting and threatening to make an entrance ever since. She was wrapped in a giant, fluffy, white hand-knitted blanket that she'd treated herself to as a gift, so it could be a kind of security blanket through this next unpleasant ride. She'd seen one in a B&B she had stayed in up north last week and instantly looked it up online and had now taken it with her on tour. It was like being cuddled by a giant mum. Her actual mum had been brilliant as always, totally there for her and giving her all the love and security she needed. Esmeralda found herself increasingly valuing the time she had with her mummy. Friends were beginning to lose their parents. Her dear brethren had lost their dad in a boating accident earlier that year, and it was utterly heartbreaking. He was an incredible man and in times of gloom she would now think of him and imagine what he would chose to do in any given situation and try to emulate him. He was a Quaker and, like her mother, only chose to see the good in people and the world. Somehow she hadn't managed to pull off quite the same outlook. Perhaps she needed to re-find god?

Can't do the Christian God though. Too much of a feminist for that bollocks. I did pray to the Goddess yesterday... But it felt hollow. She's forsaken me too.

Esmeralda was sitting in the remains of her old world and she pondered on how much things had changed. She was curled up on a dusty sofa bed, in the only warm room she could find, known as the snug. It was the only space with a cosy electric fire in an otherwise rattling and rotten, but adorably characterful, theatre. She was staying there with the actors she had been touring with for the last two years, as their producer. They were presenting a musical comedy about science to rural communities around Nottinghamshire and Lincolnshire. Esmeralda had contacted the owners of the theatre to see if they might be able to put them up for a few nights for free, as she knew them well and that there were plenty of beds at the old theatre.

She knew the theatre and its owners from being fellow fools in the company of fools she'd produced, trained and performed with many years ago. They'd lived on the road together, touring and training with their Master Fool in his unique and unusual theatre technique. They had practiced for ten days every month, in a different location somewhere in the UK or Europe, every month for ten months of the year. They had learnt every word of Richard II and had created an incredible production of the play, as an ensemble, where they had used no props, no costumes, just their bodies and imaginations, creating the world of Richard II around the audience, like the audience was in a dream bubble of the play, akin to the ballroom scene in *Labyrinth*. People who had seen it said it had reminded them of reading a book, where the reader dressed the action with their own imaginations. They'd said that they could recall armour and flags, horses and weather, from the production they saw, but all they had seen on the stage had been the actors in black costumes. They spent three years developing the piece, learnt all of the words to the whole play so that they could all play all of the parts, and about twenty people had seen it. Towards the end of their time touring together, someone from a trust that the Master Fool had been part of retired from running the old theatre where they were now staying, and two of the company members had moved up to Lincolnshire to run the place. That had been four years ago now and Esmeralda had not seen them since, so it was odd being back. Mainly because so little there had changed. But *she* had. Quite a lot... In some ways.

'No. No wine for me thanks. I'm not drinking. I don't drink at all anymore... Or do anything else... I've even become vegetarian.'

'What...' he replied, looking at her in mock horror. 'You've really changed.'

She thought about the differences in the kind of theatre she was currently working in, compared to the work she had been immersed in when last she had been here. For the last couple of years she'd been working on shows to do with science and had formed a better understanding of how the universe worked than she'd ever achieved at school. And she felt incredibly proud to be then sharing this knowledge and understanding with audiences young and old, all over the country, in a fun and accessible way. Then, earlier this year, she had found herself working in an art form totally new to her, that had totally rocked her world, which was disability arts. It did everything she wanted from the art world. It challenged preconceptions, expanded the mind, made the world a better place. There were not many areas left in the theatre or the arts in general that she felt actually achieved this. She thought that most theatre was awash with naval gazing and preaching to the converted at best, outright commercialisation at the worst. Being introduced to this world of disabled artists had shifted Esmeralda from someone who knew in theory that she had no problem with disability to realising that she didn't actually know anyone with a disability and because of this she didn't actually know what life was like for a disabled person. This made her realise that she was making presumptions about people in all other areas of her life too; and that it was high time she faced everything head on rather than just assuming her ideas on people were right. This changed her interaction with everyone. Homeless people, for example, who she'd now stop and chat to for a while, rather than just handing over some occasional cash. It had opened up the world and had made her more aware of all of the wonderful people living upon it.

It was great to be back in this theatre building up north again. She was bloody glad she didn't have to live here though, because it was freezing, but she felt a magical connection to the place. First of all, when they had arrived at this theatre for the first time many years ago, having been given the theatre, the company had gone off to explore the tiny market town, which had reminded Esmeralda of the place where she had grown up in Essex, before the London overspill had moved in and changed it forever. It was also an old market town and the market square looked as if it had been built around the same time as the one she'd grown up in. During their investigations they had been amazed to discover that the Norman church across the road from the theatre contained none other than the Willoughby Chapel, a character that Esmeralda had spoken the lines for in Richard II. And there, on top of his tomb, lay a life-size stone sculpture of the dead knight himself, placed there when he had died in 1409. The serendipity was crazy. Then it turned out that Bolingbroke Castle, where Old John of Gaunt had lived with Henry IV as a child, was just down the road. They went to the castle on a kind of pilgrimage and reverentially rehearsed Gaunt's 'This Sceptred Isle' speech amongst the ruins.

Another fantastic discovery had been the wool shop. Esmeralda hadn't knitted since her Nanny had died, which meant she got very excited when she found the wool shop, as it reminded her of her Nan and inspired her to have a go at knitting again. The woman in the shop and the smell of the place totally reminded Esmeralda of the one they used to go to in the market square back home. The woman was great, full of beans, and suggested which needles to use and the correct wool. This time, some four years later, Esmeralda was very pleased to see that the wool shop was still there and the old lady in good health. She was excited to get her little mitts on the textures of the wools and to tell the lady how much she had inspired her all those years ago and that now Esmeralda had become an avid crochet queen. The old woman told her that she too loved crochet and that she wanted to be remembered as the Rabbit Woman, as she always appliquéd rabbits on her creations 'Like the pig man of Yorkshire' she said, expecting Esmeralda to have heard of him and know what the hell she was talking about, which Esmeralda adored.

Whilst there Esmeralda also popped into the witches' shop. It was filled with unusual scents, glittering crystals and an array of colourful candles hung from the walls. It was coming up to Hallowe'en and Esmeralda wanted to get some bits and bobs to help with her IVF at this magical time of year. She selected a bunch of candles and a gift for her fellow witch friend.

Driving through the eerie landscape of Lincolnshire, mists hung in heavy duvets across the harvested muddy fields, and a black cat silently stalked some poor unsuspecting field mice.

'Tom used to go out with a Witch,' said Rachel, as they talked about Tom's dream the previous night, where a woman was being burnt at the stake. Esmeralda enquired which witch had once been his witch? He told her and she knew the woman. She had suspected she probably would.

'I'm a witch too' she said.

'Yes, but she was a real witch, as in, she was in a coven and practiced witchcraft.'

'Oh,' answered Esmeralda, instantly riled that a man was laying ownership to a woman's level of witchcraft, 'Well in that case I'm more of a shaman than a witch, in that I had a near-death experience when I was a child, where I made contact with the spirit world, and it became my path. But in shamanic cultures, female shamans are called witches too, so it still makes me a witch.'

And she was in a coven *and* she practised witchcraft. She wore a ring on her right hand to prove it. But it was a secret and certainly not one for a man's ears.

MAY DAY

In the end, it was three years before they got married, so they'd had time to figure out if it was what they really wanted to do or not. They always argued a lot, but she trusted him implicitly. They were both from broken homes where the dads had been rubbish, and so it was deeply important to both of them that they didn't turn out like their fathers. And that meant a lot to her. She hadn't met anyone else who was up for committing completely, who was also trustworthy and up for taking on her host of crazy schemes. They had fun, though, and great adventures. He was being flexible and they were doing exactly what she wanted to do.

They got married and it was the most epic event of her life. Or four events, as it turned out. First of all the theatre company they were with took it in turns for each member to have a day whilst camping in a yurt in a field in Norfolk. Esmeralda and her then fiancé had chosen to have a combined day and

213

together had invited lots of friends and family to come and spend it with them. Their activity was to go for a walk. Whilst they were all out walking, a guy had appeared in a paddock and asked them if they wanted the key to a tiny old medieval church they were approaching. They said they would and, upon entering, discovered that it was covered in flowers from a wedding the day before. The director suggested that they had a foolish wedding themselves. One of the company played Elton John on the organ, two of her best friends acted as her bridesmaids and she made herself a veil and bouquet out of the left over flowers and lace work in the church. Their director married them at the altar...

'Do you promise never, ever, ever to look at another man or woman ever again?'

'I do.'

'Then I pronounce you... The most foolish people on the planet!'

Although it was a joke wedding, the director had a strong connection to the archetypes and her nearest and dearest were all there *and* it was in a church. She had felt the winds come up around her ankles and from that moment on Esmeralda had felt that her soul was inextricably woven into his.

The second wedding had been in the year 1535.

Esmeralda had been working at a Tudor re-creation since she was just ten years old and he'd been up for taking on that part of her life, too. Once they had got together he had dressed up and joined in, which she was over the moon about. He was known about the manor and it seemed only fitting that they should have a Tudor wedding the year before their actual one, as they were to have a hand-fasting. This meant that they would be married for a year and a day. It was a fabulous event. They were carried in on a horse-drawn cart, covered in flowers, with a giant sun hat crowning it, which she often wore in the mummers' plays that they performed together. An army of soldiers, drumming boys, and pipers led them in and greeted them with a twelve gun salute. They were driven onto the barn sward where Doctor Dob, who looked like Gandalf, met them by the maypole, which was in front of their beloved mummers' cart, and he conducted the service. He tied their hands together and made them exchange vows, then they were asked to walk through fire, which they did. Gifts were brought to them, including a sneaky jug of gin under the guise of being a 'love potion'. Her brother told a tale about Plato's theory on the origins of love and her brethren friend told a story about why love was blind. Then they cut the bind, everyone threw rose petals over them and then they all danced in circles.

The third wedding was at a registry office and was *meant* to be a quiet affair, but they just weren't very good at such things. It was the day before their big event and in Brighton Town Hall. All their local friends turned up to throw confetti at them when they came out. Their nearest and dearest were witnesses and a friend of theirs was an ordained registrar from Hastings, who came over especially to conduct the service, bringing with him a magical looking silver goblet that split in two, meaning they could both drink from it. Afterwards they all went to the pub and had a meal. Then they headed to the main wedding site to start setting up for the following day.

The fourth and final wedding was epic. They hired a field in the middle of nowhere, a mile or so from the beautiful Bodiham Castle, so that they could go there to get their photos taken. The field had nothing in it at all, which meant that Esmeralda had called in every favour imaginable to get it all set up. This hadn't been so difficult as she'd been working with lots of creative Brightonians for years and everyone had been happy to help out. She hired a stunning marquee for next to nothing, one that was originally from India and looked like a harem. It was a deep maroon on the outside with golden trimmings and on the inside it was golden with maroon paisley. The coconut matting was a deep red and on the floor were scattered low dark wooden tables and opulent Moroccan cushions. At one end they had a stage and at the other end a 'bring a bottle bar' and 'pot luck' buffet table. They supplied a load of free bubbly plus a mountain of beer and wine from a trip to France. They put on a hog roast and had seats for 200 people around large round tables with bunches of fake red roses and peacock feathers as centre pieces. One of her bridesmaids made 200 cupcakes and a giant cupcake that was a jaffa cake. This disappeared at some point throughout the evening before they got around to cutting it and was never seen again. They were pretty sure that one of the groom's friends from Kingston had smashed it into someone's face.

It took place on May Day and the Royals had been kind enough to announce that they were getting married the same weekend, thus extending the public holiday to four days long. The service was conducted under a maypole beneath a beautiful old oak tree. Everyone sat on gold and red chairs or hay bales and the ten bridesmaids and ten ushers all sat in couples around the maypole, circling the happy couple. He had a great big handlebar moustache and a tweed suit, with a top hat. She was thin and gorgeous and wore a Marilyn Monroe style lace halter neck dress that fish-tailed down to the ground with a lovely splashing trail, showing off her naturally curved body to perfection. She wore a fastened-on feather boa about her shoulders and a 1920's-style headdress of beads and peacock feathers on her head. Her hair was dyed red for the occasion and she had a bunch of red roses and peacock feathers in one hand and a flamboyant ruffled white parasol in the other. Her shoes were gold and white, covered in frilly flowers and had transparent golden stripper heels. Her handbag was handmade and dripping in shaky white beads. They both looked stunning. Her beautiful friend with an incredible voice sang in a wedding march, which was *Some Day He'll Come Along, the Man I Love* by Kate Bush. Esmeralda walked the wedding march on her own, with her matrons of honour ahead of her and parents behind. Her dad had given her away years ago as far as she was concerned. Their mutual friend, who was like an archetype on earth - part Jesus, part Elk, part orangutan - with long flowing ginger hair, conducted their service dressed as an angel, with big white feathery wings. And their huge black registrar friend was also there to assist and include his silver goblet again in the wedding ceremony. They did the hand-fasting ceremony once more and her brother and brethren told the same stories as they had at the Tudor wedding, then performed a mummers' play which included members of the theatre company they were part of, tying all four of the wedding services together nicely. Their friends who played modern music in a cockney knees-up type fashion on the honky-tonk piano conducted their 'hymns' and they plumped for Queen's *Don't Stop me Now,* Madness' *Must be Love* and Sonny & Cher's *I Got You Babe.* After the service the bridesmaids and the ushers danced the maypole. Then her friend performed one of her favourite cabaret acts for Esmeralda on a little castle stage that had been brought along for the occasion. They went to Bodiham Castle to get their photos taken, then came back to watch an old band who had not played together for over ten years, reform once more just for them. It was great to see the guys perform again and Esmeralda laughed with her Maid of Honour as the audience were all the same, but just much older. They realised that between them they'd pulled all the band members at one point or another. The toasts turned into a comedy show with possibly the most inappropriate speech ever told by one of the ushers about the groom; going into graphic detail about a time they'd both been on acid and pulled a couple of rough birds from the Isle of Dogs, only to then be attacked by what turned out to be a very angry mob of said ladies' boyfriends. He finished it by quoting the words of Bill Hicks - *Life is just a ride,* he said. *And if it is just a ride then this groom is at the front of it, with his hands in the air and his cock hanging out.*

Never Worn

PROTOCOL

Injection One - Esmeralda forgot they were doing the first injection that night. Completely forgot about it. They had enjoyed a gorgeous day. It was her first weekend off since August and her dear friend came over to help her chill out, by painting her nails blue with shellac - which was the first time she'd used the stuff - whilst her wonderful husband cooked a delicious roast and left them to it, whilst they gassed about men and babies and friends and feelings and all the usual flow of ladies' chit chat. They then enjoyed fine food. A thoroughly delightful evening. Esmeralda's husband was the one who then went for the baby kit as Esmeralda's friend left. Bugger. She wasn't mentally prepared for that at all and then discovered that the kit didn't have any Buserilin in it. Luckily they had some left over from the last time, which had not been opened and was within date. Fucking imbeciles. Made her

221

get a bit panicky. Then couldn't find the protocol explaining what dosages they had to do. Finally they located it. 50IU's of the liquid needed to be pulled into a syringe and pushed into her poor little belly. She had really enjoyed being thin. Her friend had jumped on her the night before cooing over how little she was. It had made her chuffed. But it was time to get fat again. Hopefully it would be worth it this time and not just a precursor to making her lose the plot. Buserilin lowers your estrogen levels and simulates having a menopause.

Injection Two – Esmeralda had been working all day and was a bit concerned about the lack of shows booked for next year's tour. If she didn't bring in the cash then she wouldn't get paid, so it's a real worry. She worked from 9am until 10pm at night. She had terrible RSI in her right arm. She couldn't type very much. Her husband was playing a zombie game on his PC, one of the online ones where if you die you start back at the beginning again and you hardly ever see anyone. It was a pretty cool game that seemed quiet realistic. He asked her what she was typing and she told him she was writing about him. They were getting on well at the moment. She was already feeling her stomach doing the reverse of what it had been doing of late, which was a very good impression of a thin person. It had swollen back up again and was back to its usual pot-bellied shape. Her nails were still perfect though. She injected her belly. It hurt.

Injection Three – Esmeralda was all ready to climb into bed in her pyjamas, when she remembered that she had to do the injection and dragged herself back down stairs again and got that lovely husband of hers to administer it. It really stung this time and the prick spot on her stomach kept scratching against her top on the way back up the stairs in a rather painful manner. But it wasn't so bad. There were plenty of people out there having to put up with much worse.

Injection Four – Esmeralda nearly left the house without the Buserilin and syringes in her bag. She was on her way up to London to perform a show to the Arts Council, and ended up nearly being late to the show. She was starting to feel the mental effects of the injections. Was picking a fight with her husband this morning and was feeling busy in her brain. Making mistakes. Also trying to do too much. No downtime. She needed to ease off the gas. First injection she had to do to herself tonight. Had to sneak in her room and do it when no one was looking.

Injection Five – She was making mistakes left right and centre, and getting stressed out, paranoid and tired. Feeling like she was on a drugs comedown the whole time. It had taken two hours longer than it should have done to get where they were going today, because of her directions. Or possibly not, as the driver missed the junction they needed, but still she beat herself up for it anyway. Did the injection that night in front of her friend who had very kindly just driven them all the way to Liverpool and back again in a day. He said that if it worked this time then he'll tell the kid when it's born that he saw it being conceived.

Injection Six – Esmeralda had completely gone to pieces. She had been for a gorgeous day at the spa with her mum the previous day and from the talking, being massaged and having not had a proper night's sleep for the last few days she had gradually unravelled until she was a sobbing heap on her mum's sofa. It was cool, though, that she knew it was the injections this time. It was familiar ground now. Didn't make it any less unpleasant, but at least she was able to hold onto the thread that she was not insane. She was genuinely concerned, though, that she was going to be mad for the whole of the pregnancy if this worked, and that she might get post-natal depression. She had decided to start looking into depression to see if she could find out how to combat it and reprogramme her brain. Was there a way of protecting herself against post-natal depression, she wondered?

Injection Seven – Esmeralda tried to do the injection with her husband there, but couldn't. She had to get him to do it, Thinking it was probably her way of subconsciously of keeping him part of the process. She had a really bad headache. Needed to ring the clinic tomorrow to let them know she was getting the side-effects again. Hoped they wouldn't have to cancel this round too. She couldn't face doing all this again.

Injection Eight – She realised in the morning that she was meant to start the Gonal F last night. Whoops. Rang the clinic and told them that she was a) getting negative symptoms again, having once more lost the plot and b) didn't do the Gonal F when she was meant to. She was rather annoyed to discover that morning, on the NHS website, one of the side effects listed for Buserlin was the following... 'depression or worsening of depression - seek medical advice if you develop depression'. No one had ever checked with her to see if she had suffered from depression before, and when she got depressed as hell from the over-stimulation last time, the clinic acted as if they'd never *heard* of such a thing before. Luckily though, today, they said to her it was good she was late with the injection, as she would not be so far along the line by the time she got the first scan and they could keep a closer eye on her. It was amazing that they were getting this for free, though, and she loved the NHS for it mightily, although the treatment was from a private clinic, paid for by the NHS.

Injections Nine & Ten – She had to go to Canterbury, to do a performance in a *Spiegeltent* as part of the festival there. They stayed in a hotel and she enjoyed having a bit of "me" time. Esmeralda took sexy photos of herself naked in the mirror, which had lights down the side of it that made her look good. If she got pregnant, it would be the last time she looked like this. She had to do both of the injections herself. It was fine.

Injections Eleven & Twelve – Esmeralda was just doing them herself now, but with her husband there. She got home and did them that night with him. Her stomach was looking pretty bruised now and she was starting to gain a bit of weight. Doing loads of swimming though. She learnt to do that spinning thing at the end of a lap, to help her go faster, which she was rather proud of. She was feeling more normal again. The second injection seemed to be cancelling out the side-effects of the first one. Gonal F is a follicle-stimulating hormone, that makes the eggs pop out.

Injections Thirteen & Fourteen – Esmeralda was feeling much better, which was ace. She got scared when doing them that night, though, that she'd been administering the wrong amounts, but they did the maths and they were okay.

Injections Fifteen & Sixteen - The horrible side-effects of the Buserlin had worn off, and she was feeling much better. That day, she applied for a

Vippassana. This is when you meditate for ten days without speaking. It's free, but you pay a donation if you can. She was booked in to do one at the end of January. This made her feel calm, because if the IVF worked, she could realign herself with her truths before becoming a mother, and if it didn't work, she could realign herself with her truths before heading back into the world she would create for herself as a childless woman.

Injections Seventeen & Eighteen – She went for her first scan that day and it was all looking normal. She had eight follicles forming on each ovary and when they took her blood they found that her hormone levels were okay. Injections were going fine. She found the Gonal F a lot less painful than the last stuff they tried.

Injections Nineteen & Twenty – She had had a flu jab as well, that day. She was beginning to feel like a human pin-cushion and the jab made her feel a bit under the weather. She had an argument with her husband that night, which made it hard to want to do the injections. At one point he was even saying to her, just cancel doing it altogether. In the end, she made him stick a needle in his belly at the same time as her having to do it. It made her feel a little bit better.

Injections Twenty-One & Twenty-Two – They had argued all day because she was annoyed at him for talking to her like that the previous night. It was a horrible day, and they both felt ill by the end of it. The injections were the last thing Esmeralda felt like doing. She finished the first Gonal F pen that night. Just one more to go. Instead of making him stick a pin in his belly, tonight she used it as an opportunity to make him take the selenium he was meant to be taking. Why did guys have to be such cocks about their health? She was doing all this, and he just had to take a fucking vitamin pill. And had he done it? Had he fuck.

Injections Twenty-Three & Twenty-Four – Esmeralda had a really lovely day, cooking for all of their friends and things had smoothed down between them. She was fed up of him though. Was also getting concerned about the amount of stuff she had planned during the week between her being harvested and the eggs going back in. She would be really busy. Thought she needed to thin out the load somewhat.

Injection Twenty-Five & Twenty-Six - At the scan that day, Esmeralda talked to the nurse about how screwed up the world is and how stupid it seemed for her to be forcing a child into it when everything is such a mess, and the nurse replied that she didn't think it mattered, as a billion years from now we will all be dead and no one will ever know we were here and it won't matter what we got up to. We might as well live our lives for today and just do what we've got to do as individuals, without worrying about the future or dwelling on the past. A wise woman. Esmeralda also believed we should always do whatever we can to make the world a better place, though. Filling the planet up with more people is not really making the world a better place; however, if you feel you are one of the good guys, you ought to at least leave your body weight behind. The scan showed that she had a good bunch of follicles on each ovary, that were above a ten in measurement, which meant they were looking good. They took her blood again and would contact her if her hormones were too high. She didn't feel ill at all this time, which was a good sign, but she was putting on a bit of weight, so perhaps they might need to start reducing her doses soon.

Injections Twenty-Seven & Twenty-Eight – Esmeralda hadn't felt very well all day. Her belly had definitely swollen up and her ovaries were hurting. Generally feeling under the weather. She rang the clinic to let them know and they said that her hormone levels from the blood test yesterday were on the high side, so to reduce her Gonal F injection to 112.5IU this evening. She did them quickly and easily without any fuss. The husband ate a whole red chilli as a moral support, which was funny and sweet of him.

Injections Twenty-Nine & Thirty – She went in for a scan that morning with the husband and they found that her ovaries were plumping up nicely, with eight proper follicles on each side and a couple of little ones forming. When you saw them on the ultrasound they looked like honeycombs. She would never forget the day she saw her ovaries swollen up to the size of tennis balls. It made her eyes water just thinking about it. This time around they were more like ping-pong balls and the nurse informed her that they'd decided to trigger her tonight, ready for collection on Friday. This really threw her at first. Her life was stupidly busy the following week, so much so that she had even been getting nightmares about it. A few desperate phone calls were required to remove all the appointments from her calendar. She lost it for a bit. She was meant to be heading off to Bedford that night for a show, but in the end they re-arranged to go the next morning at 6am instead. The trouble was, she was trying not to tell anyone what she was doing. Last time was horrific, so she would rather just let this round either work or not work and then deal with the consequences. Once the panic was over and the week had been cleared, she was able to relax and enjoy the fact that it's all going well. Her husband was actually great that day. He came with her to the scan and helped her get through her calendar freak-out. He then administered her last injection of Buserelin. When he was good he was a winner. They went for a walk that night to look at the fireworks. Esmeralda was wearing her Ewok onesie because she didn't want to get out of her pyjamas and it had turned cold. They looked over Brighton from high up on the hill and watched the glittering stars sprinkle the night sky. *In two weeks time*, she thought, *I might be pregnant*.

At 10.30pm they administered the final trigger injection. Whatever happened now, this would be her last IVF sharp, and so after it had been done they put it in the sharps box and sealed the lid. HURRAH.....

While they were sorting out the dosage of 250mcg of Ovitrelle, the telly had Grayson Perry on it, doing a programme about identity and he was looking at fat women coming out and enjoying their bodies. The husband said it was fortuitous of Esmeralda's inner fat woman coming out and her enjoying my body. Fingers crossed.

No Injection – Esmeralda had to get up at 5.30am and get in the car to go and operate the lighting and sound for two shows about Einstein in Baldock and Bedford. Both lovely places and the shows did really well. Got back after midnight.

Operation - No food after midnight or water after 7.30am. They arrived, and the, husband got called up right away. *Can you believe it,* she thought, *I go through all of this and he just wanks into a cup. It's ridiculous.* She was called into a waiting room and they took her weight - still just 60 kilos - get in there! Then they put bands around her arms saying what her allergies were and what procedures were being done. They were getting ICSI, which is where they literally pierced her eggs with a needle and inserted the best sperm. The other form is where they chuck the eggs in with the sperm in a petri dish and leave them to party. Theirs would not work like that though. She changed into a hospital gown and the anaesthetist came to see her. He was very funny and chatty, with a pencil moustache. It was Movember and everyone had a moustache. Her husband had noticed everyone staring at him all of a sudden because he had an enormous beard. It took them a while to realise that it was due to all this Movember nonsense. Esmeralda was led into the surgery and they set about lying her down on the bed, legs in stirrups. They put those sticky pads on her chest to listen to her heart, oxygen mask over her face and a drip into her hand. Then the anaesthetist administered an anaesthetic down the drip and the room began to swirl and she was gone. Next thing, she was coming to again in a tiny ward with just one bed and a set of armchairs. There was a kind nurse there to hand her some water. It reminded her of when she went in for an abortion all those years ago. But this time, everyone was being nice to her. The nurse told her they managed to harvest fifteen eggs. That was a great number. The nurse asked her how much pain she was in on a scale of one to ten and Esmeralda said eight. Her ovaries were really sore.

She was given a pain killer and began to feel better. After a while, she was moved to one of the armchairs and they brought her a coffee and an egg sandwich. She wondered if they appreciated how ironic that was. After perhaps an hour they let her husband take her home. He had bought her a bunch of flowers and a box of chocolates. She sat on the sofa in front of the telly and relaxed. When the painkillers wore off, it really hurt. She was in a lot more pain than last time, but she didn't have a fever and was not bleeding, so it was just bad bruising.

Morning after - Still in a lot of pain, she had to stick a Progesterone pessary up her bum. The clinic rang her to tell her that out of the fifteen eggs they had harvested, eleven of them were good enough to use and so they had started the procedure on them last night and today nine of them had fertilised. They would let her know on Monday how many had survived the weekend. This was all great, but was the same as what happened last time. They put a top grade embryo back in her last time and it didn't implant. All they can recreate is the 'up to sex' bit of the baby making act. After that, it is all up to fate.

Morning after the morning after – Esmeralda's mum came over and helped her to clean the house. Her dear black cat had become allergic to fleas and looked like he had the mange. He had scratched off all of his fur and was over-preening. It was sad to see. Plus, if she did get pregnant then they wanted the house to be clean and she wouldn't be able to handle flea-killing chemicals. They blitzed the house. Esmeralda was still feeling fragile, so couldn't have done it without her mum. She was amazing and Esmeralda felt unbelievably relaxed afterwards. She shat herself that day, from farting out a pessary.

Morning after the morning after the morning after - The clinic rang to say that, out of the nine eggs that had fertilised, eight of them had survived the weekend. One was looking a little slow, but there were seven good ones and it was all systems go for the transfer in two days time. Esmeralda couldn't believe that in two days she would be technically pregnant. It might not last, she may not be pregnant still in three weeks' time, but it was soothing to know that for at least for a day she would be pregnant. It was all about the minor victories. The neighbour's kids were screaming blue murder next door. Why did she want do this again?

Morning after the morning after the morning after the morning after – Esmeralda worked all day. She got really stressed out in the morning by a thoughtless friend and couldn't calm down again. Another friend offered to give her a shiatsu massage and that had helped to sooth her, but it all goes to show how her deep-seated emotions were all coiled up inside, and if something set her off, she struggled to calm down again. She went to a meeting in London. It sort of went well, but somehow she managed to end up feeling like a nobody again. She made lots of mistakes today and was struggling to be present. She was getting anxious. She woke up at 5am and her brain was full of stuff, going over and over old upsets, grievances and concerns. She got up and wrote a play. That helped a bit.

Day of the Transfer – It was time to go and make a science baby...

They arrived at the clinic and were led into the changing room and asked to undress. Her husband had to also wear the theatre blues too and Esmeralda was told to put on a hospital gown. They went in and the embryologist was there and the doctor. The embryologist went through the list of how many eggs she had, how many had fertilised, how these had been developing since they'd last spoken to them, and finally got around to saying there were just two left that can be used and none that could be frozen. Esmeralda didn't see how any could ever be frozen. She didn't think you can produce more than fifteen eggs without it tipping into overstimulation, so how could they ever expect to get any for freezing, when they are unable to freeze any out of 15 a pop? She'd produced twelve last time, too, and they hadn't been able to freeze any of those, either. Then they told her that the embryos this time were not grade A, like the one they'd tried last time had been. These ones were grade B/C and grade C, so the doctor recommended that they put two in. The embryologist didn't look too happy about this recommendation and Esmeralda's husband wasn't sure either, so they talked it through a bit more and the upshot was that this was their last go. They couldn't afford to pay £8000 themselves to do it, she didn't want to go through it again and she was nearly 36. They needed to try and make this happen now. They brushed over the fact that she had started to over-stimulate again this time, which would mean she wouldn't be allowed to have two put back in and they skirted around the history of multiple births in her husband's family. In the end, they went for two anyway. She lay back on the raised bed, and put her legs up in stirrups. A nurse held an ultrasound wand to her belly so they could see the shape of her womb. The doctor inserted a catheter and did a dummy run to check it was inserted properly, then she called over the embryologist, who brought the embryos over in syringes, which got squirted down the catheter and appeared on the screen in Esmeralda's womb. And that was that. For this afternoon at least, she was carrying twins.

ODIN SPEAKS

Odin spoke to Esmeralda directly one night. This was obviously rather exciting. He told her to listen, which was funny, because she didn't at first. Whilst in Spilsby, she'd visited a witches' shop she knew was there and bought herself four candles; a green one for fertility, a white one for spirit, a red one for passion and a blue one for wisdom. In a ceremony, once she'd returned home, she created a small shrine in their hearth. It consisted of two replica casts of the famous prehistoric Venus statues, a doll of a woman that a young girl sold to Esmeralda in Egypt, after they'd landed in her father's field, having just flown over the Valley of the Queens in a hot air balloon, and a small Russian doll set. They represented the Goddess, to whom Esmeralda was praying.

She meditated on the candles and etched runes upon them. On the green candle, she carved the rune Geoff, which looks like this X and represents a spiritual gift. She lit this and placed the candle in amongst the statues of the goddesses, positioned it to the north, which represents the physical realm and the earth. On the white candle, she etched the rune Thurisaz, which looks like this ᚦ. To her, this rune represented the hawthorn and the shaman. Once this candle was lit, she placed it to the east with the wind, in her spiritual realm. On the red candle, she etched the rune Mann, which looks like this ᛗ and means man. This represented her husband, and she placed it in her emotional fire realm, to the south. Finally, on the blue candle, she etched the rune Ing - which was her rune, the first one she ever drew, when she was 13 years old and taking her first LSD tab in an old stable next to a stately home, where a friend of hers had lived with her hippie family, who were all part of the Rainbow Tribe. Ing looks like this ◇ and it means transformation. It is the seed. Before she had got married, her name had literally translated as inspiring clear transformation. Now she was married, her name meant inspiring clear one who sleeps in the fields with the animals. It was ironic that her names had always suited her disposition, yet her name was currently the total opposite to the flow of her reality. She lit this candle and placed it to the west, with the water, in the wisdom realm.

At first, she sat in the circle of candles and meditated. She was very tired and had lovely music playing, so she felt herself easily sinking into a quiet state. After some time, she set about doing a rune reading. The first rune she pulled out was to represent Esmeralda and she placed it between her legs. Then she drew four more and placed them beside each of the candles, starting in the north. This was the first one she could see, as it was in front of her, and it was the rune Ansur, which looks like this ᚨ and means a mouth. It represents a spiritual message from Odin, who was a personal favourite of hers. He had led her to the runes when she was only eight years old, when she learnt to read and write them fluently off the back of a tourist brochure at the Jorvik Centre in York, where it was presented as the Saxon alphabet. Having learnt to read and write them fluently, she then used them in her journals to disguise anything she didn't want people to know about. Odin was also with her in crow form, when she made a blood offering in Lewes and apologised to the Goddess for sending back her gift of a baby, thirteen years ago. He was the first shaman she ever learnt about. And here he was, speaking to her and telling her to listen...

Of course at first, she didn't. She was too busy freaking out about what the other runes were saying. The rune between her legs, representing her, was ᚷ. meaning spiritual gift and the same rune she'd etched on the fertility candle in her physical realm, yet here it was upside down in her lap. That means there was a block there. Her gift from the Goddess was blocked. Then, to the east in the spiritual realm was the rune ᚲ which literally means pregnancy and was again upside down, so it meant the spirit of her baby was blocked from her. Behind, to the south in her emotional realm, was the rune ᛗ the very same rune as she had etched onto the candle and represented her husband, and was also upside down and so blocked. Finally to the west in her wisdom realm was the rune ᚦ - the same as the one she'd etched on her white candle in her spiritual realm and again it was upside down, and so meant that her wisdom about her spiritual path was also blocked. She was so freaked out by the reading that she picked another one out quickly, asking the question, 'well is the IVF going to work then?' The rune she pulled out was ᛁ. This is a rune that links the upper and lower worlds. It can be seen as death, but also represents birth. As she was freaking out, the first thing she saw it as was death. This made her panic so much, she leapt out of the circle and sat on the sofa shaking. It went against her instincts completely. She was convinced it was going to work this time. It might not, obviously, but she felt like it was going to.

After a while, she began to calm down and then thought about it from a different point of view. She hadn't asked a specific question when she'd pulled out the circle of runes, so in a way it was just telling her how things were. She had been blocked from her spiritual gift from the goddess and the spirit of her child. Her relationship with her man had been blocked and her spirituality had been intellectually blocked, as she loved science and was an 'atheist' on paper, but as you can see, that was also bollocks.

It then struck her that Odin had asked her to listen.

So she asked, 'Should I bother doing this IVF?' and pulled out three runes, which is a simple past, present and future reading. The following three runes came out...

ᛗ ᚴ ᛯ

These runes mean man, pregnancy, inheritance.

It was going to work. And the blocked runes she'd pulled in the ceremony were the things she needed to get in order, so that it all can fall into place.

Thanks Odin... I think.

Never Worn

THE FISHPOND

One of the most significant moments in Esmeralda's life was thanks to a fishpond; a deep-set rectangular construction, dating from the 15th century. A Tudor swimming pool in fact. The water was murky and bright green, the colour of bitter lemon. It ebbed and flowed from the continual movement of the great stalking mirrored carp whose black shimmering backs would trawl below the surface like ominous sea monsters, occasionally peering up through the murky depths with their bulbous eyes and huge gaping mouths, sucking at the air like they wanted to eat your soul. If you threw food down to these creatures then a multitude of faces would appear as if a scene from Dante's Hell, all gaping and gasping at the air, scrabbling with gluttonous anxiety.

Despite its far from glamorous façade, the fishpond was a favourite haunt during the hot summer days of the Tudor re-creation, the re-creators having spent their days in thick woollen costumes outside and under the blazing heat of the summer sun. By the end of the day, when the visitor numbers began to dwindle, many would descend upon the pond, stripping down to their white linen smocks, the women carefully keeping their coifs upon their heads whilst lowering themselves into the fishy smelling pool to cool their sweaty bodies in its cold, murky waters.

On this particular occasion, a group of friends and Esmeralda had spent the day jumping in and out of the pond, creating quite a bit of business. Her family had turned up as visitors and had taken a great many photos and a video of them frolicking in the water. Then they'd wandered off and the friends continued with their frivolities. Even though she had run and jumped into the pond countless times that day she suddenly found that she was unable to do so. There she stood, poised on the bank, skirt hitched up, body primed, ready to run and leap into the air. But for some reason every bone in her body was screaming at her not to do it. A crowd began to form on the bank opposite shouting at her to jump.

It was as if there was an invisible wall blocking her way. Like in a dream, her legs filled with lead and glued themselves to the spot. Her hearing went fuzzy, but all other senses were heightened. Colours were vivid and the light reflecting upon the surface of the pond sang to her with mermaid voices, enticing Esmeralda in, but she knew with certainty that they should not be trusted. Pulling herself together her reasoning kicked in. Hadn't she done this all day? Weren't there lots of people gathered now on the bank who wanted to see her do this? Did she want to disappoint them? What exactly was the problem? Reason prevailed. She ran and jumped...

As her body lifted into the air, her smock lifted above her head and as she hit the water her smock became an embalming net, caught around her flapping arms and wrapped itself like a constrictor around her face. She became disorientated and couldn't tell which way was up and which way was down. At first she flapped around, trying to pull the material free and find the slimy floor with her feet, but time trickled past and it began to dawn on her that she was in trouble. Becoming calm, she opened her eyes and tried to pull the shift from her body, but the sleeves and neck were tied tight with drawstring. All she could see in the dark waters was the material all around, glowing green in the depths, and dancing bubbles of her breath escaping from her shrinking lungs. She could only get the neck up to her nose and there it stuck fast. Then it occurred to her that if she stopped kicking and let herself float she would find the surface, so she stopped moving and let herself be lifted by her natural buoyancy. She could see down the sides of her nose beneath the shift and saw the surface coming into view. As her face peered up through the rippling veil of water she saw the shimmering shape of a grey old man standing on the bank. She did not recognise him but he was dressed in a full Tudor outfit of heavy brown and black wool. His small white-haired head protruded out of a great thick cloak that hung about him. Even through the water she could tell he was a frail looking fellow, but as her head finally bobbed out of the water for a moment, just long enough to call for help, her very last breath leaving her, she watched him leap into the water to the rescue without a second's hesitation. The disturbance of the water from his impact filled her open mouth and, although she grabbed frantically towards his outstretched fingers, she had no strength or air left and began to sink back beneath the water, into the darkness.

On a train with separate compartments. On my own. Looking out of the window.

A drumming sound is distracting me.

Above my head a Red Admiral butterfly is flapping violently against the glass.

Opening the window to release it, it flutters away…

A raven, black as night, screams from a gate post.

A dove, white as day, nuzzles my neck.

Falling.

A white mask, smooth like royal icing.

Darkness.

A white mask, smooth like royal icing, but smashed into a million pieces.

Darkness.

Darkness.

Arms pulled her up and she was dragged backwards through the water. She was lifted onto the bank and hands ripped the shift from her prepubescent body. Lips planted themselves onto her lips and blew. She coughed. She threw up water. She was naked.

Clothes were wrapped around her and she was led to the sunny garden. In the garden, a gentleman in jeans and a t-shirt was dripping wet. Esmeralda was confused.

'Where is the man in the long brown cloak?' she asked. There had been no man in a long brown cloak, only a man in jeans and a t-shirt. She thanked him. He saved her life.

She stayed in Tudor character. In shock. And went back to the dairy. Just carried on as if nothing had happened. Didn't want to cause a scene. Kept thinking *I'm in big trouble*. A woman from the bakery came in to see her and she said, 'You are allowed to cry, you know!' and Esmeralda burst into tears.

Her family were found and they took her home.

For three days she did not speak. She lay in bed staring with unblinking eyes at a frog mobile, bought as a present from her grandparents, left spinning above her head.

Three years later, she was approached by a bee-keeper at the Tudor re-creation, who it turned out was a pagan.

'I've just heard a story about you nearly drowning and making contact with the spirit world,' he said.

'Well, I think I saw someone in Tudor costume jump in to save me,' Esmeralda replied.

'You have had a near death experience,' he said, 'And survived. You made contact with the spirit world, which shows they have some use for you. This means that you are on the shamanic path.'

THE TWO-WEEK WAIT

Day 1 - They were very happy to discover that the two week wait is judged from the egg collection day and not the embryo transfer. Esmeralda was sure that wasn't the same as last time, but maybe it was. Anyway, they had just shed five days in one go, so that was brilliant. They only had nine days left to go. They used to recommend bed rest for the first two days and they said this to her last time Esmeralda did this, but that had been disproven, apparently, and, it seemed, from looking it up online, that this had been disproven quite a long time ago. Esmeralda came home on the train, which meant walking up the hill. It was a beast of a hill, giving her some gentle exercise that would get the blood pumping. She then sat on the sofa for the rest of the day, watching *You've Been Framed*. Laughing is really good for helping implantation and that show never failed to make her laugh.

Day 2 – Esmeralda tried to take it easy, but had loads of work to do. She got on with as much as she could, and was hoping to be done by lunchtime so that she could relax and watch some comedy. Her husband was being a real nuisance though, without meaning to be, but he kept going on and on about technology and when she asked for his help with something, she had to sit with him whilst he went through a process that would have taken half the time if he hadn't been asking questions to a spectator who didn't know the answers and had just figured it out himself, which is exactly what he did in the end anyway. Normally that would be fine as he was doing her a favour, but she ended up not watching anything properly all day because he kept interrupting her and by evening she hadn't laughed once. Then he told her he had taken out a £5000 credit card to help with paying bills and she lost it. Had to leave the house and get away from him. She'd just paid *off* a credit card and they were getting close to being out of debt. That card was more than all their debt put together. She got very angry, especially as she wasn't meant to be getting angry. Esmeralda walked until she had calmed down, then came back, and they sat together on the floor and he wrote *I Love You* on her belly. They lit her magic candles and meditated together for quarter of an hour. It was the first time he had ever meditated. She was impressed he did it.

Day 3 – Esmeralda woke up that morning to the sensation that it had all stopped. That nothing was happening any more. No more grinding feelings of implantation or raised body temperature. She had had this last time, where she felt that the chemical reaction had stopped. But her best friend, who had a successful IVF cycle, said that there was no way of being able to tell at the moment, and to not worry. She went for dinner with her dear friend and his wife that night and they laughed about how couples all have the same gripes with each other, and talked about how we had changed over the years. She said the main change that had happened to her was that her ego had been dismantled. She used to be just one big fat ball of ego, but that life had decided it wasn't going to play ball with any of her dreams and didn't make her the big famous star she thought she was destined to become. All her plans to make the world a better place and be an ambassador for women's rights and write books and all that jazz had all hung on the presumption that she'd make it first as an actress. When that didn't happen, she realised she had a lot of work to do, trying to figure out how to get all these things done *without* the fame to fund them. Her friend's wife was confused, she said she thought Esmeralda was too sweet and kind to be egotistical. Esmeralda explained that was only because she'd finally climbed down off her high horse and had come to spend time with all her mere mortals. This made his wife laugh. She was an extraordinarily beautiful woman. Esmeralda had a bit of a girl crush on her.

Day 4 – The next morning something was going on again, but it felt like period pains. Esmeralda had been really hot in the night and the dull pains in her belly didn't feel like specific implanting pains, but overall dull aches. She was not going to get upset though. If she bled, then she was having her period, but there was no blood yet.

Day 5 – She had not bled yet. Plus, that day, she lay on her bed and meditated. There was a moment in the guided mediation where the lovely lady's voice said to let yourself relax and scan through the body, to notice, but not judge. Just witness, experience and accept. Esmeralda felt like an energy bomb went off in her body and a wave of relaxation flooded through her, and she felt like she could feel two embryos fizzing away in her womb. She was sure that they were both still alive.

Day 6 – Esmeralda had a really delightful day hanging out with friends. An old chum from drama school came around in the morning, who she hadn't seen in a long time. She was one of the dozen or so friends who had lost someone close in the last year. Then she went for lunch with her girl friends from university. That felt fortuitous. She had been living with them all when she had had her abortion thirteen years ago. The baby's birthday would have been sometime around now. That would complete a circle if she was to be conceiving now.

Day 7 – Esmeralda nested, with bells on. They had wardrobes delivered. Now, for the first time in a year and a half, they had a proper bedroom without piles of boxes and clothes in the corners. It now looked peaceful and amazing in their room. Like a cloud. She was feeling confident that she was pregnant. She made love to her adorable husband and they called it baby-making sex.

Day 8 – She had been keeping busy with many jobs and running errands. Esmeralda was not feeling so sure today that it had worked. In some ways nothing had been going on since that first day she felt that it had all stopped, but she didn't get her period last week, which was now twelve days late, and that was a more reliable indication than her trying to judge it all based on her experience of getting pregnant over a decade ago and the last time the IVF got this far. She went for a Shiatsu massage and the woman doing it said her womb area seemed active and not resistant or needing strengthening, which she guessed was a good sign. On the radio she heard an old lady saying how she dreamt that she was young again, then when she woke up she almost killed herself by leaping out of bed. Esmeralda thought that was a crazy notion. Then, that evening, she went and watched a film with her girl friends. In it, the main character said that once one has children, one becomes the ghosts of their futures. Another amazing idea. She told her mum on the phone, and she agreed one must make the most of every moment. It made Esmeralda very sad the day that she realised her mum would not be around forever. She hoped the universe blessed them with a baby.

Day 9 –Esmeralda worked all day. She was enjoying pretending she was pregnant, at least. As much as she wanted Friday to hurry up so that she could find out for sure, at the same time she also wanted these next two days to last forever. At least until she did the test she could pretend that she was pregnant with twins. During the night she woke up feeling like she was getting morning sickness. She had to get up and go to the toilet, and felt very nauseous. It made her feel hopeful.

Day 10 – The last day of their wait, tomorrow they would test. Her husband was super-nervous all day. She was feeling pretty serene. She felt almost certain it had worked, in that everything seemed right for it to happen. On the other hand, she didn't feel like anything *was* happening. Couldn't judge either way. Would just have to wait and see. They agreed to do the test in the morning. This was it. Their last attempt at having a baby.

Day of Test - Not pregnant. It was negative. They were not having a baby. Odin was wrong. She was wrong, even. She was not pregnant.

FRACTALS

Let's get something straight. Esmeralda believed in science first and foremost, and if life had taught her one thing, it had taught her to relax about giving up on her beliefs. Little ones, medium sized ones and the really big ones. They were only there as pathetic superstitious tools that desperately tried to make some kind of sense of the nonsense that is the universe. She had learnt to let go of all of her beliefs. Her little ones were her day-to-day beliefs, where she thought that she was right about everything when it turned out that she was wrong. Medium-sized ones were where she believed that the universe intended for her to be a big, famous superstar but at thirty-five she'd discovered she was a skint nobody. Then there were the really huge ones, like the moment when she'd realised that she no longer believed in God. She stopped believing in

255

God the moment when she asked her dad, 'Who will you be with in heaven, then, Dad? You swore your vows to Mum in the sight of God in church, but now you're going off with my drama teacher...' The look on his face made her first suspect that the whole deal was a sham, and could be bent to fit in with the whims of men. Then she went to university and studied feminism. There was a moment in one of her lectures when the professor who she greatly admired said something along the lines of 'And it's like people believing in God' and the whole room laughed. At that moment she realised how much this omnipresent male presence had been controlling her life, making her feel watched, like she was being kept an eye on by some CCTV camera god.

But there is something beautiful that religion had tried to capture and own, yet in doing so has let it slip through its fingers like water. There is something unifying that runs through this universe. It pervades everything and yet evades us all. We are in it, so can never see it. We can only sense it and try to trust our senses. As soon as we formalise it too much and start naming it and labelling its aspects, then it vanish again. Esmeralda was all for the marriage between science and the spiritual. She saw spirituality as the female yin energy and science as the male yang energy of the same thing. In a very crude way there was a male tendency to take things apart and see how they worked and a female tendency to feel what's going on and make sense of things in an intuitive way. But obviously there is a bit of yin in all yang and a bit of yang in all yin. Nothing is binary. Science *sort* of tells us how the car works. Spirituality *sort* of tells us who made the car and why. Science without spirit creates pollution and destruction. Spirituality without science creates superstition and dogma. Scientists need a moral compass and a meaning to it all, so they don't just blow the fuck out of everything. Spiritualists need to be willing to eat their taboos and give up on things that can be proven not to be true or they start burning each other.

To practice a religion is a beautiful thing, but to believe in one is most certainly deadly.

For example; Esmeralda decided in the end to become a pagan and also follow the teachings of Buddhism. She thought Buddhism came with too many trappings, though, but the essence of its teaching was the clearest explanation she'd found out of all the religions, at the very nub. And it felt to her that science was also trying to nail this nub too. Reaching back into the very essence and source of all this... this *stuff*. Where did we come from? Where were we going? Why was this happening and how are we doing? That is why she was a pagan, because she accepted that she was a tiny little fractal in this eternally swirling dance and that she could influence it in her own tiny way, but would never obtain these big answers because the answers were too big for her to comprehend. She was but a cell in the body of a universe that she would never see from the outside. Like an electron flying around in her own arm. The only journey for her, therefore, was towards being completely happy with the situation and submitting herself completely to playing her tiny little part.

Not I, nor any man that but man is,

With nothing shall be pleased, till he be eased with being nothing.

As good old Shakey had put it. And, for Esmeralda, paganism was the only faith that made any sense to her as its focus of worship was the life giving planet of earth. She needed no greater deity than this. Another thing she liked about paganism was that it was all made up. She'd spent some time researching it properly and quickly worked out that the vast bulk of the pagan faiths like Wicca and its ilk had been made up by the Victorians, and we all know how much *they* liked to make shit up. Some loose threads of aural traditions were woven in there somewhere, but they'd been all but lost under the sheer weight of Victorian bullshit. But she liked the idea that the faith was open to interpretation and creativity. It is an artistic faith. Esmeralda had found a definition of paganism she liked, by an author called Richard North, quoted in a book by Alan Cameron, *The Last Pagans of Rome*:

[Pagans have] ...no tradition or discourse about ritual or religious matters (apart from philosophical debate or antiquarian treatise), no organised system of beliefs to which they are asked to commit themselves, no authority-structure peculiar to the religious area, above all no commitment to a particular group of people or set of ideas other than their family and political context.

A bit like anarchism, which is where her political leanings leant, paganism allows the participant to make it up as they went along and in reference to the world around them. The traditions of pagan faiths create colourful responses to the natural world and attempt to try and work with the forces that influence us all. Creativity is the essence of its practice and Esmeralda personally believed that creativity IS the essence of the universe. The universe is in a constant dance of creation and destruction. To be in an act of creation or an act of destruction is to be truly present in the moment and that is where one feels most alive and the constraints of the universe, even its physical laws such as time, disappear.

Esmeralda believed it was important that we look after the one living lump of rock we have so far discovered in the known universe. It annoyed her that there are so many films out at the moment about space, as if the only option we now have is to act like bacteria and spread our destructive ways across the universe, without learning a damn thing along the way. In response to this unbearable destruction her desire was to work in harmony with the delicate balance that kept life ticking over on this beautiful planet. Science is a tool for being able to do this and the focus of science for getting to clearer answers and pushing frontiers means there's still so many new and exciting things to discover about this earth and the universe it spins around in. This knowledge can be used to make cleaner energy, create less waste, even free us from the laws of physics and the biology that holds us in place. It's an exciting time to be alive. We need to hold the question mark up as our crucifix and relinquish perceived wisdom the second it is debunked.

She was traumatised for a split second the day she and husband decided to look into what influence the moon actually had on women. Somewhere along the lines she'd picked up that the moon affected periods. Something about it pulling the tides, and so it also pulls women as they are made of water. Sounds totally daft to her now, but it was something she believed in at the time and held quiet deeply sacred. But when her husband asked her what the deal was and she wasn't sure, they set about researching it and soon realised that of course it didn't pull periods, or women would all have periods at the same time and so would all other animals. Women don't have periods at the same time. Women's cycles are not the same as other animals and can vary from 17 days to 30 just in humans. The link is that because human periods vaguely match in length of time to that of the cycle of the moon; if two moons pass and you haven't bled then you know you are probably pregnant. That's it. There was also some vague study about the possibility of fertility heightening on a full moon as it possibly increases with the more light you get, but it was just one study and inconclusive, plus with artificial lights all around us nowadays has ceased to mean anything anymore.

For a moment, this discovery severed the bond that Esmeralda had felt with the moon. She'd spent her life feeling like she was in a better place in herself if her periods were happening on the full moon as they were going with the flow properly. But this disconnection lasted only a moment. In its place she felt a bond with all the women throughout history who had looked up at the moon and feared or longed for a baby in their bellies. She felt the influence of the moon as an archetypal entity ever hanging in the sky, watching over humanity like a great face peering into a Petri dish, studying the funny little experiment that we call life on earth. She realised that it didn't matter that her beliefs had been incorrect, she felt a further evolved human being for just letting them go. And she loved the fact her husband had led her on this journey, towards greater truth. It is interesting to keep learning more and more about this fabulous happening called life and science is amazing for that. However, in the end life is meaningless and it is meaningless that it is meaningless. Whatever we discover and learn, we will all one day disappear and no one will ever know that we ever, thought, made, did or even breathed. It's all going to just be a bunch of stuff that happened.

In her lifetime on this planet Esmeralda thought perhaps she'd witnessed one person reach full enlightenment, although her mother was also very close. The person she had witnessed was the father of her brethren from the Tudor re-creation. He had been humble, kind and generous all of his life. When he found out he had cancer, he'd become even kinder and even more generous. But he didn't die from cancer. He died from drowning in the sea. In a part of the sea that he loved to swim in, near to their favourite family holiday spot in Wales. He'd always associated people he loved who were no longer with him with areas of landscape that were special to him, so it fitted poetically that he became part of a landscape that he loved. He had already got his house and affairs in order and heard all the things loved ones wanted to say to him in case anything happened to him due to his illness. He seemed totally at peace with the world and left nothing behind but people who he had touched and whose lives he had made better, in a multitude of ways.

Esmeralda's chosen belief was that life is a game. That there are many levels and side missions, but basically you can kick around being a dick for as long as you want to but to actually get out you've got to put the effort in at some point to become one with the light, or light and dark, as it was all about distance. That over many, many, lifetimes the wisdom gleaned from lessons learned accumulated, until one day one becomes kind, emphatic and compassionate just out of sheer wisdom. One can see the struggle in the eyes of those around you and the crosses they are baring. Things change around you all the time; politicians, faiths, people, memories. They're all affected by changing circumstances and what was once up can often become down. The only thing you can trust is your own moral compass in the present and the only way out of the game is to become pure-hearted. You might not do it in this lifetime. You might not feel like exiting the game for a while yet. We're here to play after all and no one knows what's on the outside. Perhaps we are in a correctional unit. Perhaps it is better in here than it is out there. Who the hell knows? But it's the only way out, baby. And as folks get closer to the exit, they increasingly glow. Her friend's father had glowed and her mum glowed too.

She didn't assume that any of this was true. It was just her current musings as a creative entity weaving stories out of her imagination. If it could all be proved wrong tomorrow then that would be terribly exciting news, and she'd be all ears.

CREATE OR BE CREATED

They went up to London to celebrate her brother's birthday the day after they found out it hadn't worked. Business as usual. Both felt two feet off the ground and it was surreal to be back in the normal flow of life again. They ate a meal and went back to her brother's house to get wrecked. Esmeralda did a good job of not really fucking herself up. She had a jar of magic mushroom honey and some delicious home-grown weed and a dark wooden pipe. Everyone was boshing cocaine and booze, but she kept it reined in and only drank one fine whiskey at the end of the session as a night cap. The next day though, both her and her husband felt utterly rotten. They agreed they were over this now. Obviously, with Christmas coming up and New Year, it was likely they might have a few more blow outs in the foreseeable future, but as of January she was going to clean up her act for good.

As much as it broke her heart that this was it, they were never going to be having their own children; Esmeralda felt like a huge weight had been lifted off of her shoulders and suddenly serendipitous magic was creeping back into her life. Performance opportunities immediately fell into her lap and she began to make steps towards running her own theatre company. This suddenly felt like it was somehow meant to be.

'How about Alice in Wonderland croquet?' Esmeralda suggested.

'We would need a flat area with Astroturf and some big painted flowers, then two pretty stilt walkers dressed as flamingos, and two 'balls' who are folks in hedgehog onesies. A big Queen of Hearts character with a wooden painted croquet bat and actual ball, both painted to look like a flamingo and a hedgehog ball, which means she can actually play croquet properly, whereas the two punters playing will have to deal with their equipment being alive. We'll also have three playing card chaps to act as croquet hoops.'

'Or... even simpler and cheaper is if myself and a crew of say eight people in shit-hot costumes play a bunch of characters from the books you mentioned and we do walkabout in character. Would be cheaper and easier and I know plenty of folks who will be able to interact with the public well. Would need some money towards costume...'

My work focuses ostensibly on the route of performance from our earliest forefathers' attempts at explaining how they'd survived death by performing elaborate ceremonies, healing rituals and performance techniques as village shamans, through to the power of show business today. I'm exploring how theatre can be used as an act of subversion, healing and discussion, whilst continually delighting in its inherent magic, the act of creation being the most holy act of all.

I'm interested in how history and theatre are both tools for change. History offers up lessons from the past. Theatre allows for safe and sacred spaces to be formed within which issues can be discussed without fear of retribution.

I'm currently developing a new theatre company of young people, using traditional forms of performance called Mumming and the technique I trained in called Fooling, both of which are almost completely forgotten about in modern Britain, but that can be found all over the world and which ring forgotten bells in the subconscious mind of the audience. Like physical graffiti, we aim to creatively explore themes and issues that are of concern to young people today, by opening up a discourse on our streets. Using a style that seems not only innocuous, but inherently traditional and therefore acceptable, thus giving access for young people to make themselves heard in public spaces in a way that seems not only appropriate but intrinsically British.

Do one thing every day that scares you - Everybody's Free (to wear sunscreen)

She did it. She took herself to the improv group in a church hall in the centre of town. It was deeply nerve-wracking for her. All of Esmeralda's deepest wounds had theatre caught up in them, and so getting back onto her horse after years of not performing after so much heartache, meant she felt anxious down into her furthest reaching roots. Which is also what made it so exciting. The class was brilliant. Lots of elements were there from her training with The Fool and she felt privileged to be working in a circle again. She wanted to be there all day the next day, and the next, and forever and ever. Theatre was and always would be her blood. It's what made her feel most alive.

She was rubbish at it. But it didn't matter.

Esmeralda met her brother in London again the following weekend, owing to work responsibilities. Her workload had instantly piled up once more. If she had been pregnant she would have been looking now at ways of diminishing her work load and taking it easier. As it hadn't worked it was all just business as usual. Except it couldn't be. She would need to find a way to make life changes without the excuse of a baby. As she walked through Brick Lane, feeling shattered from a 6am start to work on a show she was having to operate for free as a venue had messed them around, she saw a trendy hipster chick looking super cool and well pregnant. She became overcome with grief. The sadness she felt was so deep, so painful. The despair made her feel sick. She was grieving for lives that had never been lived, for feet that had never walked upon the earth. Pure perfect entities of possibility. Esmeralda had planned how she would raise them, what she would feed them, how she would talk to them, educate them, amuse them. What secrets she would keep from them and what possibilities she would encourage in them. What rules they would set and how they would administer discipline. Where they would live, how they would dress, what they would do with their days, holidays, futures. But now her and her Husband were going to be growing old and die alone together. No one would be there to look after them. No one would be giving them grandchildren. Their futures were filled with nothing but more of themselves and the same old same old. She did feel that she was at the start of a new journey and all would come good in the end, but at this moment in time she had become flooded with sorrow.

'I might be at the end of a rainbow with a pot of gold, this could be the start of whatever it is this universe wants me for. But right now I'm so very,

very, sad. I give up. I have to. I don't know what else to do. I can't kill myself, but I have nothing left to offer. I turned up, I tried. I tried to make it as a somebody. I tried to start a family. I've worked really hard and taken a lifetime's worth of risks. I don't know what else to do? It's the universe's turn now. I'm just going to plod along and do whatever, because nothing I try to do works anyway. It is the universe's turn now to make whatever it wants out of me. I'm spent.'

DO WITH ME AS YOU WILL, UNIVERSE.

Then she spoke to her husband on the phone.

'Well, you know how you can have this couple who really wants to have a baby and is all desperate to start a family? And then you can have a kid who is really desperate to have a family and is really sad that they haven't got one? Well... we could be all like - well I choose you - and we could make that kid's life by choosing them?'

It was the first time that he had mentioned being up for adoption and she was over the moon.

It was what she had always wanted to do anyway.

What is theatre? Is theatre important? What do you think of as good theatre? What does it mean to make theatre? What would you want to say to the

271

world through a piece of theatre? What can you do with theatre that you can't do with other art forms? If you could make any piece of theatre, what would it be like? If you could be in any existing theatre production what would it be? Which characters would you most like to play? How do you want to be remembered? If you could change the world, what would you do to it?

Esmeralda went to Liverpool with the show she was working on about Tourettes. They were performing at a disability arts festival and taking part in a conference entitled Art of the Lived Experiment. Artists who identify themselves as disabled get fed up with being described as inspirational. It's as if they're there to somehow impress able bodied folks and make them appreciate how lucky they are to not be disabled themselves. Artists, whether disabled or not, are generally making work because they want to express themselves and because they feel like they've got something worth saying. Esmeralda loved watching other people's work because it opened her up to a bigger and richer world than the one she had lived in before. One where we intrinsically share so much and yet at the same time our differences are welcomed and celebrated. By looking at the world through the eyes of different people, it opens up one's own preconceived perceptions and makes one taste the air afresh. This is why Esmeralda liked hallucinogens, or travelling, or getting to know someone new. They were all vehicles for opening one up to more and more of the universe. Like parallel universes living side by side one another. Through other people she felt limitless. And she was. She just often forgot.

When the conference began discussing disability and sexuality, Esmeralda started to cry.

It was funny at the conference, as both her and the other co-producer were both invisible, because they were able-bodied. It was fair enough too, and was an interesting experience. Her co-producer described himself as an aspiring beige, in that he wanted to be able to just pass through life unnoticed. He really enjoyed these events, where he got to be invisible. Esmeralda had not been created from the same fabric as him, but life did seem to be moulding her more in this direction.

Esmeralda had her drink on. She decided that she wanted to get super-pissed. Heading to a tequila bar with her visiting young friends, she found that the delicious golden liquid slipped down her throat with such ease that no matter how much she drank there was still room for more. Somehow it wasn't even touching the sides. Esmeralda continued sinking shot after shot over at a friend's house after the bar closed and threw them out into the cold streets of Brighton, twinkling with Christmas lights. They bought a bottle from the off-licence, headed to the friends, and found the room was filled with their nearest and dearest. They had all been at a gig and were pretty steaming themselves. She threw herself onto the sofa and set about dishing out shots of golden tequila to all the team, ranting wildly in that special way tequila always made her do. That was why she loved it, it was almost like it made her channel something. They stayed up all night, sinking the bottle. They were still at it by midday the next day, when they were all due at the annual Friend's Christmas pub lunch. Esmeralda insisted that they get up and go, so they jumped into a cab and headed back to hers. She snuck in a shower then wrapped up a half full bottle of poppers and a bag of chocolates for the Secret Santa presents they were meant to be bringing along with them. She had actually ordered something better than this as the gifts, but they hadn't arrived yet, so she was forced to improvise. When she got to the pub nobody could believe she had been up all night drinking, as she looked so sparkly. To put an end to any doubts on this Esmeralda set about drinking nothing but tequila shots for the whole day and night. They ate a delicious roast, then everyone asked her to be the Secret Santa, providing her with a red Santa hat to wear for the occasion. Everyone was being very sweet to her. She felt a certain amount of pity coming from them, but it was all meant with the best intentions. One of her friends talked to her about it briefly and said that they thought it would be a very good idea for her to adopt, because she had so much love to give. That was nice. But if any social worker had seen the state of her on this particular occasion she would never be allowed near a child. There were plenty of her friend's children there and they all found her a little bit scary. As everyone left to make their ways home, Esmeralda rounded up those who still wanted to party and dragged them back to her house, much to the annoyance of her Husband, who had gone to sleep. They had bought another bottle of tequila on the way and they polished that off in her living room. Everyone had gone by 9pm and Esmeralda finally crawled up the stairs and threw herself into bed. Her sorrows were well and truly drowned.

'I'm never drinking again.'

'Famous last words.'

Two days later and she was still depressed. Which was interesting. It looked like booze was a key factor. Esmeralda had spent most of the last seven years suffering from depression. This had been in correlation with her return to hedonism after pretty much clearing up her act whilst at drama school. Seemed obvious that booze would be playing a part in the depression when she thought about it, but still, it was glaringly obvious to her after that binge at the weekend. There was also possibly another emotional breakdown lurking in the wings that her brain was blocking out. She was determined to hold it together, but cracks were revealing themselves in her overbooked diary. This seemed to be quite a good litmus test for how she was doing, noting how many double bookings were going on in her arrangements. How she'd ended up as busy as this was a mystery, especially as she'd been keeping her diary clear in case she'd ended up pregnant. Somehow though every day this week had resulted in some kind of double booking and it was spinning her out. The Christmas holidays were only a week away, so if she could just hold it together until then she might be okay. Hopefully.

Here were their options:

1. Pay to do another IVF cycle
2. Not have kids and move on
3. Adopt

Then also there was what to do next with her life. She was currently a producer, but talking on mushrooms to her friend the other night it became clear to her how much she needs to progress her theatre technique and develop her own practice again. Get back on her acting horse, so to speak.

Christmas managed to pass without too much trouble. Esmeralda made her mother cry on the train heading to visit, which wasn't a great start. It was the same old childish argument over who got what room and who had to sleep on the inflatable downstairs. She had her husband in one ear saying 'It's always us that has to move' and her mum in the other ear breaking down in tears because she was obviously rushed off her feet doing tons of stuff for everyone else and the last thing she needed was a self-centred daughter making her feel bad. Why is it that those closest to you bring out the worst in you? For the rest of the festivities Esmeralda was on tenterhooks, first of all trying her hardest not to upset her mum again and also trying not to beat herself up too much for being a godawful person. She did the washing up after dinner, didn't react to four or five jabs her mother made about how selfish she is as a person and managed not to argue with her husband, brother or new sister-in-law. Which was no mean feat, as she normally argued with all of them all of the time. The week was lovely, they were spoilt rotten as always and were stuffed to bursting with Christmas dinner after Christmas dinner - one of the few perks of coming from a broken family was the significant increase in festive spreads. They had two ducks at the in-laws before Christmas Eve, turkey on Christmas Eve with her mother and their first cousins, a goose on Christmas Day with her mother, brother and partners, a beef stew on Boxing Day at her dad's family do and a slap up meal at the Spice Market in Chinatown the next day, before going to watch a musical in the West End. This was the same every year, except that they swapped going to the in-laws with her mum's each year. Spoilt rotten. This year Esmeralda felt like she was coasting it though. Her emotions on hold until the merry go round stopped and she'd have some time to just be with everything that had happened. And this made her feel self-centred and selfish, which came out as her being self-centred and selfish. It was the frequency she was tapping into.

Then at the end of the whole run they went and saw *Matilda* in the West End. Obviously no one had done it on purpose, but the show was all about parents not being able to have children. The opening song was 'little miracles' and opened with going on about how special children are. From the outset Esmeralda began to weep uncontrollably and couldn't stop all the way through it. The most upsetting thing was that her family seemed oblivious, just her and her husband sat holding hands and weeping on the back row. She was beginning to come down with a cold and was tired, which wasn't helping, but every second of the first act was like a knife turning in their hearts. Even the characters in Matilda's story who couldn't have children looked like her and her husband. They were circus performers and he had a great big handlebar moustache, just like her husband's. And every time they came on the stage these spotlights shone into the audience, straight onto Esmeralda and her husband, who were sat right in the middle of the row. It was all creepily uncanny. Her husband said afterwards it was like there had been some kind of sick intervention. It had taken all of Esmeralda's strength to not have a panic attack and run out of the theatre. Afterwards her mum did cotton on and apologised. They then had a long chat in the kitchen back her brother's house before her mum went home. It was the first time anyone had talked to her about it at all over the whole break, making it all the more like a twisted dream. The moment it was openly discussed, though, everything came back into focus. Her mum saw how upset she was and how hard she'd been trying to keep it all together. Then it was home time and Esmeralda fell into her bed and into a fever for three days, eating naught but kale in desperation to be well again in time for her birthday on New Year's Eve.

This year there had been huge smiles, oodles of laughter, unforeseen joys, unsought for sorrows, tears of grief, screams of heartache, archetypal unions, lightening storms in pink skies, pirates, hot tubs, weddings in fields, songs around fires, Tourettes, science and injections. It has been real.

A bout of hedonism descended upon Esmeralda and her husband that had not been previously intended, but it was New Year's Eve and her birthday, and it seemed at the moment to be working as a catalyst for positivity rather than an escape from their sense of failure.

Having secured magic mushrooms for the ride, Esmeralda found that uppers were required for some loved ones with whom she was tripping, but had become freaked out by the term 'lock in' and the concept that no one could leave the birthday pub celebrations and expect to be able to get back in again. The air became thick with cigarette smoke and an element of 'Let's get involved' was required to keep up with the craziness that was ensuing before them. It was like being in an episode of *Eastenders*, but on crack. A hundred of her best friends were all in one place, openly skinning up, snorting lines off the bar and drinking mushrooms from tea pots in a central pub in town, from 11pm until 5am. It was utterly divine and it mattered not a jot that it meant she was starting the year on a comedown. The flow of heartfelt conversations filled her to the brim with love and nourishment. Incredible woman after incredible woman took it in turns to grab her and hug her and tell her what a huge impact she had had upon their lives and how something she had said or done had changed the way they saw the world. Everyone was saying they can see her stepping into an even bigger and bolder being and that they all wanted to see it happen. They invited her to go for it. By the end of the night she felt like she had the permission of all her peers to go out and take over the world. Just like she had always planned to. They didn't stop partying until 4am on the 3rd.

For a day or two she and her husband argued, but it was so clearly the effects of the drugs wearing off she didn't mind. Then one of her best chums turned up from Hong Kong and the fun started up again. Her chum came with her partner and baby in tow. The partner was also a very dear friend. He had been the photographer at their wedding and had run off to Hong Kong with her matron of honour. Their baby was celebrating her first birthday and continued to be the cutest and sweetest natured human being Esmeralda had ever met. They enjoyed three delightful days of cuddles, onesies and catching up. The upshot of the whole bender became clearer as the days went on. They lived a blessed and privileged life. And that there was no need to plan or worry about the future. They had no idea whatsoever about what lay before them and it didn't matter a jot what they dreamt up as possible futures, because the only thing you could guarantee about their future was that they didn't have a clue. Esmeralda found herself grounding into the present in a way she had never felt before. Nothing mattered and anything was possible.

That's it, say your plans out loud. God loves a laugh.

-    Deadwood

No more superstitious religions.
No more money in politics.
No more profits before people.
No more dumbed-down media & broadcasting.
No more ignorance.
I DON'T have all the answers, but I DO know what
I'm sick of.
I'M ANGRY AS HELL AND I'M NOT GOING TO
TAKE IT ANYMORE.

LET IT GO...

OR, A HOMAGE TO *BONE CLOCKS*

Esmeralda's house is surrounded by fields and isn't what she'd imagined when she was in her twenties, with its net curtains, cushion-covers, porcelain figurines and Flower Fairies. There's even carpet on the bathroom floor. It's rented and out of town in the neighbouring village of Woodingdean, where all the poorer than 'yummy mummy' mummys moved to, when they've begun to breed. It's 7.30am and time for the kids to get up for school so Esmeralda quietly opens the door to their bedroom. The early morning light filters its way through the orange curtains, casting a warm glow into the quiet room. It smells sweetly of innocent sweat and wholesome farts. Marinus is snoring gently in his bed on the right hand side of the room and Betty sleeps silently on the left. Between the beds a large wooden chest is lodged, full of toys, and on top of this sits a large doll's house that her husband salvaged from a street find and Esmeralda did up with a lick of paint. The walls of the bedroom are a neutral misty buff with a once-cream carpet on the floor, now grubby and worn. This mess is covered with an equally grubby orange rug, placed over the carpet to add a bit of non-gender-specific colour. The bedding is also orange, as is the lampshade. Over Betty's bed is a poster of *Frozen* that she's covered with sticky backed gemstones. Marinus has model aeroplanes hanging from the ceiling above his bed, that he painstakingly made with Daddy over the summer holidays following a trip to Duxford Air Show. Despite their attempts to break gender stereotypes in their children the second the kids had gone to school it had slid into their beings as if it had always been there. Marinus had also used to love *Frozen*, as much as Betty did, until he went to school. The first time he announced that he didn't like it anymore he had decided it was because the film was for girls and he justified his change of heart due to him realising that he wasn't a girl too, but was in fact a boy. Esmeralda is fairly happy with the school the kids go to. It's one of the best in the area and the reason they'd moved to the village, but it still had the usual comprehensive stereotypical views. Esmeralda would've loved to have home educated, but she just couldn't afford not to work full time. Being born's one a hell of a lottery.

Marinus was also getting bullied for his name at school so now he'd changed it to Marni. Esmeralda quite likes Marni, which means she hasn't objected, but she's also sad he's had to give up so many little bits of himself. He'd loved his name as much as he'd loved *Frozen* before starting school. His full name is Marinus Eunoia Atom Dewin. His initials spell out M.E.A.D., which Esmeralda had spent ages thinking about and had been pleased with the results when she had finally came up with it. His name literally translates as 'Marine loving beautiful thinking unbreakable wizard'. Esmeralda believes words are powerful spells and that, with her son especially, she wanted to ensure a strong spell was in place to keep him on a good path. Her daughter, on the other hand, she had wanted to infuse with strength and power and so they'd named her Betty Machete. Betty as an abbreviation of Beatrix meaning 'bringer of joy'. Machete meaning strong. Translated her name means 'bringer of joy strong one'.

Esmeralda tiptoes over to Marni and begins to stroke his soft little nose until he wakes up. He has his father's nose. A sweet little turned-up button. Although it was hard to say who he'd inherited it from, as Esmeralda also had a button nose, though her husband's family had a distinctive crease where the button starts, which Marni had inherited and Betty does not possess. He chokes on his snores in a little surprised snort as Esmeralda touches him, then he commences to wriggle around as he wakes up. His eyes flicker open and his arms fling out without a second's thought and grip Esmeralda around the neck. He hugs her tightly and she can still smell the faint whiff of infancy on his young skin. He has grown up even faster than Betty did and Esmeralda knows it will be all too soon before he's leaving home and moving in with some girlfriend she doesn't approve of. Of course she'll try and approve, but it's a child's prerogative to rebel. And Esmeralda was fine with them rebelling, almost intrigued to see how they'd do it. No one wants a *boring* child after all. Though that's probably how they'd rebel against her. By becoming very straight and boring.

'I'm just going to wake up Betty,' whispers Esmeralda gently into Marni's still sleepy ears and untangles herself from his grip, transferring herself over to Betty. She looks down at the wonder that is her daughter. She always knew she'd have a daughter first. She'd had no interest even in having a son until a daughter had been obtained, but now she had one... She knew at some point their relationship would flourish. It had been the same with her and her own mother. Dad had been the interesting one to Esmeralda. She'd been a daddy's girl through and through. Esmeralda believed it was a prerequisite to being a strong independent woman. Think, act and associate yourself with men and with being a man. Women are weak and boring.

Fair enough. She wanted her daughter to be a tomboy and adore her daddy. The day she really clicked she was a woman and had no choice in the matter would be the day that their relationship would take a new turn. Until then, her daughter Betty was a beautiful sparkling island on the distant horizon and upon which Esmeralda was definitely not invited to step foot. Esmeralda stroked Betty's arm to wake her. Betty no longer liked her nose being stroked as she 'wasn't a baby' and as Betty stirred Esmeralda jumped out of the way so as to avoid any early morning conflict. Betty had a short fuse and everything Esmeralda did was wrong. Having leapt out of the line of fire she instead went over to the curtains and gently pulled them open. It was a gorgeous early summer's day and the sea glistened in the distance past the green rolling Sussex Downs. She loved this view.

'If you go to the equator,' said Marni over breakfast as he pierced his sausage and juice dribbled from the prong holes, 'you can stand with one foot on one side of it and your other foot on the other. I'm going to go there one day. And there's a lake in the Alps where half of it is in Switzerland and the other half is in Italy. I'm going to go there too...'

'You'll adore Switzerland.' Esmeralda smiles before she swallows down her toast and dabs her lips with a tissue. 'I think I've been to that lake. It's called Lake Majorie. Your Grandma and Grandpa once took me to Lake Majorie on a family holiday'

'When they were still together?' butted in Betty.

She seemed obsessed with the fact Esmeralda's parents had split up. Like it had been her mother's fault somehow and evidence of Esmeralda's failure as a human. She didn't seem to have clocked that her father's parents had also split up and that her grandfather wasn't her biological grandfather. It was a subject they'd broach at some point, when her husband was up for dropping a peg or two in his daughter's esteem. Which didn't appear to be any time soon.

'We camped by the lake, which was fresh water, nestled up near Mont Blanc. Me and your uncle would swim in it every morning and let the fish nibble on our toes.'

She slurps some tea and recalls the speedboat rides they'd enjoyed with her father whilst they were there, before he'd fallen from grace.

'Why don't we ever go abroad?' moaned Betty, nudging a baked bean about her plate.

'Well, your father and I haven't got a huge amount of spare cash.' replied Esmeralda trying to cover up her own disappointment at a life without adventure.

Travelling had been pretty much her favourite thing in the whole world. After sex. And she didn't do either anymore. Her gypsy blood was always at its happiest when she was embarking on a new journey.

Esmeralda dabs her lips again. 'Is it swimming club today, Betty?'

Betty nods and forks a tomato. 'My kit's in my bag.'

'Whatever the problem is with Robin Hood's Bay' says my husband, 'I myself am looking forward to going back. We can go to the Jorvik Centre again and see if it's still as smelly.'

My husband reaches for the ketchup.

'Oh my god it stank.' laughs Betty, always enjoying whatever her daddy has to say.

'It sure did,' he laughs back, ruffling her hair.

Betty would literally kill Esmeralda if she ever dared to do that.

Esmeralda does the washing-up. Betty and Marni are running around the house getting washed, putting on uniforms and packing bags. The husband is getting ready for work. Esmeralda also has to get ready for work, but apparently she's the only one who has time to also do the washing up around her other activities. Secretly, Esmeralda is hoping one day they'll offer to give her a hand, or maybe even start getting in a cleaner, so that she doesn't have to spend every waking hour doing something for other people, but this suggestion does not seem forthcoming yet. They don't appear to be aware of how much she has to do. Increasingly she feels like their irrelevant slave. She rinses the glasses first and then wipes them with a dry cloth, like she used to do when she worked as a barmaid in a pub, to stop them getting streaks. Suds drip off the wooden chopping board, and she lets them drain next to a lethal carving knife. A song called *Empty Chairs* by Don McLean plays on the cassette player: The husband told her to choose anything so she chose this tape. She was feeling a little melancholy today for some reason. The lilting notes would normally put her off first thing in the morning, but she loves this album: his voice is like the wind swerving through a weird day.

'Cool choice,' says her husband, passing through the kitchen barefoot and kissing her on the back of the head. 'I haven't heard this for ages.' Inside, Esmeralda glows.

He goes outside with his tablet. Esmeralda remembers she watched a programme called *This Year's Top Ten Hottest New Apps* yesterday, so maybe she can impress him later. He leaves the patio door open so the smell of grass drifts in. Then Marni comes in and puts his school bag on the table and starts doing up his shoes.

'When you're done, I'd like to show you my homework, if that's alright, Mum?'

'Okay,' she says, wondering what her son is learning about now. Marni takes his school bag and goes to join his dad out on the patio. Esmeralda checks the time: eight thirty. They need to start leaving the house now.

'Betty!' she shouts up the stairs, 'It's time to go...'

'Alright,' screams Betty back at her, 'Why are you always hassling me? For God's sake!'

Esmeralda sighs. She was expecting that response. Instead of rising to the bait though she instead turns around and carries on with the washing-up, and Don McLean moves on to *Starry Starry Night*. It's a delicate, serenade-the-moon sort of song. Through the window, down the short garden, foxgloves and common mallows sway a bit. The lawns and flower-beds are pretty as a picture on a tin of shortbread. She'd asked the landlords when they'd moved into the house if it would be okay for them to do something with the garden, which had just been a plain lawn. They'd said she could and she'd bought in a bunch of bulbs and topsoil from ASDA. It was looking lovely now and buzzing with the sound of insects. The washing-up water glurps down the plug-hole, a teaspoon clatters in the sink, and Betty comes bounding through the kitchen and storms straight out into the garden. Esmeralda keeps her cool and shrugs. She slips on her boots and coat, then steps out behind them, pulling the patio door to and locking it behind her. They're all sitting on plastic chairs at the bottom of the garden looking at their smart phones, behind them is the back wall where the gate leads out onto the most direct route for them to get to school. Her husband took the same route as them to catch his bus into town for work.

'Let's go, then,' she says, and they all get up and walk out of the gate.

Betty and her dad lead and Marni walks beside Esmeralda. He shows her his homework. Bees graze the herby hedges, the sea sparkles in the distance, and the traffic drones away below them along the main road into Brighton.

'That's looking good' Esmeralda says to Marni, who has shown her his drawings of the anatomy of ants, which are actually really rather clever. Though he is less creative than Betty he is still an artist in his own right. Then Esmeralda notices the light from the sea seems to be glistening through Betty's body, as if she's become translucent or maybe it's a trick of the light... She takes a proper look, because obviously she can't be see through ... But she is.

'Betty. You've gone see-through.' Esmeralda shouts, but Betty doesn't react. Esmeralda sort of brushes off the thought as nonsense, but then she looks down at Marni and she realises she can see the grass they're walking on through his school uniform. *What's wrong with them?* she wonders.

'Marni...' She shakes his arm, but realises that she can't really feel him and after a moment her hand no longer grips an arm, but is flailing around in the air. It's like a magic trick, like the ones those guys do on the telly, but this isn't funny. Marni has become unaware that she is there and is fading away with every second. Esmeralda leaps back with a terrified scream and almost falls over. Her husband has walked on so far ahead that he can't hear her, as if he's late for his bus, and he doesn't react when she calls to him. Betty doesn't stir either. Frantic now, Esmeralda runs towards them - and sees Betty is almost invisible now. Only the skin on her hands and face remain. Esmeralda's hand is unsteady as she reaches out to touch her face. Her hand goes straight through and the same shaky scream pours out of her. A bird in the pink roses threads sharp and shiny notes together, as Esmeralda's mind starts throbbing and woozing. But this serves up one possible explanation: she has food poisoning and is hallucinating. Possibly, but it didn't really make sense. Esmeralda had taken a lot of drugs over the years and had endured several bouts of food poisoning. She didn't currently have any of the symptoms she was used to other than feeling sick with fright. Which was fair enough given the circumstances. Then she thinks, *Stop thinking, Esmeralda – call for help now* - it's the morning run, there are people everywhere. She runs down towards where the faint suggestion of her family appear to be, who are still walking along, but are barely visible now, along the cliff top walk on the other side of the main road into town. The traffic is crawling at its usual morning pace and she easily slips past the cars onto the pavement and looks back and forth along the route for help. She notices a woman, or perhaps it's a man, watching her from a bench a few metres away, but she's looking for another mum, a familiar face who might be able to help her. To tell her what's going on. The gears of what's real slip. She turns around and there he/she is, next to her on the pavement. She knows him/her. The cat-like eyes, the sharp black suit, the perfect nose – it's the androgynous being from her poem about desire. The archetype she'd renounced after that disastrous relationship with the unworthy one.

'I – I – I – I'm – I'm in need of help, I – I —'

'You need my help with Betty and Marinus?' The he/she's voice is full of hate. There's a small sort of flickering in its eyes like nothing she has ever seen. Did it just say, 'Marinus'?

'Where is Marinus? I think I need an ambulance.'

'I've given them a clean death.' This isn't an empty threat. Whoever he/she is, it's killed Betty and Marinus, or made them vanish, or whatever it's done. It doesn't make any sense.

'I – I – I – don't understand,' Esmeralda falls to the floor and curls up into a terrified ball and begins to cry, 'I –'

The creature takes a step towards her. 'You deserted me, Esmeralda.'

'I don't know who you are, and I just want to go – please, I need to save my children –'

'You renounced me and left me for dead...' It re-angles its head. 'Yes, you know who I am. So tell me how does it feel now to live without your desires?'

Esmeralda is shaking: 'Swear to God, I – I've no idea who you are.'

It reads her, suspiciously. 'Tell you what. Those two children of yours; they're not quite gone yet. Use your deep desire now, you might save one. Go on. It's what a true slave would do.'

Far, far away, a dog's barking, a seagull screams... the thing's so close now she can smell it. The smell of sex, success and addiction. Esmeralda's voice has gone all anorexic.

'So can I call a doctor then?'

'You can't heal them yourself?' asks the thing.

Esmeralda manages to shake her head.

'Then you'll not need an ambulance. You'll never see them again. Run away. Go on. Run. Let's see how far you can get.' She doesn't trust this monster or her ears.

'What?'

'There's the road – go. Run, you rancid little thing.' It steps away to offer an escape route. She's expecting a trick, she doesn't know what, but then it comes back and leans in so close, she see the smoothness of its skin, and its big golden cat's eyes, with long thin pupils, that are not round like a humans, and it shouts at the top of its lungs: 'RUN BEFORE I CHANGE MY MIND.'

Through the row of traffic, past the swaying bushes, up the grassy hill, she runs. She runs like she has never run before. The sun's in her face and the house is not far. Halfway there, when she get to the trellis thing, she looks back: but it's not running after her, like she dreaded, just standing there, a few steps from the side of the cliff, where she had last seen Betty and Marinus – who are gone now and she doesn't know where. Perhaps they are back at the house and this is all a bad dream so run run run run run run, but, run, but, but, run, but … But she's slowing, slowing, how, why, what, her heart's straining like crazy, but it's like the brake and accelerator are being pressed at the same time but whatever's slowing down isn't inside herself, it's not poison, it's outside of her, it's time slowing up or gravity pulling harder, or air changing to water, or sand, or treacle … She's had dreams like this – but she's awake, it's daytime, she knows she is awake … But, impossibly, she's stopped, like a statue of a runner, one foot raised for the next stride that'll never come. This is mad. Fucking insane. It occurs to her she ought to try to scream for help, it's what people do, but all that comes out is this grunty spasm noise... and the world starts shrinking back towards the cliff edge, hauling her along with it, helpless. There's ivy on the bushes, she grabs it, and her feet lift off the ground, like she's a cartoon character in a hurricane hanging on for dear life, but the pain in her wrists makes her let go, and she falls to earth with a bruising whack and is dragged along the ground, scraping her elbows and bumping her tail-bone. She swivels onto her back and tries to dig her heels in but the grass is too hard, She can't get a grip, she sort of trips herself upright, onto her feet, and a pair of butterflies flutter by, up-current, like this unfightable force only works on her. Now she's back at the cliff edge, and the drivers in the cars can't see her. The pale faced she-man stands waiting for her on the pavement and she knows it is this creature that is doing all this, it's pulling her back, then it's like 20,000 volts shoot through her and she's tossed hard to the edge of the cliff and she's there looking down at the rocks below, deciding on whether she should jump and end it all. Her children are gone, or never were. They never were. She knows it now. The daymare ends with the realisation that Betty and Marinus are not going to school and never have been to school. Their school shoes have never been worn. None of this is true. It's all a fantasy. A desire. She pulls herself up from her grip on the grass at the edge of the cliff and looks up at the bench. The creature sits there, swinging its folded leg, having a merry old time.

Esmeralda pulls herself to her feet. She stumbles towards the monster.

'You can't have everything Esmeralda', it sneers at her. 'In this world you don't get to have your cake and eat it. If you want to be a slave to me then it's a full time position. You don't just fob me off and then expect to get what you want.'

'But this wasn't what I wanted' Esmeralda whispers. 'My dream was to be an actress. Having children was Plan B.'

'Plan A, Plan B. Whatever crappy filing system your pathetic little head wants to give these mundane desires, they all belong to me. And you'll not be getting any of them. You deserted me Esmeralda. You little bitch. So now you get nothing.'

Esmeralda feels the bottom fall out of her stomach. Her children, her future, her dreams, are all erased. The poles that held her tent in place are removed and she is nothing more than a floppy blank canvas. Her ears begin to throb as her brain feels like it is trying to push itself hard out of her skull and her heart breaks into a thousand shards. She is nothing except failure. The creature laughs and she pulls herself away from the revolting sound of its total victory over her and semi-circles sideways back to the edge of the cliff, where she sways, staring down with dizzying stomach churning dread at the rocks below. Only a fool would step off into the unknown. Away from the ordered events of life. You are born, you go to school, you go to university, you get a job, you get married, you have children, you grow old, you die. There is safety in prescription. Behind her is order, but the order has gone wrong. In front of her is utter unknown. And through the shrill laughter of this torturous evil cretin she hears the silence of the void and somehow there is comfort there... And she steps off.

The laughing stops abruptly as if it hadn't seen this coming and as she steps out off of the cliff and into the unknown she feels a sense of total freedom. It is terrifying, but she's committed now and the sound of the creature behind her is a scream of angry disappointment as she begins to fall. But sometimes when you fool... you fly.

Never Worn

BE HAPPY

Loading her body and bags onto the coach, Esmeralda snuggled in amongst the pilgrims on her way to the centre and listened attentively to any snippets of news about the experience to come.

'Which course are you doing?'

'I didn't know there was more than one course. It is my first time.'

'There are two courses, running simultaneously. One for new and old students and the other is for students who have been at least four times.'

'Are the courses very different?'

'No, they are exactly the same, only the course for more experienced students is quieter.'

She had to admit it, she was feeling really nervous.

Esmeralda arrived at the centre and was shown into a normal looking canteen, where a queue was already formed for enrolment and she joined it, checking out the other women and men milling around the hall. They all seemed normal enough. Then a little old lady in full sari, who looked like she had just been teleported over from India, made her way along the line of ladies and welcomed them, telling each of them that she prepared the food for each day and that they can expect to experience a wonderful time at the centre.

Reaching the end of the queue Esmeralda sat down and found out the timetable and the number of her room for the week, which she would be sharing with one other woman.

She arrived at her room to find a very smiley Polish lady already sat on a bed in their small cell. She had short dark hair and was melancholic and very humble. They laughed about the craziness of the situation and settled themselves in. It was a simple room, very clean, and the two narrow single beds were comfortably equipped with thick duvets, a single pillow and a white woollen blanket. The beds were separated by a bedside table, upon which sat a little lamp, and at the foot of the bed they were provided with some shelves and hooks for clothes. Simple, but everything that they needed for the week ahead. The striking thing about both the canteen and the little room was the cosy warmth, which had been Esmeralda's greatest concern.

Meditating for twelve hours a day in a freezing cold room had lacked appeal.

They all reconvened in the dining hall and were given a rundown of the week ahead and an explanation on what was required from them. Before they began they had to agree to five precepts. These were...

to abstain from killing any being

to abstain from stealing

to abstain from all sexual activity

to abstain from telling lies

to abstain from all intoxicants

They also all had to observe Noble Silence from the beginning of the course until the morning of the last day. Noble Silence meant silence of body, speech, and mind. Any form of communication with fellow students, whether by gestures, sign language or written notes was forbidden.

They may however speak with their teacher whenever necessary and the teacher would also call on the students from time to time, to check they were understanding the technique, but that should also be kept to a minimum. On the whole everyone was required to cultivate the feeling that they are working in isolation. The morning gong would be at 4am and the first group meditation would start in the main hall at 4.30am, where they would mediate for two hours. At 6am they would hear the gong for breakfast in the dining hall, which would last an hour and would be followed by an hour's rest. The 8am gong announced the second group sitting in the main hall, which lasted an hour and was followed by two more hours of meditation practice either in the hall or in their rooms. At 11am there would be a simple yet nutritious vegan lunch, followed by another hour's rest. 1pm meant practice in their room or in the hall for an hour before another group sitting for an hour in the hall followed by two more hours practice in the hall or in their rooms. The 5pm gong sounded the start of tea, where new students could take a piece of fruit or two, but old students could only take lemon water. There was to be no eating after 5pm. 6pm marked another group sitting in the main hall, followed by a discourse from the main guy who started the whole courses, he talked to us in the form of an hour-long film in the main hall, which was then followed by the last hour long group sitting of the day. After this there would be half an hour to get ready for bed. Lights out was at 9.30pm. Each day, for ten days. It was an eighteen hour day and twelve of them would be spent meditating. At the end of the meeting the divide was drawn between the men and the women's sides of the dining hall. They were to have no more contact with the opposite sex until the end of the course. Then they were told to return to their rooms and that the Noble Silence had begun.

They filed out in silence and gathered together their bits and bobs back in their rooms, ready for the first gong. And what a lovely gong it was. The beautiful ringing cascaded vibrations throughout the entire body. At its first chime they began to pour into the great hall. They each had a designated prayer cushion and blanket in a large purpose-built room with very low lighting, a creaky roof and the sound of wind howling around the hall reminding you of the outside world. The men were on one side of the hall, and an aisle separated them from the women's side of the hall. As they were told to keep themselves to themselves it took a whole week for Esmeralda to actually see any of the men clearly, but she could hear them. Farting loudly. At the back of the hall were large piles of spare cushions and blankets that they could help themselves to. They got comfortable and then the teacher's assistants silently entered the hall. There was a male teacher for the men and a female teacher for the women. They sat on raised meditation stalls at the front, facing the students, and the woman especially was incredibly serene. She sat and closed her eyes as the man introduced them both and explained that they were married and here to run the course and answer any questions that might arise. They then told the students to close their eyes and begin.

A bass voice began to boom out over the PA system. It was of a man chanting. It was the worst chanting Esmeralda had ever heard. It kept tailing off as if he was Am-Dram acting out a death scene. She nearly started laughing it was so awful. *They had to be kidding?* She thought. It went on for quite some time and for much of it Esmeralda began to think she had made a mistake. That this was going to be silly. But she was here now and there's was nothing for her to do for the next ten days except for meditate, so she got on with it.

The hall was dimly lit, snug and comfortable. The acoustics were muffled by the carpet and cushions, but there was a delightful clacking that came from the wind howling against the roof, that sounded like ventilation shafts lightly flapping open and closed. The weather outside made the inside even snugger and she grew accustomed to her tiny little square of sanctuary in amongst all the other women in the large hall. She was pretty good at meditating, not that good is really a word one can use to describe mediation. But what she meant is she had practiced a fair bit during all the IVF, as it was the only thing that stopped her from completely losing it. Also, from the years of living on the road as a Fool she had learnt to sit still and relax into prolonged periods or reprogramming. There were younger women at the retreat who clearly were not used to this and acted as if the centre was forcing them to be there, which is how people normally behave when they first start doing this kind of work. It takes a while to realise that the only person who brought you there, is keeping you there and is going to get anything out of it, is you.

The week was hard work, but it was also glorious. It felt like curling back up inside of a womb. The food was nutritious, delicious and plentiful. The breaks seemed long and regular enough. Esmeralda soon discovered that time went much faster and she got more reprogramming done if she did all of her meditation in the main hall. Some of the sessions you could do in your room, but she always ended up staring out of the window instead of meditating, and this made time slow right down. Meditation is active, sitting doing nothing for an hour is boring. Soon she spent all day every day in the hall, except for at meal times or breaks when she would walk around the small patch of forest set aside for such use, behind the hall. Or if she was in a lot of pain, she would go back and lie down on her bed in the small cell and press a hot water bottle against her back.

That was the interesting thing. It was painful and difficult work. Not only were you physically sitting still for prolonged periods of time, but also you were battling with yourself in your head. Telling yourself off for not meditating properly, then telling yourself off for telling yourself off. She began to develop ways of talking to herself differently, like seeing her consciousness as a little girl who, instead of shouting at, she asked to come and sit in her lap and gave her a cuddle instead. This calmed her mind much more than shouting at herself. And the big discovery was that it was a lot less painful if she really did sit completely still. This was an area of physical experience she was used to after all her years performing on the stage. When you are in front of an audience and not allowed to move, you go into the stasis of dynamic stillness. It feels powerful, ninja-like. For most of the week she did not do this. She was in a lot of pain. Her RSI was thawing through her damaged nerves and her muscles felt like wax slowly dripping down over her skeleton and as it unravelled it was awfully painful, but it felt like good pain. However, after five days, when the dripping had ceased, she was left with the root of all the pain. Three searing points in her shoulder, one at the front in between her collar bones, and two at the back, on the inside edges of her shoulder blades. It felt like a tripod passing through her shoulder and no matter how she tweaked her sitting position or moved her shoulder around, nothing would stop the excruciating pain. This went on for the whole ten days. Then finally, in the last meditation session, when she had worked really hard all week and felt like she had successfully ironed out a lot of the depression crease and had found some genuine peace and stillness, she decided in the last session to just relax and have a think and not worry about meditating.

Her mind began to wonder and she found herself reliving a great injustice that had happened to her husband and herself. A whole group of friends had been lost because a guy had accused her husband of stealing something, which he hadn't. The guy had lost his temper, appearing at them with a red face and foaming at the mouth, then out of nowhere he had suddenly launched himself at her husband and throttled him, leaving fingerprints on his neck that remained for days. She should have gone straight to the police and charged him with assault, but he was an old friend and she had never seen him like that before. She was sure that as soon as he calmed down he would apologise. But he didn't. And not only did he not apologise, but he somehow managed to turn their whole massive group of friends, whom she had known since she was a little girl, against her and her husband. It felt like a witch-burning and was undoubtedly the cruellest thing that had ever happened to her. Esmeralda had never had any enemies until this guy covered his back by making up lies about her and her husband. It had broken her heart. As she relived this memory, the clarity of her mind from a week of meditation meant she relived step-by-step exactly what happened, in real time, recalling every word that was said, every action and every feeling. And at the end it she was filled with rage at the absolute injustice of it all. She was so angry with that horrible man for everything he had put her and her husband through and suddenly she realised that the searing pain she'd been feeling in her shoulder all week had grown and was now filling up her entire body, like she was on fire. And in a split second, she realised that there was nothing she could do about it. He didn't care, he'd convinced himself that he was right and that her husband and her are bad people. The friendships were all irreparably lost and there was no way on earth of being able to get it all back again, so she simply had to just let it all go. And she did. In one big breath, all the pain, anger and upset left her body. It was the deepest, most soothing breath she had ever expelled and as she did so the pain lodged in her shoulder released and melted from her body. She was free. And it occurred to her that all this time she had literally been carrying around a chip on her shoulder.

In the break after this meditation session she wandered out into the forest. It was encrusted with frost and the sun had begun to thaw it slightly, so it looked as if the fairy kingdom had covered the forest with sacks of glittering fairy dust. The grass, cobwebs and delicate crocus heads sparkled so beautifully it made Esmeralda begin to weep with joy. She felt liberated. It had been hard work, but the week had loosened her free from her bonds and she felt liberated from her past, present once more and full of joy. And she now knew that no matter how hard things got, way before she would ever consider suicide again, she'd become a Buddhist nun first and spend her life doing this work. Because it was a wonderful thing to do.

When the course finished and she rang her husband she chose her words carefully as she didn't want him to react negatively towards her, knowing how open and vulnerable she was feeling, so instead she said to him that the things she had realised over the week had been all of the things that he was always saying to her anyway. And she was sorry that she had not listened to him in the first place.. And it was true... He was always telling her to get back in the room and be more present. He was deeply relieved, as he'd feared she was going to come back having decided she wanted to leave him, so he felt huge relief at her not only loving him more than ever, but also liked the idea that she was going to listen to him more. Their conversation was bubbly and full of love.

The week had given her time to think about her husband and their future together. They had been through so much and a lot of unpleasant things had been said and heartache shared. But two things came up from the mediation. First of all was the ethos that you did no harm to others. Only treat people how you would like to be treated yourself.

And she would be devastated if he ever decided he didn't want to be with her anymore. Why on earth would she want to devastate him then? And, whilst she had been meditating, she had seen a vision of their love being like an oak tree that they had spent all this time and effort growing together. If she left him then that tree would be an old dying ugly waste of time. But if they carried on and worked through this difficult period in their lives, then this tree would be a beautiful, gnarly, twisting, majestic delight, with some scars to show, some tales to tell, but solid and strong and full of wonder. She knew from the hairs on her head down to the tips of her toes that she loved him with every cell of her being and she would never leave him. He was a favourite human being on the planet.

SPRING AWAKENING

Snowdrops tinkle in frost encrusted forests,

Crocus crowns push hard against the rock-solid soil.

Lapping waves of sun kissed days advance and retreat like the sea,

Hidden amongst the receding tide of frozen breath and bitter snow.

Heavy-scented summer notes carry upon the howling wind and rain,

Occasionally catching numb nostrils with their sensual promise of sweet refrain.

Robins bob in courtly dance,

On relay flights with new-found sweethearts.

Blackbirds forage on forest floors; doglike and without fear.

Blue tits call brightly from high-up perches...

'Pick me. Pick me. Pick me.'

And a little round wren leaps in fright,

313

Rudely disturbed from its ivy hiding place.

Upon the bare horizon woodpeckers mechanically drill their migraine inducing homes,

Whilst overhead, squirrels saunter saucily across bare branches,

Picking off winter's last remaining berries.

In clear frozen nights the owls call their hopeful greetings,

Across cold empty fields, left dormant since last year's toil.

And so it is, in near-silent stillness.

Spring delicately unfurls her uncompromising splendour,

As winter rails in unforgiving fury against its inevitable ending; his last death rattle.

BACK IN THE ROOM

Then, after all that, when Esmeralda returned to Brighton, she arrived at the station and immediately missed an opportunity to show compassion for a fellow human being and broke one of the precepts. Needing the toilet, she dragged all of her heavy bags to a cafe and went to settle in. But when she asked where the toilets were she was told that they didn't have any. The place was practically a pub, serving food and everything, and it didn't have a toilet. This annoyed her. Instead she had to go around to the station's public toilets, which were the ones where you have to pay, but she couldn't see a change machine and she didn't have the right change for the barriers. An old lady was stood next to her and Esmeralda turned to her and said...

'How am I meant to go to the toilet? I don't have the right change.'

'Nor do I' said the old woman in the most pitiful voice, but in her anger Esmeralda didn't hear. In a flash she had already responded,

'I'm going under,' she said and she ducked under the barrier, both missing the fact that this woman could have done with her help and at the same time that she was committing an act of stealing, all in one swift move. As she sat on the toilet, she instantly felt awful, like the whole week had been pointless. Then even worse, when she came out, she saw the change machine had been on the wall right behind her the whole time. In her anger she hadn't seen it. And she could have given some change to the old woman if she had of spotted it. But... She had to let this go. Not because it didn't matter, because it *did* matter, but the important thing was that it is good that it mattered to her, it didn't mean she should give up at the first hurdle. This was not a quick fix. Nothing in life ever is. She was starting on her journey along a path she would be traversing for the rest of her living days, and would never reach the end of. No one will ever be perfect. All she could hope for was that the tenth, twelfth or hundredth time something like that happened to her, she'd remain calm enough and compassionate enough to not make some quick selfish decision rooted in anger and misery, but remember to be honest and helpful to other human beings who are in need of some love instead.

'*In the streets, all over the world, people gathered in vigil this evening, holding aloft pens and wearing stickers saying 'Je Suis Charlie', which means 'I am Charlie' to show solidarity with our right to freedom of speech and to pay tribute to the victims of the attack on satirical magazine Charlie Hebdo. Ten journalists were killed by gunmen in Paris this week for having drawn a cartoon of Mohammed...*' reported the news on the TV screen in the corner of the cafe. It felt strange to be back in the 'real' world again.

'I will not be made to participate in a new holocaust. It is scaring the hell out of me how people and the press are demonising Muslims.'

'It is beginning to feel like Nazi Germany isn't it.'

'Well before any human being shoved another human being inside an oven, a whole bunch of propaganda and brainwashing went into making sure that people no longer saw Jews as human. We are doing it now to Muslims, and it's working. I don't think we are many years away from a collective permission to exterminate Muslims. If I was them, I'd be taking out as many of us as I could.'

The positive twist she had got on all of this, though, was that she'd been taken down a peg or two and that can only be a good thing. She had more pegs then an OCD housewife's washing line. She'd learnt that you don't always get what you want, but if you try sometimes, you just might find that you get what you need. She'd learnt that life is what you make of it and the greatest weapon a person can have is an ability to turn anything into a learning experience. She'd learnt that it is all too easy to become a victim of depression and that it is possibly impossible to get over it again fully. She'd learnt that time flies once you've passed adolescence and one day you wake up to discover that it has all somehow passed you by without everything going completely as intended. She'd discovered that the mainstream had no use for her, but that she had too much wit to be an outcast. She was seeing that she needed to learn to use her power in a subtler and less acknowledged way than the one she had been expecting. Her path turned out to be that of the silent healer, rather than a starlet of the silver screen. She was only just getting used to this revelation and was a million miles away from being a silent healer, but hoped to be able to get there before she died. And she'd learnt that falling apart and being thrown into the unknown didn't kill her In the end, it had only made her stronger. She'd learnt that the road to enlightenment is a quiet and humble one. She was nowhere near enlightenment, but was learning to shut up and listen.

Really crazy shit was going on in the world. Even though times were scary and she believed things were going to get a lot worse before they got any better, she believed there was only progression before them and that in the end the future always held an inevitable improvement. Life is a spiral. We keep going through good times and bad, like summer and winter, seemingly always making the same mistakes, but each time we do still move forward. Fewer people live in poverty now than ever before, there are better human rights, longer life expectancy, fewer wars, less infant mortality. Things always get better, but in a cyclical, spiralling manner.

'A wise shaman once said to me that the two things to watch out for in life are fear and ego. Don't let fear run your life, or your ego take control. I've just had a horrid seven years, run by fear, which sucked, but now I feel I'm out of the other side, the depression has finally lifted and I feel brave and strong again... But I am scared now of finding myself feeling like an egotistical bell end once more. I hope one day I can find a happy medium.'

'I would just like to say that you have been looking extra specially lovely recently. I also understand that you have been eating a lot of cheese. Is that your secret?'

He texted her. *You are little naughty bits of human, spliced together in a suggestive fashion.*

Esmeralda and her husband went to find out about adoption. They watched videos, did Q&A sessions and spoke to people who had, themselves, adopted. It was very inspiring, but the upshot of it was that they knew they were nowhere near ready. Or possibly not ever going to be suitable. They were young anyway, 38 years being the average age of an adopter. He was 39, but she had only just turned 36. There was the problem of them needing to have their finances sorted, with cleared debts and savings. Being able to drive would help, but the main issue was that the perceived wisdom now is that you tell the child they are adopted from the offset and never pretend otherwise. The social services are continuously in fairly close contact, in that you'll need to keep a door open by keeping in touch with the child's family, in case the child ever wants to make contact with them again in the future. Which was all fair enough, but this approach meant that you seemed a bit more like an extension of the social services rather than a family. She guessed they must know what they're doing. It must be less emotionally stressful to just always be told you're adopted rather than one day discover you are, but she hadn't been expecting the level of contact that continued with the social services once the adoption had gone through. But the main obstacle was that the young people were very scared of change and were in great need of stability. That was the biggest issue for Esmeralda. She had no routine. Not just did she have no routine, but she despised routine. The only time she had tried to do a normal job she had cried in the toilets every day. It didn't feel like what they had to offer was going to work with what the social services were looking for or what would be right for the child. Which is crazy, because they would be such awesome parents.

Her husband didn't take the news well though, that it looked like this was it, there were no more options. As soon he got outside of the adoption centre he went straight to a shop and bought himself a pack of rolling tobacco and made himself a fag, thus undoing all the clean living that had been strengthening any tiny sliver of a chance they might have on conceiving naturally. Esmeralda was furious and they screamed at each other into the night. She was angry with him, but also she could see his point of view. It was pretty much impossible for them to conceive naturally, to the point where they might as well just get on with their lives and enjoy themselves. But this then flagged up a bunch of interesting questions. I mean, in all honesty, what is the point of being married if there is absolutely no chance of having children? And this is not a hypothetical question. Esmeralda genuinely needed to think about this. If they weren't having kids, why were they married? Obviously because they love each other. But what were they going to do with themselves now for the next forty years? And if he was going to smoke and drink like a twenty year old, then it was a pretty good bet she would be living a whole other life without him after he'd passed away, but without anyone else there, or any financial security, or anyone to look after her. It was all a bit scary.

Esmeralda sat in the stifling warmth of her friend's huge houseboat, moored quietly on the still, illuminated waters of Surrey Quays. Canary Wharf twinkled at her on the horizon and the shaggy dachshund called Loopy nestled up to her, substituting Esmeralda's cuddles for the love of her real mummy, who was the other side of the world in Canada, waiting for her visa.

Just like her mum and her bestest friend, this man had been a very special soulmate to Esmeralda. He was almost a secret. Very few people remembered him from his wild days in Brighton. Even during his recent fleeting stay back in her little city of sin by the sea he had been a recluse. He was a maverick who didn't like large crowds. A few of her friends were like that and she found herself drawn to them. Somehow warmed by the hermit in their soul. She knew she could talk to him about her concerns before the off. He was someone who genuinely listened to what she was saying and would unpick and analyse what was really going on underneath. Obviously this was heavenly for our little egocentric heroine and, although fighting back tears for half of the conversation, relished the attention. It wasn't wholly one sided though. She made him laugh three times in the conversation by saying things that surprised him. He loved being surprised, what with him kind of having everything sewn up in his logical yet emotionally wise world. He was surprised when she told him the latest chapter in the saga that was the story of her Father. He loved the fact he'd convinced himself he was gay and then changed his mind. Laughing, he said,

'I feel like I know your father now,' he smiled, 'Is he a hopeless optimist?'

She nodded, and he sat back satisfied with his deductions.

He also offered her some sound advice about her husband.

'He is in pain,' he explained. 'He just watched you go through a process that he had no control over and could do nothing to help, and it's all ended up being for nothing. He is also going to be mourning the ideas of the children he thought you were going to have together. If he is drinking and smoking again, it is because he needs to let off some steam. Sounds like you have been doing the same yourself. It sounds to me like you need to cut the poor guy some slack.'

And he was right. She had drunk a bathful of tequila, whilst letting her hair down. He had every right to do the same.

'There is nothing noble in being superior to your fellow man; true nobility is being superior to your former self.' - Ernest Hemingway

'The next election date has been set. It's for May next year.'

'Okay; if the Tories get in again, can we go burn down everything that Murdoch owns?'

'Don't even joke about it.'

'But they won't get in, though, will they... Surely the country isn't *that* stupid.'

Noel Fielding just totally checked me out.

He checked me out once too. He likes a saucy lady.

'Which nudibranch would you chose to be?'

'Oh that's hard. There are so many great ones.'

'Today I learnt that nudibranches have disposable penises and they eat poisonous sea creatures and imbibe their toxins, therefore becoming toxic themselves.'

'Wow, disposable penises and toxin imbibing. What skills. I learnt about Mungo, a Filipino mung bean soup. I made it and it is delicious... and vegan. I'll have to make some for you, if you fancy a break from being a carnivorous poisonous gobbler.'

'That sounds delightful. I'll give you another call next week and we'll make a date.'

'Big love gorgeous.'

'I love the words mung and bean. But not as much as I love you.'

'Magic and logic must live side by side, or they'll destroy each other.' - Flight of the Dragons

'Do you know any global warming deniers? I've got a Christmas card that needs holding up next to my window.'

She wrote out her New Year's Resolutions:

1. Become vegetarian

2. Learn to drive

3. Commit random acts of kindness

4. Roar less, purr more.

3. Stop using exclamation marks and the words 'very' and 'really'.

She wandered into the kitchen to make breakfast. She still loved her muesli in the summer and porridge in the winter, but this year everyone had gone crazy for the magic bullet, a juicer that was quicker and easier to use and clean up afterwards than all the massive monsters of equipment for juicing that had come before it. Her favourite morning smoothie was a banana with almond milk, a spoonful of peanut butter, ground almonds, a sprinkle of cinnamon and a splash of maple syrup. Shoving this all into a plastic cup and screwing on the lid, she turned it upside down, pressed it hard onto the base and the blades sprang into life, whisking the whole lot up into a delicious shake.

She drank this as she went about unloading and loading the dishwasher. Her husband and the lodger did help out a bit with the housework, but she did the lion's share and every day without fail it made her hate them both a little bit more. It occurred to her that it was a microcosm for the macrocosm for the world. Men think they have some kind of right to have everything done for them and be treated like they're somehow in charge, whilst everyone else lets them get away with. If this *status quo* somehow was just the natural way of things and led to harmony in the world then it wouldn't really be a problem, but it doesn't lead to harmony. It leads to people feeling exploited and hating the men who are exploiting them. It also stops everything functioning as well as it could. The world is dying before our eyes. And it has died under their watch.

That's the kind of thing that whirls around our Esmeralda's head whilst she is doing the housework before making a smoothie.

However, having said this, slowly but surely Esmeralda began to notice the effects of her meditation retreat and daily practice easing itself into permanent habits. For a good few weeks she did not argue with her husband. Then the weeks became months and the months became a year. It was incredible. Gently and calmly the meditation began to soften her soul.

'There's something satisfying about turning up to a theatre show in London, only to discover the programme includes me in the 'Thanks to...' section.'

'We just ate so much melted cheese I ain't gonna shit right for a week.'

'I feel like I was born in the wrong time. I've always felt like that.'

'I did too, you know, until recently. Then I read a study that was about how those of us who are now over 30 are the last generation to recall a world before technology. The study showed that young people have 40% less empathy than previous generations. It went on to say that our task, as folks who remember a world without technology, is to ensure that empathy, community and time without screens are all passed on to future generations. Or they'll be owned by their devices (and those who control them). They'll be unaware of their own resilience. They'll find it increasingly difficult to be present and increasingly ignorant to the power that exists in them all joining forces, and how this can topple any oppressor. We are the storytellers my friend. And the world needs storytellers... Now more than ever.'

'Many families who are 'old money' and run our country, and who are against trade unions, made their fortunes five hundred years ago by banding together into guilds, so they could ensure decent

prices for their products and avoid exploitation...
Just saying.'

'Behind every great fortune is a great crime.' - Balzac

'The guy who teaches me hot yoga,' announced
her friend, 'looks just like Jeremy Clarkson. It's
hilarious.'

'Have you noticed how they have a bookshelf full
of books in the waiting room at the station in Hove...
Actually.'

'Well in Brighton we have a piano at our station...
What a bunch of middle class knobs we all are.'

'Imagine how screwed up it would be if a tobacco
company sued a government for banning smoking
and won.'

'Yep, that would be fucked up.'

'Well it's happened. More than once.'

'Did you know our national debt increases by five
grand a second because the government isn't
levying enough taxes to cover the costs of running
the country? Am I being stupid, but isn't that kind of
the point of the government?'

'You're being very political at the moment.'

'I personally think if you are not political at the
moment then you should be ashamed of yourself.'

'When you wish good things for other people it will come back to you tenfold. But when you just wish good things for yourself, you'll often feel like you're not getting the things you want.'

'Oh Mummy, you are so wise.'

'I've finally figured out how to remember the spelling for necessary. A beautiful friend of mine helped me to work it out the other night.'

'How?' She asked.

'Cunt eats sperms... sperms are plural, so now I can remember which order the c and the s go in and that there is one cunt but more than one sperm.'

'Genius!' She laughed.

'The Greens only have a 5% lead at the moment, so please try to get to the polling station tomorrow.'

The Tories got in.

Owing to the hideous result today and inspired by Josie Long, in the next five years I promise to:

1. Endeavour to meet and speak with as many fearful people as possible and let them know without blame that we are all in this together and I've got their backs.

2. To keep living life to the fullest and celebrate its many nuances, colours and creeds.

3. To share with and serve others.

4. Fight every step of the way to keep all that is precious in our wonderful country alive, like butterflies, the forests, the NHS, our human rights and support for the vulnerable.

5. Stay... And shout.

'Loving you is easy, because you are beautiful.'

'You are the most beautiful human being on the planet and I am so lucky to have you.'

'I just love and trust you.'

'There's so much dog poo on our street I decided to take affirmative action, so I covered a massive pile in glitter and stuck a sign in it, which read *'You can't polish a turd, but you can roll it in glitter'*. I think that might help.'

'I just lost my phone and my husband switched it on remotely from his work and made it ring from the bathroom. He is the best geek ever.'

'I had a dream we had to get married because you stole a dead bat from a school.'

'I had a dream last night that I came around to visit you two at your house, to play with your pet rabbit. You lived in a bungalow on a road that looked like a house on Ramsay Street.'

'Today appears to be a beige food kind of a day.'

'I've just realised that the only way to tell if you have become middle-aged these days is when your friends start posting photos of themselves jogging on Facebook.'

'British trains can't cope with snow on the tracks, leaves on the tracks, and now too much sun on the tracks. They just need to develop an aversion to snowdrops and they'll have covered all the seasons.'

'It's not every morning you wake up to the Sydney Opera House introducing itself to you by email.'

"I think the pain of not being able to have children is similar to the pain of losing your parents," said Esmeralda to her friend who had lost both her parents in the last few years. "When you lose your parents you are losing your past. When you can't have children then you are losing your future."

'What's wrong with us?' exasperated Esmeralda, 'Why do we have to keep learning life's lessons over and over again, never learning from the past?'

'Be the person you needed when you were younger.'

'What, Mr Blobby?'

'Today I realised that if you leave a pile of important papers for long enough they stop being important, but if you leave them a really long time, then they eventually become sacred.'

'Someone I love was in the Paris attacks last night.'

'Are they okay?'

'Yes, they were a hero. My God, though, it freaked me the fuck out. Life is so fragile and short. We must make sure we don't take each other for granted. You never know when one of us might be gone for good.'

Who'd have known that bestiality could bring so much joy? #piggate

'Do no harm, stop others from doing harm and do what you can.' - Scarlett Thomas, Popco

'Last year I saw an unusual number of white feathers and it was a year of great loss. This year I have seen an unusual amount of rainbows and it's been a year of great blessings. Life really is a series of swings and roundabouts. The only given is that things will change.'

'What are you off to see tonight then?' asked the manicurist.

Esmeralda's mum replied, 'The Suffragette'.

'That's to do with women, isn't it?' asked the woman doing Esmeraldas nails.

Esmeralda and her mother proceeded to tell them about the suffragette movement.

'Don't need to see the film then, do you,' laughed the woman.

Esmeralda didn't want to judge the young woman, so when she got back she checked to see if the Suffragettes were still on the national curriculum and they were still there, which she was relieved to discover.

The Last Hurrah... We're All Going to die:
Shirt off, half naked,
At the great office party of life.
Sweaty, horny, reckless and arrogant...
Happy to throw caution to the wind
And burn the fucking place down.
The future is gone,
The past is ignored.
We're all going to die...
So let's drink tequila,
Screw our bosses,
And shit in the drawers,
Because there's sod all we can do about it now.

World Childless Week... was created as a way of highlighting the experiences of people who are unable to have children. Not to be confused with those who are childless by choice – the "child-free", as some say.

- Barbara Ellen

Esmeralda thought about this for a while. She was childless, in that fate had dealt her and her husband the horrific blow of infertility, but they were also child-free, in that they'd eventually accepted the situation and had then come to the conclusion that not having children was not a bad thing. The non-stop holidays and still possessing an impeccable vagina more than made up for it.

'On the one hand...' said one of her oldest friends, who had been told all her life that she was infertile, but had then almost accidentally got pregnant the first time she had ever tried IVF, 'is having a kid...' she weighed her hands out like scales, 'But on the *other* hand is everything else. Having a kid is the most amazing thing in the world ever, but if you *don't* have kids, you *do* get to do everything else.'

'I think it's a total con," said her mentor, "I walk through the Pavilion Gardens in the summer, which I've nicknamed *The Field of Broken Dreams,* and I look at all the yummy mummies sitting there watching their toddlers and their eyes are full of despair.'

Plus there is an ominous feeling that hangs in the air, Esmeralda thought, *that any babies born now are destined to be nothing more than cannon-fodder.*

'I was hoping people would stop asking me after I reached a certain age, but I'm not so sure they will. Now I'm 40 I think people see it as their last chance to persuade me to have kids, before it's too late. We are child-free by choice; I can only imagine how hard it is fielding these questions for those who that isn't the case...'

'An older lady I know,' replied Esmeralda, 'who is also childless like me, told me this bullshit never ends. First of all it's all questions about having your own children, and then it's all about the grandchildren. It never stops.'

'Oh great,' she snorted, 'It never ceases to astound me how intrusive people's questions are and how thoughtless people can be...'

'Interesting, that,' replied another friend of hers, a woman she'd met through work and had instantly hit it off with, "As a single parent, the drone of similar questioning applies too. As if it's completely acceptable to pick apart women's life choices so easily and publicly.'

'Also, there's a stigma on *only* children,' piped up a friend of hers whom she had once been a 'fool' with, and who was still a dear friend. (They were sitting watching her beautiful blonde daughter playing on the swings) 'Which is not even apparent until you have just ONE?'

'I would agree,' her old chum interjected, as they sat enjoying a pint in the Edinburgh bar at the Fringe Festival, 'I have never understood why it is anyone else's business. As a single parent, I have spent the last 12 years or so having people tell me how I should have lived my life.'

'Which one of you is it, that's the reason you can't have children?' asked the woman Esmeralda had known but seconds. What other medical condition allows a complete stranger to ask you all about your most private life and genitalia? It made Esmeralda's blood boil. If the woman told her that all she needed to do was relax and stop thinking about, it she was going jab her fingers into both her eyes.

'For Christ's sake!' snapped Esmeralda angrily, 'In other words, whatever life choice you make as a woman is WRONG!'

And so it is.

The moment they stopped trying for children, or hoping they might get pregnant, as soon as the last drop of hope slipped through their fingers, everything changed. For the better. Their tempestuous relationship became significantly eased and the following year passed by without a single argument. Something they never dreamt could be possible. Esmeralda kept mediating and this helped with curbing her quick temper and ironing out her depression, but more than that, they just cut each other some slack. No, they were not having children, but they were now free to love each other without any of the trappings of how a marriage should be or what society expected of them. They were free to be politically active and fight for a better future for the lives of all their friend's children. And they were surrounded by friend's children. And all the children thought that they were amazing. Esmeralda was everyone's fairy-godmother and they thought she was imbibed with magic. And these little people were growing into dear friends in their own rights. Esmeralda got to keep her figure and her fanny intact. And they both got to feel incredibly self-righteous about the fact that neither of them could drive, they didn't have a dog, she was now vegan, and they didn't have kids. It's official... The imminent demise of the planet Earth was hardly their fault.

Esmeralda believed that the outside world is a sign language telling you how things are going on in the inside. If your life is full of magic and beautiful people, then things are probably going okay. That's why karma does exist. If you're a dick to people then shit stuff will happen to you. It doesn't mean shit stuff doesn't happen to good people. Of course it does, all the time, but if your heart is in the right place then you'll find a resolve in and a way through that gives the shit a positive slant. It might take years sometimes to pick your way through, but nothing lasts forever, including the shit times. For Esmeralda it felt like she had suffered seven shit years. This Saturn Returns quarter had been a shit one. She'd been depressed for most of it, had struggled with fertility for five of them, argued with her husband for most of it, her career had appeared to go down the drain and she'd felt suicidal. What was the point in living? She'd become one big fucking failure. By my goodness was she glad now that she had hung in there.

Suddenly their whole lives had changed for the better, just from deciding not to do any more IVF and that it was fine that they didn't have kids, more than that, it was great they didn't have kids. All the shit that had happened to them suddenly made sense. Both their careers blossomed. She'd ended up performing at the Barbican and the BBC Television Centre before it was sold off. She was in the biggest zeitgeist show of the Edinburgh Fringe Festival and it crossed over into the international festivals and took her all over the world. None of that would have happened if she'd killed herself. Or if she'd got pregnant. Her husband finally managed to get out of the call centre he'd been stuck in for three years and was now doing a job he loved, fixing computers, for his own company, as his own boss.

And they had fallen hopelessly head over heels in love with each other again. Their sex life drastically improved as soon as baby sex went out the window, spending their money on sex toys and skimpy outfits. She went to the gym and enjoyed getting back to having a tight and trim figure. They partied and enjoyed sleeping in on the mornings. They spent their money on travelling and having fun.

People don't realise that it is hurtful to tell someone who can't have kids how they know someone or other who as soon as they stopped trying for children got pregnant. They don't know that as a couple struggling with fertility issues you get told this stupid fucking story every fucking day. They don't appreciate that over the seven years that

Esmeralda and her Husband were having sex, that there were regulars times when they were not 'trying', were 'relaxed', weren't 'worrying about it'. They think they are being inspiring, but the truth is they are being massive douchebags. What about all the women who don't EVER have children? What about the couples who NEVER conceive. There are thousands and thousands of these examples too. Esmeralda felt proud to be an alternative narrative, that from now on friends could tell couples they met who were having IVF that there was also this other couple they knew about who tried and tried and tried, weren't successful, and subsequently lived extremely happy and fulfilled lives enriched with dreams that came true once they stopped trying, that they couldn't have fulfilled if the IVF had proven to be successful.

She was glad that she got to be that person. And with a warm glow of a job well done Esmeralda saved her document, shut down her laptop, closed the lid, put on her raincoat and opened her umbrella. Stepping out of the cafe into torrential rain she felt satisfied with a job well done.

Stay strong. Nothing lasts forever.

Never Worn

EPILOGUE

If you have ever suffered from depression, felt you have failed at life, experienced the heart crunching pain of infertility, found turning thirty a bit of a ball ache, or simply possess a curiosity for learning more about the human condition, then perhaps these pages have offered some comfort or interest, from one sufferer of misery to another. And if you have been through these things and have found yourself in tears reading the pages within, then without meaning to sound like a pretentious twat, I'm sending you a literary hug.

And if you need to talk to someone, or feel you need help, please feel free to DM me on Twitter @kriyaarts or go to www.kriyaarts.co.uk where there are also lots of links to organisations who might be able to help you.

ACKNOWLEDGMENTS

Thanks again to the wonderful Mish Maudsley for another beautiful cover design and to Rachael Beaumont for once more reading through and feeding back on my first draft. Thanks to everyone who was there for me during this very difficult period in my life; to my Mum for all her strength and love, my beautiful husband, to whom I dedicate this book - and who *is* allowed to read this one - although he's still decided not to, and to my best friend Saffron, who went through the same journey as me and understands the pain I've gone through better than anyone. Thanks for making me godmother to Nell. Huge love to anyone I know, or don't know, who is going through a similar experience. I hope this book provides some fortification, even if it is just in knowing that others out there know your pain. I know your pain and it is huge. Don't let it kill you. There are plenty of reasons to be happy if the unimaginable happens and you're never successful. Lazy Sunday mornings and holidays to exotic climes take on an even greater glamour when considered through the eyes of a thwarted mother. It's a small victory, but a victory nonetheless.